Mark Watson is the acclaimed author of four novels, most recently *Eleven* and *The Knot*, which have been published in twelve languages. He is also a stand-up comedian and has won numerous awards in Britain and Australia. He regularly appears on TV, has had his own cult Radio 4 series and been named the Edinburgh Fringe Festival's highest achiever of the decade by *The Times*, having performed a series of legendary 24-hour shows. He has a home in north London, but mostly lives in hotels. You can find Mark on Twitter *@watsoncomedian* and read more on his website: *www.markwatsonthecomedian.com*

Praise for Mark Watson's novels

'A beautifully observed, touching and funny book of considerable power' A L KENNEDY

'A pitch-perfect tragicomedy of ordinary – and not so ordinary – family life' JONATHAN COE

'Hugely recommended. Gentle, compassionate, unusual and thought-provoking' CHRIS CLEAVE

'Brilliantly hilarious and hilariously brilliant' STEPHEN FRY

'Funny, sharply observed and unexpectedly moving' *The Times*

'Unnervingly accomplished' *Observer*

'Intelligent, humane and desperately funny' *Independent*

'A witty, sharply observant writer' *Stylist*

D0257117

Also by Mark Watson

THE KNOT
ELEVEN

MARK WATSON

HOTEL ALPHA

PICADOR

First published 2014 by Picador
First published in paperback 2014 by Picador

This edition first published 2015 by Picador
an imprint of Pan Macmillan
20 New Wharf Road, London N1 9RR
Associated companies throughout the world
www.panmacmillan.com

ISBN 978-1-4472-4333-5

1 3 5 7 9 8 6 4 2

A CIP catalogue record for this book is available from the British Library.

Printed and bound by CPI Group (UK) Ltd, Croydon, CR0 4YY

Visit **www.picador.com** to read more about all our books
and to buy them. You will also find features, author interviews and
news of any author events, and you can sign up for e-newsletters
so that you're always first to hear about our new releases.

PART ONE

⟳ 1 ⟲

GRAHAM

The Hotel Alpha was in flames. Fire had broken out in a top-floor room and was ripping through the place, threatening to gut the building I had devoted myself to for twenty years. Yet there I was, a quarter of a mile away, gliding along in the Mercedes, oblivious.

It was a warm evening in the summer of 1984 and I had just ferried a guest to Heathrow Airport. As I swung off the Westway, heading back towards the hotel, people were everywhere: gathering outside the Globe pub, dawdling and laughing at zebra crossings until I honked jokingly at them to get a move on. I never spent much time outside myself, but I could see why this sort of weather was so popular. There was the delicious feeling in the air of a long, luxuriant evening still to unfold. It would have been impossible to believe that, not five minutes later, I would be facing the worst catastrophe of my career.

As soon as I pulled up and saw that something was wrong – a melee of people in the forecourt, some fleeing, some trying to peer inside – a part of me felt as if I had known for twenty years that this moment would come.

Not that I could have anticipated the fire, of course: just that, in some superstitious chamber of my brain whose existence I barely acknowledged, there had always been the fear that the paradise of the Alpha could not last forever. It was a similar impulse to the one which obliged me to imagine the loss of my wife Pattie or my children, a way of somehow safeguarding against the worst by picturing it. The Alpha was only a building, of course; yet it had, from the moment I had arrived here twenty years ago, come to feel like a blood relative. If I were away for any length of time, I would begin to have the most absurd fantasies that it might have disappeared; that it would prove to have been a vision, a dreamed world.

Perhaps that is why, amid the panic which began to flood into my limbs as I leapt from the car, there was also a vein of cool determination.

I dashed into the building through the mahogany doors I waxed and burnished each week, across the chequerboard floor I sometimes got onto my hands and knees to scrub – to the amusement of the cleaning ladies – as I could not bear to see it marked or muddied. I stood by my reception desk and looked up at the balconies running all round the hotel, stacked one on top of another like the layers of a cake. The top balcony was already obscured by a cloud of black smoke, and people were stampeding down the staircase. Our antiquated smoke alarms were rattling, and a competing swell of voices rose in horror or a sort of guilty fascination.

At this time, many rooms would be unoccupied, the guests dispersed around London's countless night haunts. But not everyone would have escaped from the top floor, I knew. I fought my way against the tide of people moving towards the doors and round those who were standing and gawping up at the thickening cloud. Across the atrium to the back stairs I went. The heat and the screaming and the panic were all on the other side of the wall, but I could feel it all like pinpricks on my skin as I leapt up the stairs two at a time. At the final bend, the gateway to the top floor, I ran into Howard York.

This was a man who was credited with being able to make anything happen. For these twenty years he had been one of the crucial figures in my life and – as it sometimes felt – the life of London itself. He had bought the Alpha as a very young man and conjured up, from its neglected brickwork and empty space, the most notorious hotel in the city. People came to him, and to the hotel, for solutions to their problems; for things they could not get elsewhere. When he was in the room, there was a sense that anything was possible. Conversations stalled as he walked by; onlookers nudged each other; reality braced itself to bend into whatever shape took his fancy.

But now there was no trace of the magician or the raconteur

of a thousand nights in the bar, the supreme salesman and romantic, all the glittering versions of Howard we were so used to. Now he looked like a lost boy. There were tears in his eyes, and his face was as red as raw meat. He had no shirt on. He grabbed my wrist, his grip tight with a desperation which might tip into violence.

'Room 77, Graham,' he spluttered, breaking out into a cough, '77, 77.'

One of us had to fight through the smoke and try to stop what was already a calamity from becoming a tragedy. One of us or both of us. Or we could both stay where we were and trust that Howard's luck would hold once more.

∞

It had held pretty well so far. But then, in Howard's own opinion, luck was not a whimsical force which flitted in and out of lives. It was a commodity: something you could make or buy. This was one of the first things I learned about him.

We were both in our mid-twenties when we met, but unlike him I did not know quite what I was doing with myself, and the question was becoming rather urgent.

I had gone into the army under the influence – I should more accurately say the orders – of my father, himself a brigadier. I was well suited to military service, he thought, in that I respected authority and kept my shoes very clean. He had overlooked that I was ill suited to it in other ways: namely that I loathed the cold, could not run quickly, could not pitch a tent, hated mud, did not care to sleep in dormitories, and above all did not wish to kill other men.

When I put all this to my father, he eventually allowed me to leave the forces, but he never spoke to me again. I would have to fend for myself, and for my wife Pattie. At first I greeted this prospect with a certain bravado, but this was beginning to flake away after a couple of years of poorly paid and unreliable work.

I had been a tailor's assistant, an 'apprentice barber', which meant sweeping hair off floors, and, when I was fortunate enough, a silver-service waiter at the Grosvenor House hotel and the Ritz. In these places I felt something like a sense of belonging, surrounded by the heavy wood and marble, chandeliers and vases and telephones, the mock-classical bas-reliefs. Grand hotels were fussy and old-fashioned in a way I recognized I was myself. But the work they offered was sporadic. We were, as they say, scraping by.

Pattie never complained about our dingy flat or the fact we had ham and oven chips for dinner every night. In a way, her patience made matters worse. It was shaming to see her poring over the classifieds section of the *Evening Standard* on my behalf, or hear her talking about getting a loan and going to secretarial college. When she came across the ad which was to change my life, I was almost too grumpy to hear her out.

'What about this one? Listen. *Outstanding head concierge wanted ...* '

'I am hardly "outstanding", am I? And I've never worked as a concierge. I don't even really know what—'

'Shush! *Wanted for London's best hotel,*' she went on. '*No experience* – there you go! *No experience necessary. Efficiency and integrity important, as well as a sense of adventure.*'

'I'm efficient, I suppose. But I wouldn't say I had a sense of adventure.'

'Oh, I'm sure you can get one,' said Pattie. 'Do you want me to write you a letter or will you do it?'

'Where is it? Which hotel?'

Pattie laughed. 'Well, this is the funniest bit. *NB Hotel does not exist yet.*'

I had allowed my mind to play for a moment with the image of myself, smartly attired, at the front desk of the Dorchester; but at this final sentence I felt the picture dissolve. 'It must be some sort of joke,' I said, 'and I'm damned if I'm going to mess about with the typewriter to apply for something which ... '

'Well, this is even odder!' she said, continuing to pay my moodiness the scant regard it deserved. 'You don't even have to apply. It says: *Interested parties to report to Howard York, 11 a.m., May 1st.*'

'It'll be an April Fool or something,' I muttered.

'April Fool's day is in April, you silly man. And then there's an address: *Hotel Alpha, Curzon Mews, off Euston Road, N1.*'

I recognized the address and realized that the new hotel must be the establishment once known as the Royal. It had been a magnificent railway hotel in Victorian times, but endured a miserable retirement as an emergency sanatorium and a government records office, finally closing altogether in the fifties. I had heard about it from the one friend I made in the military, a retired colonel who had been sequestered there for several weeks after getting typhoid in India. He had described the magnificence of the interior: a huge central atrium designed for horse-drawn carriages, the balconies, the ornate and now neglected rooms. He had mentioned the eeriness of it, this place that had once teemed with extravagant life and was now full of illness and death. I had walked past the unloved building on a foggy day a few years ago and wondered briefly how long it would stand there before someone demolished it. But now, quite the opposite had happened. Now there was to be a new hotel, the Hotel Alpha.

'Well, perhaps I'll think about it,' I mumbled.

The day went on as normal after that: I went out to buy ham, we listened to the radio and cooperated on *The Times*' crossword. The first of May approached and I pretended not to be thinking about it; but the more I did so, the more the words 'Hotel Alpha' seemed to swim around in my head.

On the eve of the interview, Pattie ironed my suit and chose a tie for me, and we rehearsed possible interview questions.

'What do you think are your best qualities?'

'I … well, modesty forbids me to, er … '

'No it doesn't,' she scolded me. 'Don't you dare be modest tomorrow.'

'Very well,' I sighed. 'I am punctual and reliable, have never missed a day of work, have an excellent memory … '

'And you're the loveliest man I know,' Pattie finished for me. 'Don't forget to mention that. Now, what are your hobbies and leisure interests?'

'I enjoy crosswords and am a keen fan of rugby.'

'That's not good enough either,' she said. 'You need to stand out. Pretend you're into morris dancing or something.'

'Oh God, what's the use? I may as well not turn up. There are bound to be … '

Pattie laid a finger on my lips. She had a flower in her hair, and there were ink marks on her fingers.

'You will be marvellous,' she said, 'and if you don't get the job, nobody's going to die, are they?'

I slept poorly, and – not knowing what else to do with myself – got the bus to the hotel first thing in the morning, arriving almost two hours before the advertised time. The hotel's massive, weather-beaten brickwork was as I remembered it, but new windows had been fitted, and an imposing pair of mahogany doors bore a silver 'A' rendered in art deco style. I gazed up at the cedars which framed the forecourt. They had the advantage of me: they had been here many generations already, seemed to know how things would turn out. Behind those doors, the trees seemed to say, exciting things are about to happen. You might be a part of them, or they might just as easily go on without you.

A queue began to form in the hour or so before midday, and the longer it became, the more my spirits flagged. The great majority of the forty or fifty men communicated youth and ease. Although I was only twenty-five myself, I felt like a relic with my case and my wartime hairstyle. I was not like these people who blew out cigarette smoke with an insouciance modelled on pop stars and chuckled slyly at each other's remarks. They would know the bars to direct guests to, or the shops to be seen at on Carnaby Street. They, not I, were what this establishment would need.

As I struggled to suppress these pessimistic impressions, my attention was drawn to a commotion. A man in a tatty old overcoat had wandered into the traffic, whisky bottle in hand. He hesitated for a moment, arm uplifted as if to conduct some invisible orchestra, and then slumped in the middle of the road, forcing cars to swerve round him with a fusillade of honks. A bus gave a low bellow like an animal whose lair had been invaded. I glanced about. A few of my fellow interviewees were watching curiously, even with amusement; others were fussing with their hair or checking wristwatches. Nobody seemed to be concerned for the fellow who now lay there motionless. Without stopping to consider it, I dropped my case and darted into the road.

'Are you … would you like some help?' I asked.

'Very kind,' he said in a voice quite as composed as my own. 'Get me to the pavement, will you?'

I reached out an arm and helped him to his feet, then escorted him to the kerb.

'Brave of you, coming into the road like that,' said the stranger.

'I thought they would probably stop short of actually running me over.'

'Quite right.' He fixed me suddenly with a look of wily appraisal. 'Cars don't want to run you over. Snakes don't want to bite you. Planes don't want you to miss them. Do you know what I mean?'

I said that I did, though in truth I thought he might well be as mad as a dog.

Then the stranger did something which I would never forget. He shrugged off his overcoat to reveal a smoking jacket in purple crushed velvet, then reached up and removed his ratty, straggling hair in one grab. Beneath the wig was a raffishly parted mop and I was suddenly looking at a man of around my own age.

'I'm Howard York,' he said. 'You were the only person to help, there. Out of all these.' He gestured at the line of strangers, many of whom were now looking on in bemusement. 'What's your name?'

'Graham Adam, Mr York.'

'You're hired, Graham Adam,' he said.

I lost my speech for a second; but only a second. 'Are you sure, sir?'

'Not sir,' he said, 'Howard. And yes, I am. Go inside. Find a lady with very long brown hair. That's my wife, Sarah-Jane. I'll explain to these other chaps that their interview has already taken place.'

I passed the queue of candidates in a daze and found the young lady he mentioned; she was waiting in the atrium with a raised-eyebrows sort of smile on her face.

'Welcome,' she said with a Yorkshire inflection, 'and well done. He insisted on doing it this way, the silly fool.'

She took my arm – I was too befuddled to consider it rather forward of her as I might otherwise have done – and began to show me round the hotel. I took in, as if dreaming them, the individually appointed suites, the vast cellars with a cache of half-century-old wines, the stately smoking room. We discussed wages, though I would have signed the forms placed in front of me even if they had proposed to pay me in biscuits.

Released at last from these people, if not from the spell they had cast on me, I wandered westwards and called Pattie from a phone box opposite the green bulge of the Planetarium. I went into a pub, ordered a whisky, and on impulse bought a round for twenty strangers. In Regent's Park I finally succumbed to my emotions and did a little dance behind a statue, perhaps observed – from the windows of white mansions – by rich people who thought I had gone out of my mind.

∽

My first duty was to send out invitations to the party for the grand opening of the Alpha. The guest list ran to hundreds of people, some of the names so famous that even I had heard of them. We were also taking our first room bookings. Howard York approached this in a very odd manner. He instructed me that if anyone phoned for a room, I was to say that we were booked solid for the first three weeks, but they should call back later that evening in case something had become available. It was not so much that I minded telling a white lie – Howard was my boss, and I would do whatever he asked – but that it seemed extraordinarily rash. Why would a brand-new establishment decline business like this? Might I find myself out of a job in six weeks?

Almost everyone did indeed call again, though, and when – this time – a room was miraculously found for them, they sounded so grateful and relieved that I almost believed in the lie. Word got around that it was already nearly impossible to book a room at the Alpha. Enquiries doubled and trebled, the Bakelite telephone on my desk was ringing every other minute, and the fiction of the hotel's unstoppable popularity was quickly willed into fact.

The party worked in much the same way. Though many luminaries had been asked to attend, plenty more went uninvited, the distinction between the two groups being quite arbitrary but inevitably coming to seem meaningful to those involved. Soon those in the latter group began making strenuous attempts to get themselves an invitation, and all the more so when a couple of fashionable magazines carried gossipy articles speculating upon who had, and had not, 'made the list'. Howard, I was already realizing, had something of a gift for making things appear in print which he wished to be seen as accepted facts. At the same time there was this mischief, this relish for chaos, about him: he might spend half a day engineering a brief appearance by Mary Quant, but he also invited complete strangers, including a man whose dog ran up and tried to bite him on the Euston Road. On the day before the party, the hotel's cellars were equipped to cater for the court of King Solomon himself, but it had ceased to be clear whether we were expecting fifty people or five thousand. Pattie was away from London visiting friends, and so I spent the whole day helping to get things ready.

'How long do you think it will last?' I asked Sarah-Jane, watching in concern as she reached on tiptoe from a stool to drape an arch of fairy lights above the reception desk. 'And would you like a hand with that?'

She turned, her face a little flushed, and hung the string of lights round her neck to amuse me. 'Perhaps I'll just wear them like this instead. As for how long it will last – I would expect the unexpected.'

'I suppose I'm a bit of a stick-in-the-mud,' I said, 'but I prefer to expect the expected.'

Sarah-Jane's face lit up with a laugh. 'Well,' she said, 'it might be all over by midnight, but it might go on till one o'clock, or – good God – even two, Graham. We'll pay you overtime, of course.'

'It isn't a matter of wages at all. I just like to be prepared.'

But within an hour of the mahogany doors being flung open and the first inward surge of arrivals, it was clear that this was not an event one could be prepared for. The atrium throbbed with the energy of bodies; around the balconies went the echo of laughter, sometimes shrill and demonstrative as if designed to show the laugher's cleverness, at other times almost wild. Champagne corks came out like shots from a popgun. I went down to the cellars many times for fresh supplies of liquor; I set down plates of salmon and cream cheese and prawn cocktails and whisked away the remains only moments later. The Hotel Alpha was full of noisy joy: the building was like a person returning to company after a long period of sickness.

The slice of the heavens visible through the skylight went from heavy purple to an ambiguous lilac and finally a pale blue-white, and still no end to this party was in sight. People were in any number of the bedrooms; as I stood on the top balcony I could hear raucous song from the end of the corridor, and in a room closer at hand a young couple was collaborating on something rather different. Everyone in the building but me was under the influence of alcohol or some other drug, I realized. Further singing and shouting floated up from the atrium, like noise from a wireless far away. Some people, in their lurid party clothes, lay across the chessboard floor as if they had crash-landed there; others wandered like wobbling insects from one area to another. In the middle of it all I could see Howard unveiling one of his party pieces: balancing a chair on his forehead. His arms shot out to his sides for balance, but from where I stood it seemed as if he was gesturing to his audience *Look at me!* I glanced up at the skylight again and it was suddenly difficult to believe that anything of substance existed beyond these brick walls.

At nine in the morning I went home. The air outside was cold and thin and there was a dreamlike quality to the people I saw going to their places of work; even to the heaviness of my own body in its unchanged clothes. I let myself in, slept for a couple of hours, bathed and headed straight back to the Alpha, having telephoned Pattie at her friends'.

'How was the party?'

'It was … well, it is still going on, as a matter of fact.'

'Golly,' said Pattie. 'I hope they know what they're doing, these people.'

I could not reassure her on that score. As I got off the bus and strode along Euston Road, past people who glanced indifferently at the grin which had stolen across my face, I had no way of knowing whether the Alpha would be continuing its rise to instant notoriety. For all I knew, police might have thrown everyone out; the place might have reverted to its former ghostly state, even vanished altogether. I need not have worried, though. The doors with that angular 'A' were as marvellously solid as ever, and behind them, bedlam was at an advanced stage. Howard and Sarah-Jane, loosely flanked by other couples, were dancing the Lindy Hop to the beat of a jazz quartet in ragged tuxedos who had appeared from somewhere. There was still a drink in everyone's hand; the balconies, the bar, the smoking room still thrummed with activity. The police had come earlier in the night and been sent away again. Sarah-Jane had opened the door, naked other than her socks, to a nervous young constable.

'Shouldn't you put something on, madam?' he had suggested.

'We've got music on,' said Sarah-Jane, putting out an arm to usher in the policeman, who stayed for a couple of drinks before going meekly on his way.

There were no clocks on display, and the only sight of sky was from that glass panel: not just the time but the very idea of time seemed to disappear. The hourly boundaries collapsed like the timbers of a roof we were all falling through. It was not until the second midnight that the party began to break up, addled guests making their way out onto the Euston Road, blinking and staring as if they had been trapped in a cave for weeks. Each one was seen off with a slap on the back and a merry word of farewell by the still buoyant Howard, including the man with the dog, invited on a whim, who had ended up staying for seventeen hours.

By this time I had begun the job of cleaning up, going round the balconies and entering room after room with a certain trepidation. I gathered up cans and bottles and somewhat less recognizable items which I held by the edges, putting everything in a black bag which got heavier and heavier on my shoulder, as if I were Father Christmas in reverse. Despite the mess, no damage had been done, I was relieved to see: already I felt for the place as if I owned it myself. As I made my way down to the atrium, I passed Howard and Sarah-Jane. They were lying in the very middle of the marble floor, gazing all the way up to the skylight and sharing a cigarette. Thinking me out of earshot – or perhaps not caring – Sarah-Jane propped herself up on an elbow and said: 'We've fallen on our feet with that one!'

They were talking about me, I realized, feeling my ears turn red.

'He's the business,' Howard agreed, 'but you make your own luck, Captain. Captain is your nickname from now on.'

'Why's that?'

'Because I have decided it,' he said with mock grandeur. I glanced back, and then away again as he leaned in to kiss her on the nose. She rested her head on his shoulder and the two of them lay there, the great amphitheatre of the Alpha around and above them. The silence which had fallen felt temporary. The feeling I had experienced these past couple of days – of being the lucky invitee at a party which should have been beyond my

19

aspirations – was one I never really lost in the years that followed. At least, not for a very long time.

∞

There was no longer any doubt in my mind that Howard would
find guests to fill the hotel. What we would do with them was a
different matter. He knew how to build up a business and throw
a party, all right, but he had very little idea about running a
hotel. That was to be my job.

At least, it seemed to be. My job title – 'concierge' – was
rather vague: Howard had adopted it, like 'bellboy', from the
American thrillers which had tempted him to put his family
fortune into hotels in the first place. The position would be
what I made it. And so I made it a considerable one.

I ran the front desk, and what a desk it was: a great slab of
Dutch walnut which felt almost as big as the original tree must
have been. On the desk was the Bakelite telephone, an oversized
ledger with creamy white pages and a fountain pen, and a till.
In the desk's many drawers I kept useful things: foreign phrase
books, train timetables, leaflets for local attractions and so on.
When the phone piped up, I took the reservation and wrote the
name in the ledger, which was actually an artist's pad designed
for sketching. Pattie and I had divided each double page carefully into 77 squares, so I would always have a plan of who was
where. At nine o'clock on the fifteenth of May, 1963, I checked

in the first guest with a set of rules I had plucked from thin air, but which became our gospel.

'Breakfast is from six until ten. There is a games room and a smoking room, though of course you may smoke in your room as well. For a restaurant reservation ... '

The room keys, hung on a rack, were all attached to A-shaped wooden fobs which Howard had commissioned and shipped at breathtaking expense from Switzerland. I loved to reach one down and put it in a guest's hand; to take their cash and ring it up in the till, or file the cheque carefully in a drawer, ready to be taken to Lloyds Bank on the Friday. I had command of the hotel's dozen staff; I wore a smart grey suit and people called me 'Mr Adam'. Pattie noted that I had taken to whistling as I left the house.

'I've never known you so happy, Graham!'

It was truer than she knew. What I had found was something I had sought all my life without being aware of it: a thing I was really good at, a place where I was in command. Howard and Sarah-Jane were in charge, of course, but I spoke to them on what seemed like an equal footing. When Howard suggested that breakfast be moved forward to seven – 'it's easier on the chefs, and I don't trust people who are dressed at six in the morning' – I said as a compromise that we ought to serve guests in their rooms at the earlier time, but begin restaurant service at seven.

'I suppose,' said Howard. 'At least in their rooms they don't need to have their clothes on.' And he laughed, as usual, at my face, which rarely knew what to do with remarks of that kind.

It was as if I were in charge of a giant train set, like the one I had as a boy before my father – in one of his rages – threw it all on the bonfire. The more loops and twists I built for myself, the more ingenious I became at navigating them. I began remarking to guests that, if there were anything they wanted, they only had to call down; and I looked forward to those calls, to the challenges they presented. What time does the train leave from Euston for Liverpool Lime Street? Are any restaurants open nearby at this late hour? Sometimes there were more taxing questions: could I clarify one of the rules of chess? Might I summarize the news headlines that morning, to save the caller from getting out of bed? I soon found it was not enough to look up the information – not enough for me, that is. I wanted to be able to answer instantly.

And so I memorized train schedules; I built up a mental telephone directory of Howard's many useful friends – maître d's and nightclub owners and theatre impresarios. I learned the streets of London as well as any taxi driver; I could bring to mind the different time zones of the world, or the address of the place where you could get crumpets at one in the morning, or the names of people who had stayed weeks before. When someone forgot to take their room key out and came shame-facedly to the desk for a replacement, I would recall their name and room without their having to say it.

I had always had a precise memory; as a child I used to challenge myself to learn lists of monarchs or Underground stops in order, to take my mind off other things. But I had never thought of it as being particularly valuable. In the army, the only function of my memory was to remind me how much better life was before I signed up. In the Hotel Alpha, memory was an asset: it helped to get guests what they wanted. And that was one of the only instructions Howard gave me. 'Find out what people want. Make it happen. That's what the Alpha is for.'

His idea of what that meant, however, was rather more elaborate than mine, as I was to discover as the months and years went by.

One day in 1965 I was given the keys to the hotel's Mercedes and asked to drive a man to Heathrow 'just a little bit faster than the speed limit', as Howard put it.

'That is, of course, illegal,' I pointed out.

'Oh, not *very* illegal,' said Howard impatiently. 'Now the thing is, my friend is in danger of missing his flight.' He indicated a nervous-looking Spanish fellow who was pacing up and down, uttering the odd word I did not care for.

'When does it leave?'

'In twenty minutes.' Howard made it sound as if this were no more than a minor concern. 'But I've told you, Graham: planes don't want you to miss them. You get him there, fast as you can. I'll do the necessary to ensure that the plane doesn't take off on time. When you get there, go to British Airways' desk and say my name, and it should be fine.'

I put on the driving gloves which Pattie and I had bought in Savile Row in order to protect the beautiful ivory of the steering wheel, and started the car. When we were close to the edge of the city – not far from Fuller's Brewery, its white brickwork glistening in the wet night and lent a molten appearance by the floodlights – the man began to talk to me about Esperanto, a project for which he was trying to raise money in order to popularize it. It was very often near the brewery that passengers first struck up a conversation. If they were new to London, this was the moment at which the city began to assume its distinctive shapes and dance around them; if they had been to Heathrow to drop someone off, it was around now that they began to realize the person was really gone.

Esperanto was a language gaining in popularity, said my passenger, and in fifty years it would be spoken by half of the world's population.

'Well,' I said, 'best of luck with that. What is the … Esperanto for "good luck"?'

'*Bonan sancon*. The "sh" sound, it is just one "s", with a little curly line which sits on the top.'

'*Bonan sancon,* then!' I repeated. 'But then, we might be better off saving up your luck to ensure you make this flight …'

'Ah, the flight will be cool,' said the Spanish gentleman, 'thanks to old Howard-you-like.'

I had no idea how he knew this nickname of Howard's – a popular play on his insatiable energy and his ability to get what he asked for – but it sometimes seemed that everyone knew everything about him. Everything, at least, that he wanted them to know. And when we got there, things did indeed go just as my boss had said. At the check-in desk, his name provoked a knowing wink and nod from the lady in a blue blouse, and I was informed that the flight was taking off an hour later than anticipated. I did not ask, on my return to the Alpha, how Howard had – as he always put it – 'made this happen'. It was none of my business.

Occasionally I had legitimate reason to question him. There was once a man whose name stayed in the ledger for five pages running: SAUNDERS, in Room 34. He was late to check out, presenting himself at one in the afternoon, and when I wrote out the bill and gave it to him, he looked at it as if I were being rather unreasonable.

'Look, the thing is,' Saunders said, fiddling with the cuff of his leather jacket, 'it's going to be difficult for me to pay that.'

'May I ask why?'

'Well, to be completely honest, I haven't got it.'

'You don't have enough money?'

'I haven't got a penny on me.'

'A cheque, then, or … ?'

'I haven't got a penny,' repeated the man, flashing me a yellow-toothed grin of apology.

I wanted to box his ears. It felt as if he had taken a great liberty, not just with me, but with the hotel: if people were going to stay here and eat and drink with no notion of how they might pay at the end, we might as well open a soup kitchen. Howard, however, felt differently.

'What about if you write out an IOU,' he suggested, 'and you come back whenever you can and pay it?'

'Really, Howard,' I began, 'this seems very … '

But the matter was done. They had shaken hands on it. Saunders, his travelling case swinging by his side, was off to play the same trick on another hotel. I looked at Howard in disappointment. He swept a hand through his thick hair and grinned.

'He'll be back.'

I did not believe he was right, but three years before I would not have believed that a hotel of this order could spring out of the dust, and that I could have a part in it. I muttered something to the effect that I was sure it would all be fine in the end.

Howard slapped me on the shoulder. 'It will be. It always is.'

His habit of seeing things in the simplest, most crudely optimistic terms sometimes exasperated me, but it is hard to argue with optimism when it so often proves itself right.

∞

As time went by I stayed later and later at the reception desk. Sometimes I was home at midnight, sometimes even after that.

Pattie would leave me a plate of ham and chips, which was still all I ever wanted: I had tried an egg once or twice, but found it unbalanced the meal. I ate quietly, went up to bed, where she would already be asleep, and in the morning there would be time for a few words over breakfast before I went to the bus stop and began to breathe in – even before arriving there – the warmth of the atrium, the busy hum of people heading out to mysterious appointments or bedding down in the bar.

Sunday was my day off: on those days Pattie and I went down to Greenwich to look for antiques in the market, or spent quiet hours pasting her photographs into albums. In our late twenties we had children: first a daughter, Caroline, and then our son Edward. Pattie took to motherhood with such alacrity, it was as if she had been a parent all along. She rose at five in the morning when one or other of the children cried out; she chose clothes for them, washed their nappies with sleeves rolled up to her armpits, sat at their bedsides to read them stories. The children provided her with what the Hotel Alpha had given me: a shape for life to assume.

Sometimes, as a deserved break from the household routines, Pattie would come for dinner at the hotel, and once – it must have been in my fifth or sixth year – Howard made a big performance of inviting us out to the Ritz with him and Sarah-Jane. He was on vintage form that evening, dressed in heavy platform shoes and a floral-patterned shirt; he juggled the cutlery and asked for a wine which was not on the list but nonetheless appeared shortly afterwards. Pattie, however, remained uncharmed.

'There's something not quite right about that man,' she declared after we had got into bed.

'What do you mean?'

'I don't know. Too good to be true. Something like that.'

I might have said so too, not so long before. But in my time at the hotel, my understanding of what could be true, and of how good things might be, had changed. The more you asked from life – I had heard Howard remark – the more it could provide you. I said something of the sort to Pattie, and she shrugged and said she was sure the Alpha was lovely, and Howard was perfectly all right when you got to know him. After a while she fell asleep, and the conversation was not renewed in the morning.

The more the hotel came to mean to me, the less we discussed it. Howard and Sarah-Jane and the Alpha made up half of my life; my family the other half. But the two sides remained separate. When I set foot in the Alpha each morning, I forgot what was outside the doors.

ᴏᴄ

It was not until the late seventies that the Yorks had their own child: a boy they called Jonathan David, who immediately came to be known as JD. There was plenty of room for him in the Yorks' household, which was the back half of the Alpha: five floors of rooms invisible to guests, accessible via a concealed door and a passage which now rang with the sound of the baby's wailing. Sarah-Jane wore pullovers and jeans instead of the frantically patterned dresses she used to favour. Howard – who was almost forty when JD arrived – responded to the change by travelling more; or perhaps it was simply that, by now, he was in great demand. He had written a book about the hotel's success; he lectured all around the world on business. He was sought after for conferences, invited to the opening nights of musicals. We continued to be one of London's most popular spots. We entertained Henry Kissinger and the Rolling Stones. A football team, which had won the FA Cup that afternoon, brought the trophy into the atrium and handed it round filled with champagne. This sort of thing happened every other week in the Alpha.

If he enjoyed being a celebrity, Howard was also increasingly conscious of the responsibilities it brought. The hotel had always lent a hand to deserving or merely cash-strapped folk, as we had to that man Saunders who was let off his bill; we had tabs that were never called in, we gave away free meals. Sometimes this was, of course, strategic. Mike Swan, the editor of the feted *Swan Hotel Guide*, never paid a penny for anything when he made his visits, and we always received the highest possible recommendation in his books. But more often the handouts were purely philanthropic. If someone appeared at the front desk in need of shelter, I was instructed to let Howard know at once: almost always, they found their way onto the guest ledger. This had happened a few months before the fire, in 1984.

The guests were a mother and her three-year-old son, Charles – though she called him Chas. 'Guests' had always struck me as a strange word for the people staying in a hotel: it implied that they were invited, when in fact they had invited themselves. In the case of Chas and his mother, even that was putting it too strongly. Life had blown them here: how, exactly, I did not want to ask. Obviously the husband had left, money had run out. The child had matted brown hair and large, light brown eyes; as his mother spoke to me, he flitted about the atrium, stopping to look at a flag which had been set up for the visit of an Arab dignitary. He reached out a hand and touched the flag as if it were precious, glancing over at me to see whether I minded. I winked back.

'We've got nowhere to go,' said the woman, who was wearing a faded black dress with a hole in one shoulder and a pair of cut-off jeans.

We put them in Room 77, on the top floor. I got used to seeing the lady, whose name was Roz Tanner, and took rather a shine to Chas. My own children were teenagers by now; I brought in rubber balls and jigsaw puzzles they had long outgrown, and watched as Chas, a studious little chap, cantered across the floor after a ball, or sat studying a puzzle. This went on for a while. Roz helped out in the Alpha Bar when Chas was asleep, or waited on tables in the restaurant. Howard and Sarah-Jane got to know her; she became part of the place, in the way people had before. In the way we all had. We talked about finding her a permanent position.

That was the first thing on my mind when, in panic on the back stairs, Howard screamed the number 77 at me. As if a reel of film were unspooling, I saw the past twenty years unravel before me, from that magical afternoon when Howard escorted me past the queue of candidates through the doors, right up to the moment just now when I had parked the Mercedes on the forecourt.

The moments were melting as fast as they always did in this place. Roz Tanner and her little boy were trapped in their room; the room was in flames; the whole of the Alpha, and everything it meant to us, might be about to go up with it. Howard clutched at my wrist; tears were bulging in his eyes. There was a moment- ary chill in seeing this man, my hero, so pathetically stripped of his powers. To look at him in that moment, anyone would have said that fortune had finally caught up with him. But that would have been to underestimate what the man was capable of, what could happen if he wanted it to.

ɔ 2 ɕ
CHAS

As it was quicker than typing, I 'wrote' this by dictating into a computer, which transcribed the words onto the screen with something close to one hundred per cent accuracy. Close, but never exactly. Various people have checked over it, but there's no knowing that they didn't add something here or there, or change something not quite to their liking. This is the problem for a blind man when relying on interpreters. Machines aren't quite accurate enough because they don't have feelings. Humans aren't quite accurate enough because they do.

ɕ

I grew up in strange circumstances, to say the least. I was blind, my parents were not my real parents, and I lived in a hotel. Until the age of almost five, I had no way of knowing any of this was strange. There was nothing to compare it with. I didn't wonder about others' lives any more than any five-year-old does. There was just mine. It consisted of listening to Sarah-Jane walloping pots and pans about as she cooked dinner, pressing the occasional button to join in with JD's computer games, sitting at the front desk with Graham, who said 'ha, ha!' when he laughed as if the words were written out in a caption. It meant being tucked in at night by Howard, his scent of cigarettes and leather jacket and a subtler smell of nights out in a world I didn't understand yet. After he left the room there was always a momentary sad pang and then the rustle of JD on the top bunk above. There was the xylophone of the slats that held his bed above mine, the sigh of his mattress as he shifted his weight about, and then the miraculous coming of morning: the smell of toast, Sarah-Jane's threats to 'knock someone's block off' if they left their shoes where I could trip over them.

Shortly before my fifth birthday we visited the zoo, and the afternoon ended badly: a wasp got into my ice cream and stung the inside of my mouth. My memories are pixelated by pain. I cried out through a throat that felt as if it was filling with blood. We went to Accident and Emergency – the Royal Free in Hampstead, I've found out since – and a practice nurse took Howard's name and mine and then asked:

'And are you the father?'

'Er,' said Howard. 'Not the … not the biological father, no. Adoptive father.'

At that specific moment it made little impact on me. I recall

33

the cold of the nurse's hands and her speech about how brave I had been. Back at the Alpha there was a song and dance, as Graham put it, because an angry wife had hurled her wedding ring high into the balconies and nobody could find it. It was only that night that I snapped out of sleep with a sense of dread.

The inside of my cheek was throbbing. I wanted to go back to sleep, but there was no way of knowing how to get there. The realization that I was always going to be in darkness descended on me with a sudden and terrible force. I began to cry. As ever, there was no way of charting the night to know how much of it was left, but after a while there was the rattling of the bed slats and a good-natured muttering, and I heard JD's feet on the steps that connected the bunks. He slid into bed beside me, pushing me against the wall.

'What's the matter?'

'How come I'm blind and you're not?'

There was a pause.

'Why are you suddenly asking about that?'

'I just want to know.'

'There was a fire,' said JD after further hesitation, 'and your eyes got burned.'

'Where? Here?'

'Not in this bit, but in the hotel, yeah. You were staying here with your mother. She died. Howard saved you from the fire and now you live in our family.'

Another pause followed this barrage of big facts. JD cleared his throat.

'Are you going to be all right now? I mean, have you stopped crying?'

'Yes.'

'Cool. So is it OK if I go back to sleep?'

I stared into the invisible. I had known forever, of course, that I could not open my eyes, that there was nothing in front of me, but perhaps never quite understood that it was not the same for other people. Snot massed treacle-like in my nostrils and I wailed. JD stirred and complained, but didn't wake this time. Eventually the door creaked and Howard was on the edge of the bed, the outdoor smell of him invading the room.

'What's up, mate?'

'I'm blind,' I said, 'and you aren't even my dad.'

'How do you … where did you hear that?'

'I heard you talking about it in the hospital. And … '

Howard scrambled in next to me and laid a big arm across my chest.

'We'll have a chat tomorrow,' he said. 'We'll have a family talk about this. For now, you need to get some sleep.'

'Can you help me get to sleep?'

'Well, mate, one way to do it is to count sheep.'

'There aren't any, are there? And I don't know what they look like …'

'You don't need real sheep. Just imagine these funny things

coming one at a time. Baa!' He produced a noise which made me giggle. I lay there counting. Before long Howard himself had fallen asleep, his snores falling into a two-part melody with JD's above and his heavy arm still round me like a seat belt. I continued to inch my way mentally up the pile of numbers. There was something appealing about the task, about the way it could never end. No matter how many numbers I clambered past, there were still more to get to.

The following day began like any other. I gathered my clothes, in their unknown colours, from the Clothes Place, and collected my preloaded toothbrush from its designated spot. At breakfast Howard whistled and tapped spoon on teacup like a drummer with the hi-hat. The radio wittered in the background – people with a voice like Graham's talking about Margaret Thatcher and the Soviets. In the kitchen, Sarah-Jane baked cakes and sang a song about the way to treat a lady. I almost began to wonder if I'd dreamed everything. But in the afternoon, when Howard came back from his meetings, the family talk took place.

It was all as JD had said. Fire had destroyed the top floor of the hotel three years ago while my mother and I were staying here. Howard hauled me out of the smoke. He took me to a hospital, and later surgeons patched up my face over a series of operations, but my sight couldn't be restored: the retinas had been too badly burned. While I was recovering, Howard used his many contacts in the media to appeal for my father to come forward. It didn't happen, and so the Yorks had taken me on. I had been raised by them on these five floors, the shadow side of the hotel.

'I always really, really wanted another little boy,' said Sarah-Jane, taking my hand in hers. The familiar chunk of her wedding band pressed against my middle finger. 'Someone to keep JD company.'

There was the thrum of the washing machine from another room, and – at the other end of the passage – the faint sound of people clattering suitcases along the marble floor, calling to each other in voices which floated up to the skylight. It was rare that we could hear anything of the hotel from here. This was not normally a quiet household: normally sentences jousted for space like drivers cutting in from different lanes. The lack of noise unnerved me. I looked forward to the talk being over.

'We love you very, very much,' Sarah-Jane went on, with her flat Yorkshire vowels. 'We want you to think of us as your mum and dad.'

I nodded, but of course I already had been thinking of them that way; her insistence on the idea made me faintly uneasy. I resolved, more or less on the spot, that I would never ask about my real dad if it was going to cause trouble. Unconsciously I was also deciding that I wouldn't go into the real world outside the Alpha any more, since if it was full of wasps which could sting you, it might be full of all kinds of other invisible menaces. I'd be perfectly happy with what was around me. What was more real than that?

'There are things in life we don't understand, Chas, old mate,' said Howard with a weighty hand on my shoulder. 'All we can do is make the best we can out of it. And Sarah-Jane— Your mum and I are going to help you have a great life. All right?'

'All right,' I agreed, my face upturned so – I hoped – I was looking right at him.

In bed that night, I thought about the way things had changed. I'd learned more about myself since last bedtime than in the rest of my life put together, but in a lot of ways things seemed reassuringly unaltered. Howard was still the person I turned to. This was still home.

∝

In my sixth year, there were some attempts to give me an education. I went briefly to a 'blind school', where we had to sing a song about a dog called Bingo, the lyrics of which seemed to change each time I got the hang of them, and where a boy engaged me every playtime in a game which involved him pretending to shoot me dead. I asked if I could leave the school, and was given a tutor called Mrs Hopkins who taught JD how to guide me round the hotel, just behind my heel and to one side, his elbow looped in mine. She encouraged me to learn Braille, which I submitted to for a bit, running my hands over the bumps with a scepticism which the tutor struggled to defuse.

'Reading a book this way would take ages.'

'Well, it needs patience, but ... '

'It would take a hundred years.'

'But it's not just books. Imagine you needed to read a ... a sign or a notice.'

'Like what?' demanded JD.

'Well,' said the tutor – I caught the swishing sound of her skirt as she crossed her legs, 'say you were at the British Museum. I think – I'm pretty sure they have Braille there. So you could find out all about the ... They've got ever such a big dinosaur.'

'But why would he go to a museum in the first place,' asked JD, 'if he can't see anything?'

That was the end of Mrs Hopkins. Others followed, but a lot of my early education came from the family. Sarah-Jane, at night, read salutary Enid Blyton fables about the dangers of stealing gingerbread. JD reported passages from his books about the Hardy Boys, a pair of young detective brothers who thwarted experienced criminals and 'gave a low whistle' when a clue came to hand. At every opportunity Howard brought me to the front desk, where I could sit with Graham and listen to the hotel's heartbeat ticking on.

Before I knew what any of it meant, I came to understand the rhythms by which the Alpha renewed itself each day. There were the hefty shouts of the housekeeping ladies who wheeled their trolleys around; there was the flurry of footsteps from the morning check-ins, the gathering murmur of lunchtime, and in the afternoon the clink of ice in glasses. There was the delivery of newspapers each morning by a wheezing man who always said 'I'll have a little sit-down after this', and there were the scuttling bellboys who conveyed the papers to guest rooms, where they would be taken in and read over breakfast or left to languish. Mid-afternoon would bring a lull during which Graham and his assistant, a West Indian lady called Agatha, pored over their respective reading matter: autobiographies of rugby players, and the Bible. I would listen to their conversations, conflating each voice with the speaker's smell: Graham's the whiff of Brylcreem, which made me imagine him shiny and sharp, and Agatha the softer puff of talcum powder.

'What's it mean, Graham, "fornication and indecency"?'

'It means … well, misconduct of a physical nature.'

'You mean filthy lust and desires and so on?'

'Er, yes.'

'Why you looking so worried, Graham? You think I ask you to demonstrate?'

'I should be – in the words of that wretched song – so lucky.'

There was no music in the Alpha. For long periods there were only these conversations to break up the silence, low exchanges streaked with Agatha's booming laughs, like rocks lobbed into a river. Sometimes the phone would trill with a new booking, or Graham would call one of the shops which supplied our bar and restaurant. 'And the postcode is N1 1HA. 'Yes: H for hotel, A for Alpha. We had it made specially. Ha, ha!' He always thunked the receiver back into its cradle with an emphatic noise which made me imagine telephones were around half the size of people.

At about the time JD came home from school, guests began to check in again. Graham went through the formalities, rustling his papers; Agatha sorted out their luggage. The two of them had a game, running since Agatha arrived, which involved guessing whether a man, woman or couple would check in next. She had an almost mystical ability to do this, and was leading by several hundred points. 'I hope to get level by, say, the year two thousand or so,' Graham predicted once.

'We still gon' be here, are we?' Agatha cackled. 'Old people sitting on our behind, with the guests needing to give us assistance and not t'other way round?'

'Well, where else would we go?'

When I was seven or eight, Howard suggested that Graham and Agatha try reading me extracts from the papers. Before long this was one of our favourite afternoon pursuits.

'Tensions in Peking continue to run high,' Graham reported one day. 'That means – er – well, people in China are not very happy about some of the things that are happening there.'

'Which one is it? China or Peking?'

'Ah, well. Peking is actually in China. It is what we call the "capital" of China. Every country has a capital. London – where we are – is the capital of England.'

'Barbados, Bridgetown,' Agatha added.

When Howard came steaming like a train into the atrium that night – there was the grand leather smell, there were the stalled conversations as people pointed him out – I was eager to pass on my findings. 'More trouble in China,' I announced, 'in Peking, which is the capital.'

'I'm sorry to hear that, mate.' I heard the crack of a ring pull as Howard opened a can of beer; he took a first noisy gulp. 'But very impressed on the capitals front.'

The idea of impressing him intoxicated me. Here was a chance to show that I could do something beyond merely being there, consuming other people's energy. I enquired about further capitals and Graham raided the smoking room for a book, which he slammed down on the reception desk with his usual pleasure in the solidity of things. Agatha made a performance of spluttering as dust was blown off.

There was a list at the back of all the world's capital cities, as well as national flags and maps. Those were no use to me, of course, but the cities were: they required no extra understanding, they were just words. I had them read out to me and began to memorize as many as I could. Albania – Tirana. Afghanistan – Kabul. At first it was beyond me to lock down more than ten or so before they began to wriggle away, but Howard taught me a memory trick.

'Draw everything a little picture in your head. You don't need a real picture,' he added hurriedly. 'Just something to remember it by. So, Kabul. Cab-bull. You could think of a bull riding in a cab.'

'Tirana,' JD pitched in. 'You could think of, like, a piranha fish just getting hold of Albania and ripping it to pieces and all the blood and bones coming out everywhere.'

'Bridgetown,' Agatha contributed, 'think of a bridge goin' through a town.'

'Hard to argue with that one. Ha, ha!'

This knack of association gave my brain a little more elasticity each day. I had no idea what a cab looked like, or a bull, or a piranha fish, but I concocted my own versions; and I couldn't begin to imagine what the cities in question looked like, what any city looked like, or anything in a city, any of the people who would be there. But as theoretical cities they existed all the same. Piece by piece, my brain erected a world of sounds and half-ideas. It was not quite the world everyone else lived in, but it was one I had made for myself.

'Sofia is the capital of Bulgaria,' I recited at a defenceless JD, who was waiting with impatient sighs as his computer clicked and hummed, trying to load a game. Sometimes it got there; at other times the effort overwhelmed it. 'Quito is the capital of Ecuador. San Salvador—'

'All right, all right,' he groaned. 'I believe you.'

'Don't you do this sort of thing at school?'

'Nope.' JD slung his shoes against the wall with a clatter.

'Well, what sort of thing *do* you do?'

'You're as bad as Mum.' The computer was having a good day, it seemed: the game announced itself with a tinny three-note signature tune. The action began, bleeping aliens being seen off by the primitive booms of missiles. It was hard for me to get excited about these games – the threat of alien invasion was nothing to someone who hadn't yet come to terms with humans – but I liked to hear what was going on. 'I mean, we just do – you know – times tables and stupid stuff.' JD put the controller into my hand. 'Your go.'

'What are times tables?'

'Press the button! Press the button!' There was a low boom from the speakers; I had slain an alien. 'Well done. Times tables is, you know, three twos are six. Four twos are eight.'

'Five twos are ten,' I carried on. 'Six twos are twelve. Seven ...'

'Oh God,' he said, 'now you'll be doing this as well.'

∞

There was little Howard liked more than a new thing to show off, and what better than this: a star attraction he had created himself. He called me into the smoky clamour of the Alpha Bar to impress his friends. They called out sums, they demanded to know the capitals of West African republics, they whistled and clapped. JD and I were given Coke and our bedtimes were miraculously deferred. 'Is he amazing or is he amazing, eh?' Howard asked.

'That question makes no sense,' I pointed out, and everyone laughed, Howard loudest of all.

'Just go easy, will you,' I heard Sarah-Jane warn Howard one night. 'He's not a performing animal. It's not a circus.'

'The Alpha? Of course it's a circus. It's always been a circus, Captain.'

I would never go to Tirana, or watch a circus, or count ten red cars going by on the road, but here in the hotel, none of that mattered. Eight eights were sixty-four, the capital of Belgium was Brussels, and that was all you could say on the subject, whether you were blind or could see. Here, it didn't matter about all the mysterious things – *green, beautiful, check-in desk, suitcase*: all the cards held by every player but me. Pure words, facts, were reality. The more of them I picked up, the more of a life I could have. And it could all happen without ever having to venture the other side of those mahogany doors.

On the eve of my ninth Christmas I was taken into the smoking room for the first time. The room's atmosphere evoked a quality of mysterious antiquity which made me feel as if it might only exist at Christmas. I ran my finger along the spines of ancient books; there was the warm, wily smell of whisky as Graham decanted it into glasses. JD boasted that he was going to take his whisky in one go and spluttered violently. Agatha had lit a candle. The smoke-trail wrapped itself around my nostrils, dusting all the other smells as if in icing-sugar. Howard was thumping out an impatient rhythm on a tabletop.

'Come on! Let's make this happen!'

A large package was set down. My hands roved over a number of flat boxes.

'CDs?'

'Twenty-six CDs,' Howard said, 'the entire *Encyclopaedia Britannica*, read by Mr Howard York and Mr Graham Adam.'

'Considerably abridged,' Graham put in. 'Ha, ha!'

'One CD for each letter,' said Sarah-Jane. 'Quite a big effort by Santa Claus, this was.'

'Lovely!' said Agatha.

'Oh, bloody hell,' JD grumbled, 'I hope "Santa Claus" brings you some headphones too.'

As for me, I could hardly speak at all. Here in front of me was everything I could ever want to know, and now I would not even be dependent on anyone to deliver it to me. My small world shrank even further in that moment: all I needed now was the corner of our bedroom where JD's stereo was plugged in. But thanks to Howard, it felt bigger than ever.

∞

JD had started at secondary school that autumn. He acquired a new vocabulary, consisting largely of scathing adjectives (sad, spasticated, dumb) and points of anatomy (boobs, dick) which he slipped casually into conversation. He got into ice skating. He went to see *Teenage Mutant Ninja Turtles*, and later *Home Alone*, the premise of which terrified me. When he thudded down onto the bunk above me at night, I had less idea than ever before of what he might be thinking. And so I concentrated on what I knew. The CDs were stored in a rack, and Sarah-Jane made sure they were always in the right order, from A to Z, so by counting down I could pick whichever one I wanted. I learned to spring the stereo's CD tray open, to slide a disc in, and press the button in the bottom right-hand corner which made it play. Sometimes I spent a day listening to a CD four or five times from start to finish. The acquisition of facts became my main hobby in life.

One day an American couple trudged into the atrium, defeated by an ambitious sightseeing agenda. As they approached, the hotel's welcome team was grappling with the problem of a persistent fly. Insects had worried me ever since the distant day I was stung by one, and to be safe I had drifted to the other side of the atrium, though not too far away to hear the debate which continued.

'Give me that paper – I smash him to Hell,' Agatha proposed. 'I fed up of him, man. Give me a headache.'

'You've already tried to swat it, or "him" as you generously refer to it,' Graham said. 'You swiped at it six times. You were about as accurate as a donkey with a briefcase. Ha, ha!'

MARK WATSON

'So, Mr Clever, how we're gonna catch the fly then, if we don't swat him?'

'We will swat it,' Graham said, 'but with patience. We must set a thief to catch a thief.'

Agatha whooped. 'What's that mean? That's in the rugby?'

'No, no,' said Graham, 'all I mean is, to catch a fly, you have to think like a fly. It thinks that it can linger here as long as it likes and nobody will notice.'

The Americans were in earshot now. I could hear the man's laboured breaths as his wife said that it had been a little too hot.

'Yes, better off out of it, by all accounts!' Graham sympathized.

'It was too bad we didn't even get to see Big Ben.'

'You will have seen it,' Graham assured her. 'It was that very big clock.'

I edged back towards them and cleared my throat. 'Big Ben is actually the name of the bell, not the clock.'

Graham chuckled. 'We've made a rod for our own backs, I think! Chas has the *Britannica* on compact disc,' he explained to the guests.

'What a very grown-up young fellow!' marvelled the American woman.

'It was finished in 1858,' I went on, 'and has become an international symbol of London.'

'It sure has,' muttered the man appreciatively, 'it sure has.'

'They use the chimes on the news,' I concluded, 'but I'm not

48

usually up that late, and the style is some kind of Gothic, but Howard coughs over that bit.'

'Well, isn't that something!' said the woman, and the two gave me a little round of applause. I only wished Howard could see this, but he'd find out. He always knew what was happening.

'And how many times have you been to Big Ben?' the American lady asked.

'Oh, I haven't been,' I explained. 'I don't go outside.'

There was a sticky little silence and the Americans began to mumble about what a pity it was, and how brave I was, and eventually the man put a damp ten-pound note into my hand. I thanked them, although they had misunderstood. I had no craving for the real Big Ben; the virtual one of facts and figures was mine already. There was the noise of something slamming down and Agatha's big, rounded laugh as – I assumed – Graham began to scoop up the remnants of the fly.

I was new to the emotion of pride, and the first fall was waiting on another warm afternoon not far away.

JD, who had recently gone grumbling into his uniform for the start of a second big-school year, was off on a camping trip with some mates. Autumn always brought conferences and seminars and student groups to the Alpha. They collected noisily in the atrium, chattering in their different languages. It took both Graham and Agatha to deal with them, which meant my precis of the day's papers had frustratingly been interrupted. I knew about the war in the Arabian Gulf, that the Soviet Union was breaking up, and yet all this international turmoil was on hold while Graham directed teachers-in-training to the toilets. I'd almost decided to go back to my room and cheer myself up with a CD, but suddenly Howard was there. I heard the imperious tread, his laugh that made you long to join in without even knowing what was being laughed about. There was a woman with him. Her heels rang against the marble floor as if someone were setting about it with a tool.

'Graham,' he said, 'this is Lara Krohl, who is going to be handling PR for us from now on.'

'PR … ?' Graham hesitated.

'Public relations,' said the woman in a hard, clipped voice. 'I liaise with media, plan press events, and so on.'

'I see,' said Graham. 'Well, it's a pleasure to—'

'Just at the moment – ' Lara Krohl rode over his sentence as if it were something left lying in her path – 'I have a client in Room 34, and he's being disturbed by some noise from next door. Can you sort that out?'

'I'm sure we can help,' said Graham.

'If you could get someone up there ASAP,' said Lara Krohl. There was a flattened, slightly robotic inflection to her voice which I decided to investigate.

'Are you South African?' I asked.

'This is my son Chas,' Howard put in.

'Ah.' If Lara knew of my reputation in these parts, as I liked to believe everyone did, she was very cool about it. 'Yah,

I was born in South Africa, but I've lived here some years. So, anyway ... '

'What would you say your capital is?' I asked. 'Johannes-burg? It's a complicated political situation, isn't it?'

'Wow,' said a woman behind her, somebody who must have been waiting for service. She had a low, husky voice. 'That's pretty impressive. How old are you, Chas?'

'Nine and a half,' I said, crediting myself with a bit of extra age so as not to be underestimated and moving briskly on. 'South Africa is one of the few countries with more than one listed capital. Not surprisingly for a place where nothing is simple.'

'Amazing,' said husky-voice. 'Which school do you go to, Chas? To a special school? I only ask because I'm training to be a teacher myself.'

'I'm not at a school,' I informed her. 'I study at home, here. I'm an autodidact.'

'Are you ever,' said the lady softly. 'God, that's ... that's impressive.'

'And why are you interested in South Africa?' asked Lara Krohl without any such sentimental affection in her voice.

'He knows all the capitals,' Howard bragged. 'Seriously, you've never seen anything like this kid. Give him a country, watch him go.'

'Lesotho,' said Lara Krohl.

The feeling was like one I sometimes had when I reached

in vain for a toothbrush or toilet paper or any of the thousand things it was beyond my capacity to keep track of. I groped around mentally with heat rising at the back of my neck and oozing into my face. I thought of Howard's disappointed expression; perhaps even his embarrassment.

'I'll get it in a minute ... ' I mumbled.

'It *is* a tricky one,' she said.

But there were no 'tricky ones'. I knew them all. I would have recited Lesotho's capital twenty, thirty times before. This was just a freak malfunction. I could hear in her voice what she thought: that Howard was deluded in showing me off, that everyone humoured him. It felt as if the hotel itself were being shown up by my failure. All this in front of Graham and Agatha; and in front of the stranger with the low, beautiful voice.

'I'm sorry,' I said, 'just give me a minute ... '

'I wouldn't have a clue, myself,' chipped in husky-voice, hoping to cheer me up, but again it was cold comfort – it was what you would say to someone who'd failed. You wouldn't *have* to know, I thought. You could look it up. But someone like me has to know.

'Well, I'm off,' said Lara Krohl, 'but I'll let you puzzle that one out, and I'll let Howard explain the problem with the room.'

And without a goodbye to anyone she was clacking away towards the main doors, leaving the riddle in my hands like a heavy box I couldn't put down. I stood there listening to the reproach in each of her steps. My ears felt fit to burst with blood.

Howard began to talk to Graham. Husky-voice explained to Agatha that she was here for the conference, but a little late. My pulse was pounding in my neck. I saw, or imagined I saw, a sketchy patch of light, like a flare, and adrenalin propelled me away from reception towards the cold of the doors. Maseru, Maseru! The word draped itself like a snake round my neck. Lesotho: Maseru. I'd never had a memory-trick to fasten either down. Look where that laziness had got me! And yet, if I could catch Lara Krohl up, I could still salvage the situation.

Egged on by that thought, which overpowered everything that would normally hold me back, I went, head-down, through the doors and – for the first time in my life – outside alone.

Immediately after the main doors was a small forecourt, I knew, where Graham's Mercedes glided to a halt as he chauffeured Howard home. The flush of angry energy carried me past trees; I felt gnarly bark with an outstretched hand. As I stepped out of their shadows, fear pierced me. This was London itself. Foreign noise crowded in: the chattering and laughter of groups, people for whom being here was the most ordinary thing. I turned left at random, walked a little way, turned right. Cars came into the air with an unpredictable honking and a flaring of engines. Lara Krohl could be half a mile away by now, and in a matter of moments I realized not just that chasing her had been ridiculous, but that I was already powerless to retrace my steps. My skin swam with sweat.

London, stretching in every direction, was a room with no

walls to feel by, a room that went on as limitlessly as the sky above. I slumped down against the base of a building, shaking. What would happen to me now? Would police come? Would they call the Alpha and get someone to collect me, or was there some other procedure for people who had been stupid enough to run away from their homes?

My stomach was ready to squirm out of me onto the pavement. I rested my head on my knees and cried.

'Hey, mate. What are you playing at?'

At the grip of his hand, my shoulders went limp.

'I'm sorry,' I said, 'I'm sorry. Don't make me go and live somewhere else. I—'

Howard yanked me to my feet and I pressed myself into the cocoon of his homely smells, blocking out everything else, all the fumes and fury. 'Chas! Bloody hell!'

'I wanted to find her,' I tried to explain. 'It was Maseru.'

'I'm sure it was, mate,' Howard muttered, 'but don't scare the shit out of me like that again, all right?'

'All right.'

He mussed my hair and slung an arm into mine and clattered me back the way I had come, through the big doors, into the cool of the atrium whose sound of small activities had never been so inviting.

'Oh, he's here!'

It was the husky-voiced woman. My face felt heavy with embarrassment.

'It was Maseru,' I told her. 'I just didn't get it in time. I feel really stupid.'

'I can tell you, Chas,' she said, 'you are very far from stupid.'

'I'm never going to get anywhere if I forget things like that.'

'You know,' said husky-voice, 'there's a lot more to life than memorizing stuff and repeating it. Intelligence is about the way you look at the world. That's what I try to teach people. Not to learn stuff blindly – oh, I'm sorry.'

'It's fine,' I said, grateful to be put on the front foot. '"Blind" is just an adjective.'

' … well, anyway,' she went on. 'I'm Ella, by the way.'

It was only now that I registered the smell I was to associate with Ella from then on. It was a little like one of Agatha's Christmas candles after it had been snuffed out: a low, wispy, somehow suggestive perfume which matched her voice.

'All I was saying,' Ella resumed, 'was that I think you've got a fantastic future ahead.'

Howard's palms were slapping rhythmically against his jacket pockets.

'Tell me, if you don't mind,' he addressed Ella, 'what do you do? You're a teacher?'

'In training. I'm here for the conference. But I've missed the first session, like an idiot.'

'And you qualify when?' asked Howard.

'Another year,' she said, 'and then of course I have to actually find a position.'

'Hard work, I should think?' Howard remarked. 'Not a lot of money at first?'

Ella laughed. 'Well, I didn't exactly get into this profession for—'

'How much would you want,' said Howard, 'to come and teach Chas full time? One to one?'

There was a silence. I held my breath. Behind us, Graham and Agatha chortled as somebody was dispatched to the lifts and one of them racked up a point in the checking-in game.

'I …' Ella began, sounding rather stunned.

'Chas, would you want Ella to tutor you?'

'I'd love it,' I said, 'but … '

'And Ella – I feel like a vicar here! Do you take this man …?' Howard rewarded his own gag with a hearty laugh. 'Ella, if I made you an offer, would you think about that?'

'I … well, of course I'd think about it,' said Ella.

Much later, Ella tried to explain to me how startling a moment this had been. She'd arrived that morning for the third of four days listening to talks about the theory of education; she was some way away from being qualified, let alone from having what you would call job prospects. Now here was Howard York, a famous man, his hand on her shoulder, looking into her eyes in a manner which tended to extract a yes. And the question was: did she want to chuck in all of her plans here and now and come with him?

'Why don't you think about it for the rest of the day?'

Howard suggested, but I was beginning to recognize this tone of voice. I hadn't asked to be tutored, though I was dizzy with wanting it now, and Ella hadn't applied for a job, but she too was being tugged into the stream. Howard was going to make it happen.

ɔ 3 ɔ

GRAHAM

I have heard it said that adversity is the truest test of character, and that the greatest people turn disaster into opportunity. Perhaps Howard had heard it too, or perhaps someone like him does not need to be told. In any case it was no great surprise that he converted a moment of terrible panic – Chas's brief escape from under my nose – into one of the soundest decisions he ever made: the appointment of Ella Flanders, after an interview of around thirty seconds. Even shorter, in other words, than mine.

The way he saw it was – as usual – perfectly simple. Chas needed a regular tutor who could keep up with him. Instinct told him that Ella was the right person, and his instincts were generally right. 'She's just the ticket, Madman,' he said – the nickname being a play on my surname and less-than-excitable nature. And sure enough, she was.

Soon after I first came to work for him – after a hastily organized party bloomed into another miraculous success – I had commented that Howard's knack for conjuring tricks was not limited to card-shuffling and balancing acts, but extended to life itself. 'No such thing as magic, Graham,' he said. 'A magician is just an actor impersonating a magician.' It was an unusually cryptic remark for him, but as he had been drinking gin, I let it pass.

Now, after the fire, I thought I had an idea of what he meant. Howard's successes might look like magic, but they were not. In fact, there was no one word that explained why things always seemed to come true for him. It was not precisely luck, charm, or faith, or any nameable combination of them all. He was just Howard: that was all you could say. And when being Howard was not enough, he had found certain ways round it.

∞

The biggest disaster of all – the fire – somehow became, in his hands, an opportunity. The top floor was to be rebuilt, and the hotel would be 'bigger and better than ever' as he put it in an advert which ran in several daily newspapers. This was rhetoric, of course. The Alpha was no bigger after the repairs: it was, naturally, exactly the same size. And it was questionable whether it had actually got better. All the same, it was back. It was back, all right, and I was grateful.

The months following the fire were very trying. We remained open to guests, but they were not always open to coming. The death of Roz Tanner had left a series of wounding memories: the unearthly cries of Chas for his mother as he was carried away from the scene, the bundle of her body being taken away, the bouquets of flowers left in the atrium by strangers; Chas's frequent requests, over the months that followed, to see his mother, and the catch in Sarah-Jane's voice as she explained that this could not be. And behind all this there was the endless drilling and hammering and scraping on the top balcony, the effort to eradicate what had gone on there: an effort which guests often acknowledged with a wary glance skywards, as if ghosts might fly out any moment.

At night – I had taken, in these pressing times, to staying later than ever – Chas's wails would float along the corridor from the Yorks', and I would hear Howard and Sarah-Jane arguing. Since Chas's father had not surfaced, they had (in Howard's view, at least) no choice but to be responsible for him: all the same, given the damage he had suffered, I wondered how wise this was. There was no merriment in the Alpha Bar; the pages of the ledger stood white and bare, great swathes of rooms lay empty. After handing over the desk to the night staff I would sometimes sit in the smoking room with a glass of whisky, listening to the emptiness and feeling that, no matter how bullish Howard might be, something had been lost that we could never find again.

But he was right, and I was wrong. Chas seemed to be crying less often. Howard would bring him into the atrium on his shoulders and encourage him to walk a few steps here and there, a strong grip on his little arm. Sarah-Jane had reconfigured their house, with a strict place for everything Chas would need; JD took Chas to the bathroom and slept in the bunk above him. Psychologists told us that he might well be young enough that he would have no memory, in the end, of what had happened; that his life, in essence, could start again from this moment.

And that was also somehow true of the Alpha. It was not enough to restore it; we had to show that the fire had been – as Howard put it – 'a blessing in disguise'. It sounded preposterous, but he meant it. Money was spent on reupholstering and scrubbing, new artwork was acquired, new celebrities were strongarmed into appearing in the bar. And I was to have a full-time assistant.

'Are you sure we ought to be recruiting,' I asked Howard, 'at a time when we have just had to spend all this money on—?'

'That's what insurance is for,' he said with one of his grins, brushing his hair out of his eyes. The hair was greying a little now – we were all middle-aged – but it suited him, introducing a certain gravity which played well alongside his boyish features.

'But the insurance, surely, only covered—'

'Let me worry about that, mate. You just get that post advertised.'

I wrote out the classified ad under Pattie's proud supervision, photocopied it and sent it to all the quality papers. We received more than a hundred CVs in the post; and each carefully written submission seemed to confirm what Howard had said, that the Alpha was still in business. Eventually I chose a shortlist of ten and arranged to interview them all in the smoking room. This is not a normal hotel, I tried to explain to each. We do not leave squares of chocolate on guests' pillows; no crooner sings Billy Joel songs at squirming couples in the restaurant. Some of the younger male candidates, the ones who came in with business cards and cufflinks and a university-minted confidence, were taken aback. Didn't we understand that every hotel had music in the lobby, and air conditioning? I did indeed. We were not like every hotel. That was the point.

One candidate seemed to understand. Her name was Valerie Davey. She was lean, stub-nailed and hard-handed, economical of speech; somebody you would put your life on to get a duvet clean. 'I ain't precious,' she said. 'You tell me what to do, I'll do it.' That seemed good enough for me, but there was one final person to interview. I had done quite enough talking by now, and I was almost hoping she would not show up, but there was a forceful knock at the door at precisely the minute arranged, and when Agatha Richards entered the room I soon forgot my fatigue. When she was in a room, you knew all about it.

I thought at first glance that she was the fattest person I had ever set eyes on. But as she unbuttoned a shapeless black overcoat to reveal another just the same, and then another, it emerged that she was simply one of the most swaddled. It was very chilly outside – I had been out, briefly, to pick up some food for Chas – but this nonetheless seemed excessive. At the third coat I laughed out loud.

'I don' like the cold, man,' she said.

'Evidently!'

Off came a further wardrobe's-worth of cardigans, shawls, scarves and woollen items I could not put a name to. There were splashes of wild colour, oranges and purples.

'Sorry, took eternities!' said Agatha, finally settling her ample self into the armchair opposite mine. She was in her mid-thirties, with large dark eyes and a flat nose, great bosoms that pushed gently against the navy fabric of her dress. I could see that the dress was old and had been altered more than once at the sleeves. 'I' from Barbados,' she said. 'So cold here.'

'I was mesmerized watching your clothes come off!' I said. Then: 'Oh, Lord … '

Agatha let fly with a laugh that could have been heard on the other side of the Thames, and what an infectious laugh it was: almost to my shame I found myself joining in. We giggled for a good half-minute like schoolchildren at the back of class. Eventually she wiped her eyes, sighing. Trying to remain professional, I glanced down at her CV. It was easily the worst of the ten that had made it to the shortlist: big loopy writing like a child's, strewn with misspellings and grammatical irregularities. Yet there were a couple of sentences I had not been able to forget.

As God is my Judge, which He is, one had said, *I will always work my Best and I will not let any gest ever be unhappy while I am in the same Building.*

'I was interested that you wrote that,' I told her. 'Happiness is certainly what we try to provide here, all right.'

'I' a happy person, you know,' said Agatha. 'Not always happy at everything that'll go on. Or I' be a crazy person, right!' Our eyes met. 'You know, my life, there's good thing, God be praised, and not so good. My husband brings me to England, not a very good man, I have to run away with nothing but my son. My son, he join the army, you know?'

I did indeed know the army, I said. 'And his rank now?'

'He went to Ireland. What the hell they're even fighting about? He din' know. He was eighteen. He send me a postcard. Belle-fast. Food is awful, he says. Weather awful. Having a great time!' She laughed; her teeth were very white. 'Third day, someone ask him to play snooker. He follows them to the pub. They shoot my boy in the head. Found him on the table all in blood.'

It was a few moments before I could speak.

'He din' even know how to play snooker,' she said.

'My dear lady ... ' I began, clumsy as an elephant.

'It was a despicable thing,' she said, 'that's what the paper said, a despicable thing. Anyhow. What is it if you're unhappy, man? It's wasting your life!'

'Well,' I said, 'I ... yes. Quite so. Quite so.'

Although in theory I was still interviewing her, I had begun to feel as if it were the other way round. I returned to the subject of the Alpha. 'Howard always says that luxury is having what you want,' I trotted out for the tenth time. 'Rather than what the hotel *thinks* you should want. So we pay very close attention to our guests.'

'Oh, I' pretty good at that, man,' Agatha said.

'That's where we ... where we like to focus our energies,' I said, feeling more and more like some colonial nitwit trying to give a lecture in the heat, 'rather than, you know, some of the nonsense hotels go in for. We don't have someone standing in the lifts to press buttons. We don't ask our chambermaids to fold the lavatory roll into a point.'

'No, that's right!' Agatha cackled again, her face ignited, and it was as if the conversation of a moment ago had never occurred. 'Why you're putting the effort in, when they only wipe their behind with it!'

This was not my kind of joke, and yet I found myself harrumphing with laughter once more, and by the time Agatha left ten minutes later I dearly wanted to hire her. Yet there was still Mrs Davey. My conscience told me that she would be a safer appointment. I put the two CVs on the table and poured a tot of whisky from the smoking room's secret stash. I kept imagining Mrs Davey and Agatha Richards at home waiting for news. I could see Mrs Davey's weary face; Agatha's, stoical and good-natured. Really, I was not cut out at all for decisions like this.

But one man was, and I heard him – as ever – some seconds before he came into the smoking room. The door slammed behind him so emphatically that I thought the frosted-glass panel would jump out. 'Got a winner, mate?'

I explained my dilemma. Howard squinted as if the problem were too small to make out.

'Why not both?'

'We haven't the budget for that, surely. I—'

'They're both good, right? Good people are hard to find, Graham. There's you, me, the Captain, and that's about it. And that's if you count me as a good person.' He chortled loudly. I tried to join in, but the joke struck me as an ill-advised one. 'Take them both.'

I telephoned both women; both sounded delighted. It was a warming sensation to have been the source of that delight. They both reported for duty the following Monday; within moments, Mrs Davey was taking luggage from guests and genially bossing the chambermaids. Agatha joined me at the desk. Before a fortnight had passed it was as if she had always been there, guffawing and reading her Bible and advising guests on how to combat the cold.

'I told you to take them both, Madman,' said Howard. 'Simple.'

And perhaps it was, after all. When you were with him, you

could believe that cars did not want to hit you, that planes did not want to be missed. And that the universe, which had seemed to conspire against the hotel so dramatically, meant only good for the Alpha after all.

Long after our bookings had returned to normal, and Agatha and I were playing our check-in game ten rounds at a time, Howard pressed on with what he considered improvements. As the years slipped by, we acquired a gymnasium with a running machine and a 'relaxation area' where guests could receive massages.

Much of this seemed like rot to me. Why could people not run outside, if they must run at all? Who in his right mind wanted oil rubbed into his back by someone he had never met? It all seemed harmless enough, though. Of slightly more concern were the gadgets Howard occasionally foisted upon me. An electric typewriter would speed up letter-writing, he said. A fax machine would allow us to send menu changes to the printers', or invoices to event organizers, in a matter of moments. A credit-card machine would reduce the need to handle cheques.

'But what is wrong with cheques?'

'It's not that anything's wrong with them. It's just important to modernize.'

He was fond of these American words and the assumptions that went with them. 'Not everything modern is good,' I pointed out.

'You like to live in the past, don't you, Madman?'

'Not in the past – the present. I have done most of my living in the present so far.' (I was pleased with this response, and repeated it to myself a couple of times on the bus home, until people started to look at me.)

'If you're not standing still, Graham, you're going backwards.'

I demonstrated, by coming round the desk and standing there, that this was not true.

This was all spoken in good humour. We had never argued, Howard and I, and we could certainly not afford to start now. I might not share his eternal enthusiasm for the next new thing, but I had heard it said that the more things changed, the more they stayed the same. That was the case with the Hotel Alpha. Howard changed things, and I kept them the same. As far as I could imagine, this was how it would always be.

⚯

Caroline, now in her early twenties, was getting married to a doctor who owned a large detached house in Chiswick. As far as Pattie was concerned, this meant she had made it in life, and my attempts to talk about the Alpha tended to sputter out as she anticipated the wedding more and more keenly.

'Which do you think sounds better: *we are honoured that you chose the Alpha,* or *we are delighted that you chose the Alpha*? It's going to the printers tomorrow.' We were trooping round the stalls at Greenwich. Antique dealers, themselves on the way to being antique, prowled around their jumbles of mirrors and fire-guards and commemorative pin-badges as if any of the gently browsing couples might be about to make off with it all. There was the smell of hamburgers sizzling on the griddle of a grubby van. This place had barely changed in the thirty or so years of Sundays we had been coming. When I took Pattie's arm in mine, or we wrestled some silly purchase – a coal scuttle, a harp – back to the car, I always felt that we ourselves were unchanged also.

'Do you think lilac is all right for an autumn wedding? Or too springlike?'

'Sorry?'

Her eye had been caught by an assembly of frilly, fussy dresses presided over by a woman with a cup of soup. 'Lilac. For Caroline's wedding.'

'Oh.'

I had got so used to answering questions for hotel guests that, if a perfect stranger had come up to me at the reception desk with the same enquiry, I daresay I would have ventured an opinion. With my own wife, though, I was stuck for an answer. I muttered something to the effect that Pattie would look very nice regardless. She tutted and went on talking about the wedding. I went back to thinking about the hotel. We continued down these separate paths, watching as stallholders began to shout that it was the last chance to have a look.

In the days before the wedding, Pattie wore a permanent flush of excitement; she had her hair bobbed and highlighted and she addressed me in terms of endearment which I had thought retired some years before. On the day itself she fussed lovingly over my suit and shirt collar as she had before my Alpha interview. Finally I travelled to the church with Caroline, who was in a white dress that filled most of the back half of the vehicle: a Mercedes very like the Alpha's. As we neared the church I thought of the portrait her six-year-old self had once painted: 'My daddy is thin and important, he wears trousers and works in a hotel.' I had four, then three, then two minutes to tell her how much I loved her and what a wonderful day it would be. Somehow, all I could find to say was 'nice car, good taste!' as a feeble sort of joke, and I watched her eyes sink to the floor in disappointment.

At the reception, the talk turned to Howard and Sarah-Jane: they had been invited, but he was in Tokyo and so she was looking after the children. 'Always lands on his feet, that one, doesn't he!' observed Brian, Caroline's new husband.

'What do you mean?' I asked.

'Well. Got the hotel up and running in double-quick time, I hear. After what happened. *Triple*-quick time.'

There was an implication in his voice which I was fairly sure I disliked. It was his wedding day, however: not the day for an argument; and besides I was not the person for one.

'I'm not sure I understand you.'

'Just … I don't know,' he said, squeezing Caroline's arm. 'I would have thought it'd take longer to rebuild a hotel than that. And I hear he's actually expanded it.'

'We have,' I said, perhaps a touch stiffly. 'But it hasn't been a magic trick, I can tell you. Actually, Howard has a saying: a magician—'

'I've always thought,' Pattie cut in, and I had to steady her wine glass as it threatened to spill onto someone's toes, 'I've always thought there's something about that man. Once when we were having dinner, there was talk about affairs or something, some scandal, and he looked down at the table in a very funny way. Do you remember, Graham?'

'I don't, I'm afraid, but perhaps it's the sort of thing I wouldn't notice. As far as I'm concerned,' I went on, 'people can look at tables as much as they like, within reason.'

'Within reason!' echoed Brian, slapping me on the back. 'You're so deadpan, Graham!' There was general laughter and I thought it best to leave it there. It was not as if they were entirely wrong, after all. It was not as if Howard were beyond question. But he and I were bound together. He had found me when I was at a loss and built me into the man I was now. Where would I be without him? Languishing miserably in some office, having given mind and body to an army I despised and been put out to pasture. That was where. And so the loyalty I felt towards him took precedence over almost everything else: for better or for worse.

Besides, he had helped us in ways that Pattie was not aware of. That same autumn that Caroline got married, for example, our son Edward was in something of a funk. He had been out of university for some while, not quite settled into anything, was still living with us, and had been turned down for a dozen jobs – most of them after getting to the point of an interview. He was not much of a talker, Ed: he stumbled over words, or repeated them, and there was no mistaking that this was preventing him from being hired. Before an interview for a travel-agent job, he became particularly anxious.

'If only I, if only I … I would love to work in travel,' he said one night in the Alpha Bar. He had bony shoulders and a long spine; in his boyhood Pattie never tired of saying how like me he was. As I looked at him now, eyes turned dolefully down to his beer glass, I could remember with absolute clarity how it felt to be like him, uncertain of my direction.

'It would be perfect,' I confided later to Howard, 'if only he could master interviews. It's a pity you aren't in charge of the travel agency, or he'd just have to walk into the road.'

Howard grinned. 'Has he tried having interview training or anything like that?'

'It's a bit late for all that,' I said. 'It's this week.'

'Well.' Howard put down his glass and drummed on his

knees with that energy a project always gave him. 'Let's see if we can make it happen.'

He had me drive him the next day to the travel agency in Finchley. I sat in the Mercedes for twenty minutes or so. He emerged with one of his schoolboy grins and told me not to ask any questions. Three days later Ed phoned me. He had got the job and was thrilled. I did not ask any questions.

∞

That time at the beginning of the nineteen-nineties, when Ella had just been appointed, I recall now as the golden age of the Alpha. It is one thing to succeed in the first place, but quite another to emerge from the shadow cast by a tragedy as we did. Agatha and I worked together like lifelong conspirators. I reeled off the train times, I directed people to obscure restaurants, returned lost property, found out the results of overseas football matches. Agatha helped the man bring in the newspapers, carrying the pile on her head; she counselled a young man in the smoking room who was upset about some lady and threatening to throw himself off the top balcony. After a whisky with her, he reconsidered his plans and ended up going home with somebody else.

All this time we carried on guessing the gender of the next person to check in, and I kept the running score on a page at the back of the guest ledger – which, once more, was always full to capacity.

And then there was Ella. On the day she arrived for their first session, Chas paced the atrium for hours. He asked for the papers to be read to him, as usual, but hardly seemed to take anything in. Instead he was preoccupied with what he did not know. 'What if she asks about the Ancient Romans? I only remember about three of the emperors. I can't even remember their dates. I know they ate dormice and that's about it.'

'Funny idea to do that!' said Agatha. 'Rather have beef!'

This sort of thing went on all morning.

'What if there's some really easy sum like twelve sixteens,' he lamented, running a hand through his hair which had grown rather thick and floppy like Howard's, 'and I panic and she thinks I'm stupid and makes me sing songs?'

It was only at lunchtime that Howard put a stop to this. 'Now, look, mate,' he said firmly. 'You're not going to get the Spanish Inquisition.'

'I don't even know what *that* is,' Chas said.

'Ella,' said Howard, 'is not here to test you. She knows already you're the real deal. Right, Captain?'

'Oh, she went on and on about you the other week,' Sarah-Jane confirmed. 'She loves you. I mean – not like *we* love you. But she thinks you're marvellous.'

'Which you are,' Howard said.

By the time Ella arrived, Chas seemed more confident,

though he was still practically hopping about as she reported to the desk.

'Welcome back to Hotel Alpha!' said Agatha.

'Thank you for coming,' said Chas, and added: 'I see we're in for a '92 election.'

'Sorry?' Ella bit her lip.

'They think the Tories will put it off till '92,' Chas informed her.

'Gosh,' said Ella, 'you're well ahead of me.'

She was a very pretty young woman, with dark hair which she had dyed blonde, not entirely convincingly. She gave us a friendly wink and followed Chas into the Yorks' quarters.

'Your perfume is very strong,' he said.

'Oh dear,' Ella laughed, 'I may have overdone it.' Chas said something else, and the two of them went off laughing like old friends.

Almost from that moment it was as if Ella had pressed some button to transform Chas on the spot. She herself seemed just as happy, too: as well she might be, with what Howard was paying her. When they emerged from their lessons, they were always laughing. Chas no longer walked as if he were a soap-bubble and there were spikes all around.

That winter, a number of countries declared independence from the Soviet Union, which meant new capitals whose announcement Chas awaited with glee. A night came, a fortnight or so before Christmas, which was so cold we might have been in Russia ourselves. The bar and restaurant were down to a few late, low-volume lingerers: Mike Swan, the hotel critic, was spinning off travel anecdotes to a group of rapt hoteliers. In the smoking room was a depressed board-game inventor who was struggling to repeat the successes of his early career.

'I've tried everything,' he told me. 'I've just designed a game where you're a farmer and have to graduate from a smallholding to a full business supplying supermarkets. I mean, who wouldn't want to play that?'

'It sounds terrific fun,' I succeeded in agreeing. 'Best of luck with it.'

We did a lot of wishing people luck, I mused on my way out; sometimes it seemed to come true, and sometimes of course we never saw them again. At its first contact with my face, the grip of the night air quickly bullied all such thoughts away. It took a couple of crucial moments to retighten the scarf round my neck; as I reached the stop, I could see my bus pulling away. I scuttled down a side road towards an alternative stop. The shelter was crowded. A young man spat gum onto the pavement an inch from my shoes, and another held a Walkman which sent music hissing distractingly through his headphones. It took a few moments to notice, among this murky assembly, a buxom woman huddled in the corner.

'Why I'm seeing you here, but never before!' said Agatha with pleasure.

I explained the situation. 'How long does it take to get back to Hornchurch from here?'

Agatha grinned. 'Hour, maybe hour and a half. I got the Bible. There's plenty of it to go. There' a multitude of pages, man.'

It would be two or three separate buses, and there were people on some of these buses you would not want to spend an hour and a half with. I looked past her smile to the weary, rumpled figure I had seen before she noticed me.

'Why don't I get the Mercedes and drive you home?'

We headed back to the Alpha, where the overnight valet brought the Mercedes out of its sleep. As I eased it out onto the road, Agatha leaned forward and touched the gleaming dashboard as gingerly as if it were china. 'Lovely car. Winston, my boy, he wanted to have a Mercedes. I look into buying him one.' She laughed. 'But we had to choose a bicycle instead.'

After the rare mention of her son, we drove in unaccustomed silence. A turn-off next to a clump of winter-wasted trees brought us out by a housing block, the sort put up in a hurry in the aftermath of war. In the entrance hall it was dead dark. 'Light's gone a little time ago,' Agatha apologized. The smell of urine slunk in the stairwell as I followed her; I had to put out an arm against the wall, like Chas. We came to a door in a warped frame which opened into a single, nearly empty room. Adjacent was a kitchen barely bigger than the Alpha's lifts.

'Bathroom is upstair. People share.'

She made tea while I sat on a patched-up sofa. Music of a violent kind throbbed through the ceiling above. The radiator produced the occasional clanking noise but offered no heat. A silver-framed photograph showed Winston in his fatigues, offering a twinkling grin. There was a horror in knowing what the smiling boy in the picture did not. Perhaps it was this that spurred me on.

'Look here, Agatha,' I said, gesturing about me. 'This is not good enough. I mean – and I hate to be so frank – but for what we pay you …'

'Me and Winston live here when he first went in the army,' said Agatha. 'I had a job, you see, not far from here. I don' like to leave it just now.'

But it was more than a decade since Winston had been killed in Belfast. As I returned the Mercedes to its foxhole, and then climbed finally onto the bus to Muswell Hill, the image of the squalid little flat was still in front of my eyes. Pattie was long asleep as I visited the fridge for my ham. I undressed in the dark and lay wide awake next to her, thinking about the army, about having my clothes thrown in the creek as a prank, being called a piece of s--- for finishing last in a running race. I imagined with an almost physical pain how I would feel if Ed disappeared into such a place and never returned.

That beaten-up frame reminded me of Room 25 on our second floor. Though it was a perfectly ordinary room, it had always been the scene of odd happenings. A member of the

Rolling Stones had hidden from the police in the wardrobe there; one of our chambermaids had fallen in love with a guest after mistakenly taking a room-service tray; and most recently a man had slammed the door with such force that it came off its hinges. The door was still not quite right, and so I tended not to put guests in 25 these days. I had once recently made it available to Ella when she'd asked, somewhat shiftily, if there was any-where she could use to 'entertain a friend'. I had told her after-wards that if the unnamed gentleman ever visited again, she only had to ask for the key. And now I saw an opportunity to put it to good use again.

'Listen,' I suggested one evening, half an hour before Agatha was due to leave. 'Why don't you clock off now and go for . . . well, have a sit-down, or a bath, perhaps?'

The way I proposed it, awkwardly and out of nowhere, she was certain to laugh. 'What you're talking about? Where the bath, man? It's wrapped under the Christmas tree?'

'This room is all yours,' I said, handing over the chunky key. 'Help yourself.'

'Don' be preposterous,' she said. 'You check Howard about this?'

'Oh, he won't mind,' I said, waving her away with the sort of expansive arm movement you might have associated with the man himself. I watched her sashay through the atrium towards the back staircase with the particular momentum she had: ungainly yet possessed of a certain elegance, an inevitability, you might say. She looked back once, just before going out of my sight, and gave me a dazzling smile.

It is hard to say why it felt as if there were something covert about this, and why I gradually began to act that way. There is no doubt Howard would have approved if I had told him: the hotel's history was full of gestures like this. But he was away somewhere, and so I did not. Agatha stayed in Room 25 the next night, and the next. By Christmas this had become a fairly regular occurrence. Agatha never assumed that it would continue forever, and even if she had, it really amounted to nothing. Nobody was losing out. A room not suitable for guests was being used by someone who needed it. That was all.

All the same, it meant that now there was a secret. I had harboured a few secrets for Howard in my time, but never in twenty-seven years kept one from him. This seemed an innocuous way to end that record. It was one person in one room. But of course every room in a hotel is connected to every other.

∞

The Alpha had always had its own moods. It absorbed the various excitements and fears of the individuals under its roof and exhaled a mixture of them all. If there were a shocking or momentous news event, I could very often sense it without even leaving my desk. Something in the quality of the chatter from the bar and balconies, even the texture of the light as it streamed through the roof's glass panel and drifted about the atrium, seemed to change.

On Christmas Eve the mood was always somewhat restless; everyone was anxious to be somewhere else. Howard and Sarah-Jane spent the day putting up decorations at homeless shelters. Salvation Army singers appeared in the morning, and vanished again. In the afternoon we had the carols from King's College playing in the bar. By four or five most guests had checked out and gone to King's Cross or down to Waterloo, to be freighted across the country to their families. And on Christmas Day itself, all that remained in the hotel – apart from the Yorks themselves – would be a lonely sprinkling of strangers: visitors to London from foreign cultures, perhaps, or people with a reason to avoid the festivities. A couple of years ago a lady had stayed with us on Christmas Day to take revenge on her unfaithful husband. She lasted until five o'clock before Sarah-Jane found her sobbing in the bar and took her into their home for turkey sandwiches.

This year, Howard had planned an event for Boxing Day. The atrium would host two hundred people: fifty or so wealthy invited guests, and the remainder made up of homeless people. During the event, Howard would hold a whip-round in which the rich people would pay for the poor by means of an auction of worthless items which they were encouraged to bid excessive amounts for. As usual, I had my doubts about all this; as usual, I threw myself into preparations, telephoning the man at

Fortnum & Mason to order food, and using my joke about the postcode. We went through our biannual review of the news.

'Terrible business about that chap in New Zealand who went mad with a gun.'

'Terrible.'

'Not sure I trust that Yeltsin, do you?'

'Well, time will tell.'

'Hotel very much back in business?'

'Bigger and better than ever.'

'Well, I shall speak to you some time next year.'

When I put the receiver down, it was nine o'clock: I headed for the smoking room for a glass of whisky. But this year, somebody had beaten me to it: music was wafting from behind the frosted glass of the door, and inside, Agatha was jigging about the place. The song was about diamonds on somebody's shoes. She put out an arm as if offering me a dance in some long-gone era of politesse. She was wearing a billowing black dress with a plunging necklace; her breasts swung boulder-like behind it.

'I don't know the song, I'm afraid … '

Agatha put a finger to my lips for a moment, as Pattie used to do, and began to steer me, diagonally like a chess bishop, in a waltz. My cheeks were warm. When the dance was over, we looked at each other. My face reddened with her scrutiny.

'Thank you so much for the room,' she said. 'So nice.'

She leaned to grasp my arm again as a new song began, one about Africa. I broke free with a little more force than I had intended. Agatha looked put out for a second; then she resumed her dancing, thrusting out her hips and belly, the aliveness of her seeming to fill the room entirely. I poured out a drink and sat in the corner armchair, glancing up every now and again to see her moving as if there were a hundred other dancers in the room.

By the following afternoon I had ensured this was as far from my mind as all the rest of the year's business with Agatha. I certainly did not care to think about how she was spending the day, alone in that single room in the east of the city.

In our house all was very much as usual. Pattie began chopping vegetables almost before dawn; the smell of roasting meat filled the hall. Caroline and Brian arrived at noon. There was a game of charades, something Ed normally enjoyed because of its generally non-verbal nature; but this time he got into a terrible tangle trying to mime a film. He threw his hands around, seemed to be pedalling a bicycle, to be climbing something. The living room descended into greater and greater hysteria.

'What the hell is it!' Caroline managed to say, her face streaming.

'Oh, good heavens,' said Ed in mock chagrin, 'it's *Around the World in 80 Days*. I was miming the Pyramids, the Colosseum, the Sydney Opera House ... ' – and that was as much as he could explain before everyone disintegrated into mirth again. 'I suppose, I suppose – I suppose it was a little ambitious,' said Ed, laughing as much as anyone else.

Later, in the soporific lull between dinner and dessert,

Caroline announced that she had 'something to share'. I felt Pattie stiffen; her hand crept under the white tablecloth to perch on my knee. The news was what she had desperately hoped to hear.

'You are going to be grandparents!' said Caroline.

This was a festive announcement, all right! I got to my feet and applauded as if we were at the Proms and slapped Brian on the back and finally took Caroline by the arm.

'Perhaps,' I said, 'even if I haven't always been the most exciting father, I shall be a decent gramps.'

'Oh, Dad,' said Caroline, a little tearful. 'You've been wonderful, and you'll be wonderful again.'

That night, of course, Pattie talked of nothing else. Did I think they would have a boy or a girl? (It was difficult to say at this point, I told her.) Ought we to make Ed's room into a nursery, or wait until we knew what colour it should be? What sort of names might they go for? (Again, I felt this depended upon the gender.) Did I fancy they would have more children after this one?

If I could have seen the future, I would have told her: he will be called Christopher, he will be a boy of placid temperament, straight hair, studious bearing, a little like a young Chas; he will love coming to visit us, playing a board game featuring hippos which requires us all to pound away at levers, his favourite food will be jam sandwiches, and he will make us both as proud as Punch. The present was my business, though, not the future. I lay looking at the ceiling, registering with something like guilt my impatience to be back at the Alpha, ready for the big event.

I caught a bus very early in the morning. Agatha was already there; I shuddered to think what time she had left home. While the rest of London woke to a grey sluggishness, to hangover and anticlimax, the Alpha was bracing itself for action. We jam-packed the atrium with long tables fetched up from the cellar; ran strings of fairy lights around the balconies. Well before the notional start time of twelve o'clock, the needy had begun to arrive. Their faces were ruddy with burst veins, or else sallow almost to the point of transparency; they had missing teeth, yellowed fingers; they smelled of cigarettes and drink and of lives lived against the grain. They sang lustily and swore and belched. The wealthy guests arrived later and we ushered them to the bar, where they were glad-handed by Howard and peeped out nervously at the uproar.

Chas's favourite Christmas present had come from Ella: it was a program which allowed the computer to speak in a human voice. It meant that he could type words and have them read back to him, and so judge how accurate he had been.

'I spent the whole of Christmas Day experimenting with it,' he told me.

'Yes, the rest of your presents might as well not have existed, eh?' said Sarah-Jane, patting Chas's head. Something in the quality of her smile – a certain restraint, a bottled frustration – made me fear suddenly for Ella. Sarah-Jane might not have been

Chas's mother to begin with, but she certainly felt that way now, and she would not look kindly on a rival. Ella had done a marvellous job of getting Chas to trust her. Now she had to ensure it was not too good a job. There were things she still did not understand about the Hotel Alpha.

At about one, everyone sat down for a meal. The noise of all the diners, full-throated and anarchic, wafted up towards the skylight. Cutlery was dropped; toasts were proposed, songs sung, and when Howard rose to give an after-dinner speech there was a loud, ragged cheer which made Chas beam and Sarah-Jane roll her eyes.

After this came the auction. The first lot was a porcelain toilet-roll holder which looked like a dog, and bore the inscription *Dogs leave pawprints on your heart.*

'Let's start with five hundred,' Howard hectored. 'Am I bid five hundred? I am, because I'm going to bid it myself! Five hundred f---ing quid! For this piece of c--p! Which I already own, people!'

There was a lot more of this bravado, and everybody got caught up in it, myself included: I hardly even noticed the colourful language. Howard's audacity teased seven hundred pounds out of Mike Swan, who went up in his green jacket to collect the 'prize', while the audience whistled and whooped. Swan came back to join me at the top table, grinning at his own rashness.

'Seven hundred pounds!' I marvelled.

'Luckily,' he said, 'the old *Guide* is paying me pretty well at the moment. As long as people keep wanting to stay in hotels, I shouldn't come to regret this. Mind you,' he added, 'not sure why I bought something for the home. Hotels are my home.'

'I don't see much wrong with that,' I remarked.

The shows of extravagance escalated; there was a pair of lederhosen which fetched nearly a thousand despite the manifest falseness of Howard's claim that they had been worn by Mozart. Howard was in his element here: he bathed in the audience's laughter, looking bigger and taller and more youthful every minute. Then, as he embarked on a particularly outrageous auction – a ghastly full-length portrait of a nude by a talentless artist which brought ribald hollers from the onlookers – there was a strange electronic noise. Agatha and I looked at each other, puzzled. The noise had the insistent rhythm of an alarm.

'Hello?' said someone loudly into the falling quiet.

We scanned the atrium until we could see the speaker. It was Lara Krohl, the South African now charged with various mysterious operations to do with publicizing the hotel. She had produced from her handbag an item about the length of a brick, though somewhat thinner. It appeared to be a walkie-talkie.

'I'm at the Alpha. Yah, at Howard's thing,' she said, seemingly quite indifferent to the curious looks of the crowd. 'I'll call you back.'

She lowered the gadget from her ear and put it back in her bag, meeting the room's stare without embarrassment.

'I think after that,' said Howard, 'a pretty big bid would be appropriate ... '

Lara Krohl raised her hands in a show of good nature and made a huge offer, which was instantly matched by Howard. The two of them traded friendly insults across the room and the carnival went on. Agatha shook her head and, partly in jest, grasped the little crucifix brooch pinned to her blouse.

'I' never seen a telephone quite o' that kind! You, Graham?'

I confirmed I had not. 'And if it means that people can hold their private conversations wherever they like – well, I'm not sure I want to see it again, either, thank you.'

Agatha nodded and rolled her eyes. But most people there, I felt, had not seen the incident for what it was: an intrusion. They had looked at the portable telephone and wondered, not why anyone would wish to interrupt the whole room in such a manner, but: how can I get one of those?

꩜ 4 ꩜

CHAS

I knew about Ella's present, the computer program that could speak back to you, ahead of time: we'd chosen it together, even though Sarah-Jane said it was not the point of Christmas to do that. It was called 'Speech Pro', and after tearing off the wrapping paper I immediately badgered JD to set it up on the computer: something he agreed to when he realized the potential for entertainment from swear words. The first phrase uttered by the computer's toneless voice was 'I am a bender'. I laughed along uneasily for a while. By teatime his attention had long been stolen by some other toy, and I had the computer to myself.

Howard and Sarah-Jane were on the sofa, chuckling at *Only Fools and Horses* in a lulled, dutiful way. Sarah-Jane had thrown together the lunch remains into a buffet which only JD was interested in. I went back to our room, sat in the low chair and began to type.

Chas (third key from left, bottom row; sixth along, middle row; and so on) *York lives in the Hotel Alpha.*

It took four goes before the phrase read back by the computer sounded exactly as I hoped. When finally it was 'York' and not 'Tork' that came out of the speakers, 'Alpha' and not 'Aloha', the excitement in my stomach was about more than a single victory. I'd been typing phrases into the computer for a while now, ever since Ella had figured out that it would remove the huge obstacles that writing presented to me: the fact that I didn't know the shapes of letters, had no mental reference for the way they combined into words. I was already quite good at typing. But until now I'd always needed Ella, or Howard, to tell me whether I had got it right or not. Now I could do without anybody's help. The computer could talk to me.

∞

From her first session, when my heart skipped at the presence in the atrium of that crushed-candle perfume, Ella's role in my life was to free me from some of the rules which had bound it so far.

'So, tell me about yourself,' she said, setting down what might be a textbook with a promisingly heavy thump as we sat for the first time at the living-room table.

'I have no vision at all, not even to tell dark from light,' I recited with a sigh, 'and it's not true that your other senses get better when you're blind, but you use them better. I have this thing called imagine-seeing,' I added, 'where I feel a sight like it was a smack, or something hot. And that's about it.'

'OK, but I wasn't really asking about your blindness. I don't really give a toss about that. I want to know about *you*. What you want to learn. What you want to do with your life.'

The skin rose under my shirtsleeves and at the back of my neck.

'I haven't really thought about what to do with my life,' I admitted. More accurately, it had never occurred to me there was anything I could do with it.

'Well,' said Ella, 'time to start.'

The routine of her visits came to feel like the backbone of my life. Howard had bought me a talking watch which declared the time at the press of a button, and in the moments before Ella's arrival each morning I prowled the atrium, pressing the button again and again. She always seemed to bring the weather in with her: the heat of a summer day, the tang of rain. She let me hang her coat and scarf in the hall. The coat retained the smell of her perfume so deeply that it was almost like holding her for a moment.

We took on most of the regular school subjects, leaving aside PE by mutual consent, despite Howard's offer to get a long-jump pit installed in the atrium. He was probably joking, Ella said; probably, I agreed. When she left, after sessions which were sometimes a couple of hours and sometimes lasted till late afternoon, I kept away the heavy feeling of time by throwing myself into whatever tasks she left as homework.

Howard read me novels. I listened to performances of Shakespeare which Ella had taped from the radio. She and I solved maths problems by talking them through, step by step, the numbers suspended on imaginary scales in my head. We tackled elementary physics the same way. Soon I could analyse a poem read out to me or orally decode simultaneous equations. All this was probably some way ahead of my contemporaries. But by another measure I was so far behind them that I might as well have been wearing nappies.

It was the writing. Where was I meant to start? We spent a miserable morning with Ella holding my hand on the pen and manipulating it into feeble-feeling slopes and loops, but even then I couldn't see the letters to replicate them, and there was no visual register of words to check them against. I lost my temper and told Sarah-Jane to go away when she came in to check on us, feeling embarrassed by my incompetence as if I'd been caught out doing something wrong.

Then Ella thought of using the computer.

'Right, mister. You can learn a sequence of letters, can't you?'

'Of course.'

'Repeat after me. Q-W-E-R-T-Y-U-I-O-P.'

'Q-W-E-R-T-Y-U-I-O-P.'

'Wow, you're good.'

'It's just remembering.'

Very quickly I had memorized the standard keyboard's three rows of letters, like a spy drilled with a code. Ella led me out of the living room. It was both thrilling and alarming to have her at large in the house. I sat at the computer in our bedroom which gave out its bleeps and moans as it fired gradually into life, and used the wait to collect myself, trying not to think about what our room must look like, how childish it must seem to her, the embarrassing items that were probably lying everywhere. Ella positioned three of my left-hand fingers gently on the keys.

'Right. This is your Q. This is A. This is Z. So if you go three along from the Q, what letter are you on?'

It was easy; just a memory game. 'R.'

'OK. Type me an R. Very good. Now, type "Chas".'

I wrote VRAS at my first attempt, then CJAS; got it right on the next one. We played like this for ten or fifteen minutes. Letters, words, all writing on the page had been part of the dark ninety-nine per cent of my universe, but it turned out that they could be codified. Somebody had matched up the letters with pressable buttons. It was within my power to express whatever I wanted after all. Thanks to computers, and thanks to my tutor.

From now on, as soon as I had handed Ella her coat and listened to her near-noiseless shuffle out through the atrium, I always headed immediately to the computer, where I would practise writing words and get JD to read them back to me. We had more complex games to play now, relying on strategy rather than the slaughter of cosmic visitors: games called 'Sim City' and 'Railroad Tycoon' which made us into the commanders of a town or a transit empire. I still enjoyed this kind of thing, the earnest discussions of our fictitious subjects' needs, the clandestine sessions when we were meant to be asleep. But nothing was as important as writing those words. What I really wanted from computers was not what JD wanted, an escape to a fantasy universe. To me, the machine was pretty much the opposite: a portal to the real world.

∽

Gradually, and much to my own surprise, I started to go outside. The whole family, including Graham and Ella, attended a performance of *A Midsummer Night's Dream*. The theatre foyer smelled of money and shoe leather and buzzed with fussy discussion. The pages of the programme, raised to my nose, gave off an almost unbearably delicious smell of newness. A little hum went round the place when the play was about to start, nervous giggles and shushing. I tried to concentrate on the words and not on the smell of Ella's perfume, or the low, knowing way she muttered out her laughs.

'I can't always tell what's going on,' I confessed to JD in the interval.

'Nor can I, and I can bloody see it.'

The trip had been organized by Lara Krohl; her PR company had helped Howard get the tickets at notice so short it would have been beyond anyone else. To thank her, Howard took everyone to a restaurant after the play, and we ended up in the Alpha Bar. It was long past bedtime for me and JD, but it was a Friday night, as Howard pointed out to a half-heartedly censorious Sarah-Jane.

All I wanted was to stay near Ella, and at a certain point of the night I followed her and Lara Krohl to the smoking room with what seemed a very adult sense of conspiracy and rebellion, even though Howard had said it was all right. I could imagine-see the little flaps of flame flickering up from the matches, the clouds of smoke they blew out. They discussed Howard, Lara once or twice beginning to make observations which Ella seemed to snuff out.

'What are you going to do, Chas, when you grow up?' asked Lara Krohl.

'What do you mean?'

'Well, do you want to be a writer? Or something to do with maths? Maybe an accountant in the City … ?'

She was, as Neil Kinnock had recently said about Major, obviously not in touch with reality.

'I don't go outside,' I explained, 'so I'll work in the hotel.'

'You don't go outside at all?'

'Not really. I mean, tonight we did, but generally I avoid it. I went to the zoo once but it wasn't a success. That's why there was a fuss when I tried to chase you that time, to tell you the capital.'

'The funny thing is,' said Ella, 'you might find by the time you need a job, you can actually get away with never leaving your house. We were just talking about this, Lara and I.'

'Yah, we were,' Lara agreed. Their exchanges contained a tentative note; I sensed that it was only the smoking that had brought them together here. My cleverness at realizing this produced a sort of internal swagger. 'Give it a few years, everything is going to be on computers. Do you use a computer?'

'I can type pretty well.'

'Virtual reality, that's what they call it,' Lara interrupted. 'Someone was telling me about this thing called the Internet.'

That was the first time I heard the word. 'It's a way of linking computers around the world,' Lara explained, 'so you can all see the same thing, wherever you are. Like with TV. Give it ten years, maybe a little more – ' there was that rasping delivery of hers again, 'yars' – 'and you'll be able to ask computers any question you like. Like an encyclopaedia, but—'

'But who will have told it in the first place?' asked a humorous voice. Graham had come in, as he always did, without ceremony.

'Sorry?' said Lara Krohl with a note of impatience; I saw she was fonder of interrupting people than being interrupted.

'I imagine,' said Graham, 'that however clever computers get at trotting out information, humans will still have to tell them all that information in the first place. A computer is hardly going to review a hotel or predict the weather on its own, is it?'

The next morning, the mood at breakfast was a little subdued; for once there was no chatter from the radio, and Howard seemed to absent himself unusually quickly with a remark about a conference he had to get to. When I came out of the bathroom, Sarah-Jane was waiting. She asked me to sit down at the kitchen table. There was some faint noise from the atrium, followed by Agatha's cackle, and I wished to be there. This felt too much like the time they told me about the fire.

Sarah-Jane put her hand on my left knee.

'We always want what's best for you, Chas. You know that, don't you?'

'Yes.'

'That lady, Lara. I don't want you talking to her without me or Howard there. All right?'

'Why not?'

Sarah-Jane crossed one leg over another with the familiar rustle of skirt. 'She knows a lot of journalists. And journalists – some of them are people who might not want the best for you, like we do. They want to write things about Howard, or the hotel. So ... '

'Lara is a friend of Ella's, though.'

'Ella – ' I heard Sarah-Jane's voice inch a degree higher and her inflection slide northwards – 'doesn't always necessarily think about the ... what we call the bigger picture.'

'I don't give a toss,' I said. There was a silence pure enough for me to discern the gurgling of water in the pipes that ran down the outside of the building.

'Where did you get that expression?'

'I don't know.'

'I think *I* know,' said Sarah-Jane.

It took me half a minute to muster a reply to this, and it rang hollow in the air. I realized that she had left me alone at the table.

As it turned out, Sarah-Jane herself admitted that she'd been needlessly cautious. Lara was, as I had thought, a friend, not a foe. As the hotel's head of PR, her job was to keep journalists on our side. Howard trusted her, and Ella seemed to like her too. The matter was soon forgotten by everyone else, but it kept an unwelcome place in my memory. What was there to write about Howard, or the hotel? What did Sarah-Jane mean by 'the bigger picture'? It went in the file of things I didn't understand, a file which only seemed to get bigger.

It was disappointing to learn that knowledge wasn't the same as understanding. Knowledge I had, for sure. A year into Ella's tuition, having reached what had seemed the huge milestone of ten years old, I knew more than I would once have dreamed possible. I not only knew how many people lived in China, and what it meant that China had a Communist government, but I could make the philosophical argument that there was no way anyone could know for sure that China existed unless they'd been there. Since nobody had – not even Howard, certainly not Graham who had barely been as far as Chinatown – we had no empirical proof of it, so it made no difference if you were sighted or blind.

'Do you see what I mean?' I jabbered at JD, who was shuffling around on his top bunk, his mind quite likely on a very different subject. 'Even though other people can see, they still *don't* see ninety-nine per cent of stuff with their own eyes. They rely on others' word. They don't *know* China exists.'

'It definitely does,' he said in a sleepy voice. 'It was on TV.'

'But I mean … oh, never mind. I'm just trying to make the point that other people aren't better than me.'

'I definitely agree with that bit,' said JD.

At night, when I had taken the eleven times table up to a thousand and exhausted the mental map of QWERTY sequences, I sometimes fell into thinking about that conversation with Lara. *You'll be able to ask computers any question you like.* Until recently I would have said that Howard could answer all my questions perfectly well, and if not him then Graham, and failing that there was the encyclopaedia. Now, in the anteroom between childhood and the teenage years that were already claiming JD, I realized there were questions of a category that made them hard to look up and harder still to ask out loud.

I wondered about my father. It was odd that – as I understood it – there was a man out there somewhere who had been my dad before Howard met me. Wherever this man was, he was not in the Alpha, and beyond these walls, it didn't matter much to me if someone were down the road or in Peking. Still, it would be nice to know who he was, even if it was just a name, and whether he was interested in seeing me. It was curiosity, not yearning: there was nothing to yearn for when Howard gave me all the fathering I needed, but the curiosity would not disappear altogether. It whispered at me on long nights; it was there in the swing of the Alpha's doors, in the faint breath of the idea that one day he might walk in.

That curiosity also had other matters to wrestle with. JD now made reference to women and sex as if we were boringly familiar with the subject and had been all along. He talked in bed about how sexy Ella was.

'She wears these dresses – you can sort of see her breasts, see the shape of them. And the way she walks! You are so lucky to spend all that time with her.'

Less lucky, I wanted to retort, that I couldn't see or picture any of it. Even so, I felt that I already knew every detail of Ella that he reported to me from her smell and her voice alone. My feelings about her, over a couple of years' teaching, had developed from puppy-like enthusiasm to something tenser. Occasionally, when JD was asleep, I would run my hands over my body, the areas Sarah-Jane described as 'private parts', which were nonetheless more of a mystery to me than to her. I knew more about the Hanging Gardens of Babylon or the properties of a regular triangle than I did about my own penis. I was starting to think that wasn't the ideal way round.

As Ella became a more and more fixed part of my life, I did manage to hold the odd conversation of a personal nature. I asked one day what she was planning for her birthday on the fifth of June.

'Oh, nothing big. Going out for a few drinks near where I live with some mates.'

She lived – I knew – somewhere called Manor House, which sounded appropriately regal. I tried to imagine how going out into the world, drinking alcohol in a place of your choosing, could seem like 'nothing big'.

'And is your … your husband going?'

Ella laughed in the low and slightly indulgent way which always made me wonder whether I'd said something clever enough to amuse her, or just been comically naive. This time it was clearly the latter. 'I don't have a husband, I'm afraid.'

'I mean – boyfriend?'

'Not even.' She patted me on the shoulder and I felt the middle of my body warm in a manner that was lovely and awful. She gave an exaggerated sigh. 'You're the closest thing I've got, Chas.'

I knew this was a joke, and that it was best to concentrate on the lessons themselves and not the person giving them. I practised typing for two hours a day or more, writing little pieces about the news which Graham and Agatha had read out to me, reports for Howard to read when he came home from his conferences. I was good at it now, and fast. My eleventh birthday rolled around in spring, and the 1992 election I had sagely predicted was set for the night beforehand: Howard and Sarah-Jane agreed I could stay up and watch the results come in. 'God knows,' said Sarah-Jane, 'you know more about it than I do, pet.'

'Everyone knows more about it than you, Captain,' Howard teased her. 'You're the only one who thinks Kinnock is going to win.'

We sat on the sofa as well-educated men delivered the news in small chunks separated by great intervals of inconclusive chatting. Howard had been drinking beer, Sarah-Jane and I were on cocoa; when midnight passed, they opened a bottle of champagne and gave me a taste. It fizzed on my tongue and swam sourly down my throat, producing a grimace which made the two of them laugh. Howard ruffled my hair. 'To our magnificent son,' he said, and their glasses chinked together with mine. I fell asleep some time around two, by which time we knew that the present government was going to hold on to power, as Howard had predicted – or wished; you could never tell the difference. Sarah-Jane muttered that she would die before we saw Labour back in. Howard said she had some years left in her yet, and the couch creaked as the two of them play-fought. I curled up into a ball and dreamt woozily that I was at some sort of university, receiving a qualification which I showed proudly to Howard.

There was an Ella session planned for the next day as usual,

birthday or not. Graham and Agatha were preoccupied talking
to a man called Saunders who had come in to pay a bill he apparently owed. This had caused a lot of laughter and excitement.
'After twenty-five years,' said Graham, 'well, you can see why we
were starting to worry a little bit. Ha, ha!'

'I told you I'd drop in with it,' said the man. 'Just one of
those jobs that you don't get round to, you know?'

There was more laughter; Howard came over, as did Mr
Swan the hotel reviewer, who promised to write about the incident in his next book. Graham found the original ledger where
he'd recorded the man as a guest in the sixties. Agatha, still
hooting, went off to direct the housekeeping trollies with Mrs
Davey: the two women rumbled past me as if they themselves
were on wheels. All this was of limited interest and had distracted everyone from my birthday. I was just about to embark
on a minor sulk when the doors opened. There was that tang of
new air in the atrium, and I heard the flat footsteps that never
failed to accelerate my heart.

'Just the man I wanted to see!'

Ella's hand was on my arm, the lurking aroma of her perfume filling the space around me. 'I've got your present, but you
need to come out with me to get it. Ready?'

It rained on our faces. The pavement fizzed with a wet-
London smell I remembered from my few previous sorties.
Ella described what we were passing: grey square build-
ings, backed-up queues of cabs at lights. A siren came from

somewhere, and I flinched and snatched at her arm. She laughed, squeezing my shoulder. My dick, I thought to myself, felt like the CN Tower in Toronto: 553 metres high, built for communications and as a show of Canada's manufacturing prowess. In a doorway there was a confusion of bassy chugging pop music, and a smell of newness.

'This is Dixons,' Ella informed me. 'And we are at the counter ... '

She broke off and addressed someone. 'Just picking up,' she said. I had a prickly inkling of what might be coming.

'Put your hands out.'

I did, shifting my weight from foot to foot. A box was lowered into my clutches.

'This,' she said, 'is your very own laptop computer.'

'It can't be!'

'It's about time, don't you think?'

I was almost too delighted to say thank you properly, and I repeated it twice just to be on the safe side. Ella said we should pop to a cafe before going back, and offered to take the laptop in its bag. No, no, I said, I'll carry it. I hardly even noticed the part about the cafe until we were there and Ella was ordering doughnuts and cups of tea. The plastic bag, weighed down with its priceless cargo, stayed next to my shin where I could feel it.

As we headed back towards the hotel, it was almost too much, the cocktail of wonders: the new computer, the suddenly unthreatening hugeness of London around us, the smell of her coat and the rough touch of its sleeves. My dick hung stiff like the Hindenburg, the biggest dirigible ever built. Walking back into the Alpha, I felt so glutted with happiness that I almost expected congratulations. Instead there was trouble.

'Where the hell have you been?' Sarah-Jane demanded. 'Do you know how worried—'

'We just nipped out for a doughnut and a laptop,' I said.

'A doughnut! What about your birthday tea?'

'I'll still be hungry.'

'And what exactly is a laptop,' asked Sarah-Jane, 'when it's at home?'

'A laptop is like a portable computer,' I said. 'It's an incredible thing to have. They think in a few years it'll be really common. It means I can—'

'It must have been expensive,' Sarah-Jane said, addressing Ella. 'You really shouldn't have done that.'

'Oh, it's fine, I … I know someone in Dixons,' said Ella, 'and anyway, it's fine.'

I got the impression the two of them were looking at each other in a not altogether pleasant way, and the feeling made me uncomfortable; I brushed past Sarah-Jane and went to the living room to sit and wait for Ella. We made our way through the lesson as if nothing had happened. I asked if Ella would stay for tea.

'I really don't think … I'm not sure I'm invited,' she said with a wry laugh.

'You're invited by me! It's my birthday, isn't it?'

She leant in and kissed me on my cheek. It felt as if someone had rested a hand against my groin.

'All right then. I'll sing you Happy Birthday, at least.'

But the party went on longer than that: it went on, in fact, beyond my own bedtime. Well after dark, I was still conscious of high, edgy laughter and chatter: first just the suggestion of it in the atrium, and then a cloudburst of noise as people spilled into our living room. I heard bottles being opened, comments and giggles and mock-outraged responses. Howard's bassy voice underpinned it all. Was Ella there? Part of me wanted to slip out of bed and join them. Another part felt a resistance to the whole thing, perhaps brought on by the feeling that what had started as my birthday was now something else, something beyond me. I buried my face in the pillow and thought about my new computer, and the rest of the night went by in half-heard dispatches. There was more laughter, and – though I could have dreamed it – spikes of irritable talk, even an argument which might have been about any one of the billion subjects I was still not the master of.

I would come to look back on that series of adventures – the election night, the trip out to get the laptop, and the unspecified activities of the birthday evening – for a long time to come, because from then on nothing was quite the same.

It took a few days to register that I had crossed some sort of a border, whatever it was. We went on a family trip to Yorkshire for the weekend to see Sarah-Jane's parents; it was a lot further outside than I generally cared to go, but I was able to spend almost the whole time in my room tapping at the computer, the function of which Sarah-Jane's parents could not understand at all. We'd hired a car rather than been driven by Graham, which was unusual, and we got back too late on Monday for an Ella session, so I went to the desk for the papers. But Graham seemed preoccupied – I could tell he was writing something with his scratchy fountain pen – and Agatha wasn't there at all.

'She has gone away for a little trip,' he said when I asked. His tone discouraged further questions. Something was not right about it, and about the atmosphere of the Alpha in general. Once or twice I heard Sarah-Jane on the phone, her voice agitated, the words maddeningly out of reach. Howard seemed to be away at conferences several nights in a row.

On a Wednesday morning I took Ella's coat to hang it up and noticed with surprise the absence of perfume. There was the sound of her scraping back a chair and sitting down; she cleared her throat and put a couple of books down on the table.

'How come you aren't wearing perfume?' I asked. 'And is it a different coat?'

It was as if I'd spoken a password. Ella's hand came out to

rest on top of mine. There was no sparking of the usual circuits inside me. Her skin was cold to the touch.

'Chas, listen. In a couple of weeks I'm going to America.'

'To Washington, DC? That's the capital, even though people think—'

'To New York.'

'How long for?'

'Well, that's the thing. I'm moving there permanently.'

Water gurgled in pipes; a heavy vehicle went by on the street outside with a genial engine roar.

'Why?' I asked.

'I need …'

But Ella's voice seemed to snag on something. She swallowed very loudly. Her hand squeezed mine. I realized she might be about to cry and experienced a feeling of total helplessness, or defeat.

'Is there something I should be doing—' I began.

'No, no, no. Oh, Chas.' She kept clearing her throat, but her voice was still high and wispy and so unlike her usual one that it was like an inferior actor was standing in for her. 'There's so much which I … it's hard to explain.'

'Try.'

'I need to – sometimes in a person's life they need to change something,' she said. 'A change of scenery.'

'I don't have any scenery,' I said rather bitterly, and regretted it: Ella began to sob. I reached out for her arm and she latched on to me, rubbing my shoulder in a comforting manner as if I were the one crying. Soon she collected herself. 'I can't be doing this here,' she muttered. 'I'm sorry. I'll pull myself together. It's fine. We'll be fine.'

I didn't want her to 'pull herself together', of course; what I wanted was to understand what was going on. I handed over the strange coat and listened to her leaving in a state of miserable confusion. I waited for JD to come home from his friend's house that night, expecting to stun him with the news. But the oddness was not even half over. He had an almost equally big bombshell waiting for me.

'Agatha's gone as well, you know.'

'What?'

'She left this week. Graham says he doesn't know why. She just went.'

I thought of her big laugh and her cheery hello in the morning, all of it snuffed out as if someone had turned off the radio. It was dumbfounding.

'She didn't even say goodbye.'

'There's no law that people have to say goodbye,' JD replied in a tone of scorn.

It was true. Adults made the rules of this world and they behaved as they chose. Until I understood more, this sort of thing could happen; people could disappear from my life as easily as they could slip out of the room, leaving me unawares and chatting on to nothing.

The door creaked in a manner which somehow suggested we had been overheard, and the room was filled with Howard. 'Aye-aye,' he said quietly, 'what's up here, then? Still awake?'

There was no tap-tapping, none of his tongue-clicking. My bed creaked as he perched on the edge of it.

'Ella's going,' I said, 'and Agatha has already gone, and no one even said.'

Howard hesitated for a telltale second before launching into his speech. 'Ella has been wonderful, I know, but America is an exciting place, and she obviously feels that this is a chance she can't turn down.'

'She knew so much about computers,' I said, resenting the forlorn way my voice came out, 'things like that—'

'We'll find someone who can take care of that stuff,' said Howard. Perhaps he would, I thought, feeling the force of his confidence as he slid down the bed and disarranged my hair.

'We'll get the best computers for you that we can,' he continued, 'the – what's it called? – the Internet, whatever you want.' His voice was back in a smooth groove now: this was home territory, visions and promises. 'I'll put the word out that we need someone of exceptional quality, someone to match you.'

'And what about Agatha?' asked JD in a rising tone, a challenge. I was appalled and a little excited by the silence which followed.

'Agatha,' said Howard, 'had personal reasons for going.'

'Like what?'

Howard snapped at him. 'Personal reasons, Jonathan, means we don't ask. Now, goodnight. Goodnight, both of you.'

He shut the door hard behind him, though the use of JD's full name had had almost as jarring an impact. I waited for JD to speak.

'It's not my fault this place is fucking weird,' he eventually muttered, his voice horribly fragile.

My last two lessons with Ella were conducted in a spirit of false brightness on both sides. Or perhaps it was only an act on my side; perhaps for Ella things really were bright enough, in spite of the performance she had made of not wanting to go. She had made a huge document to map out my ongoing studies, apparently a compilation of spider graphs and plans and photocopied government information sheets which she would entrust into Howard's hands.

'I don't want you on modernism too early,' she said. 'Not because you can't do it now; just because you'll get more out of it later. History – you should choose whether you want to go into the American Revolution next, or ... well, I've written it all down. You can take GCSEs with an oral invigilator these days, and that's something else I wanted to talk to you about, or to Howard. Anyway. I've left it in the file. And we'll write. We'll talk on the phone. Please don't see this as ... as some sort of final end.'

There was a fair bit more of this, but I couldn't listen to it. The care with which she'd sketched out my future only seemed to underline that she wouldn't be supervising it in person: I felt like an evacuee. When it was time, I went to fetch her coat. Howard and Sarah-Jane had bought her a bottle of champagne. She said that she would miss this place, her voice shaking; she said it had been like a home. I followed her out of the doors, where a car was humming in wait. She kissed me on the cheek; her face was wet. Sadness was like a gale trying to blow me off a cliff face.

'You're extraordinary, Chas. Look after yourself, all right? And come and see me. We'll go up the Empire State Building.'

She must have known how unlikely this was. Even to say such a thing, the kind of cheerless platitude a near-stranger might offer, she must already have disengaged from me. The final goodbye barely made it out of my mouth. I had a feeling close to certainty that I would never smell that perfume again.

The door crunched shut and the car pulled away as if there were nothing out of the ordinary going on. I realized suddenly the scarf was still hanging in the hall, and went to snatch it down. By the time I blundered out again, of course, the car was long gone.

In the sludge of time that separated me from sleep, I tried to put together everything that had happened. I thought back to

Agatha's behaviour, what I knew of it, in recent months, and to moments with Ella, her sometimes strained dealings with my family. As my talking watch gave its discouraging updates – 02:20, 03:12 – I tried to think of a link between them, a reason that would compel them both to leave. It was hopeless. After all, there could be any number of links between everybody and everything out there: looks, gestures, guilty expressions, all the patterns and rhythms of life. All plain to see, if you were one of the gigantic majority of people who could see. I couldn't; I relied on being told. Howard and Graham and Sarah-Jane had written the encyclopaedia of my life. If there was anything they didn't want me to know, I'd never know it.

That was all as it had always been, but recent events had made it clear exactly how powerless it left me. I had come a long way by trusting the people around me. They'd looked after everything. Perhaps in future I would have to train myself not to trust them quite so much.

The faint flame of subversion soon sputtered out in the long, long dark of the night. Thinking about Ella would only be a finger picking at the wound, and so I allowed myself to imagine something I never had before: that a doctor had somehow given me back my sight, and everything was laid out colourfully in front of me.

PART TWO

ා 5 ෬

GRAHAM

'The more things change, the more they stay the same.' A comforting phrase, but less so when expressed in reverse. At the beginning of a new century, the Hotel Alpha looked much as it always had. There were the couples in the Alpha Bar, heads low in complicity, the lady's foot resting against the gentleman's. There was Mrs Davey, shunting a stacked linen trolley like a steam engine hauling freight. Bellboys scampered up and down in the lifts with their room-service trays and newspapers. Guests stopped and stared at Howard, grey hair piled as high as ever on his head, as he paced through the atrium on his way to an international flight which left in an hour but which he would somehow catch. All this was still the same. But if you looked and listened carefully, you would notice the new and strange: the electronic susurrations in every pocket of the building, delivering invisible information in ever-faster, ever less knowable ways.

Computers had entered the Alpha in earnest in 1996. Howard had been thinking for some time of converting the smoking room into a computer facility. It had always been a white elephant, he reasoned; you could smoke anywhere here. I would have argued that the room had very little to do with smoking, and was really all about the secret life of the Alpha. It was where you could get a drink after hours; where you could be counselled for a broken heart; where you could dance with a colleague in a manner which was never discussed outside the room.

None of these arguments were strong enough to hold back Howard or the drum of progress whose beat he was always so anxious to march along to. One summer morning, two men in rolled-up shirtsleeves arrived at the hotel. The leader of the two called me 'guv'nor' and immediately asked for a cup of tea. By the time I came back, they had begun to remove thirty years of history from the room; standing in the doorway with the mugs I felt as if I were the visitor. The leather armchairs had been put outside, and plastic swivelling chairs had taken their places. By the end of the day cheap wooden worktops sup-ported big white humming machines, each one sprouting an Underground-map of wires which made me think of the tubes attached to my father in the days before he died. Chas and JD, who had anticipated these arrivals for weeks, immediately began to demonstrate the benefits of the computers. You could look up anything. Any fact could be yours.

It was a couple of nights later, on my final rounds before going home, that I paused to look at the bronze plate on the wall. IT SUITE. *Suite*! I thought irritably to myself. The name ought to be reserved for our luxurious accommodation upstairs, not splashed across this newly soulless little place; but this was the fashion nowadays. The exercise room and massage tables now went by the name Wellness Suite; before long I supposed the bar would be rechristened the Alcoholic Suite. As I passed, there was a rustling from within. I recognized the sound of somebody labouring not to make a sound.

I opened the door. JD was sitting in front of one of the computers with his trousers unzipped. At the sight of me he tried simultaneously to wriggle back into them and to use the controller to change the picture on the screen: but too late. I could see, as I walked round him, that it was a naked woman, her legs apart, her face to the camera in what was almost a sneer.

'Don't bother,' I said.

JD writhed in the swivelling chair like a big, dopey animal easily cornered. His cheeks darkened. 'Don't tell my dad,' he said. 'Don't tell anyone, Graham. I won't do it again.'

'Best if you don't,' I said, 'not in here, at any rate.'

He sloped away, leaving me to add the episode to the tab of York family secrets I was already running. The photograph's subject, whoever she was, stared at me from the screen. I had been twenty-two before I saw a woman without any clothes on, and that woman was already my wife by then. This generation could now see whatever it wanted, whenever it chose to.

It took me a few minutes to work out how to get the arrow across the screen and make the image disappear. In its place appeared the message which now greeted all our guests when they began to use the computers, or 'logged on' as Howard had tiresomely taken to saying. The screen was white, with a little oblong box you could type words into. *Enter keyword – search for anything!* it urged. Slowly – on account of my long fingers' reluctance to find the right letters, and a more general reluctance brewing in my stomach – I found myself tapping out: 'Hotel Alpha'.

The computer pondered, with a few clicking and grinding noises, and then offered me various fragments of text. With another effort to manipulate the pointer to the right part of the screen, I eventually selected one.

The Hotel Alpha, the computer announced to the establishment's longest-serving member of staff, *is a five-star hotel in the Euston/King's Cross area of London.*

On it went like this for some time, and I gathered that if I wished to, I could choose any of these phrases and learn more about it. I could open a whole new article, for example, on Euston; and from there I could ask the machine about something else again, and so on. But there was more than enough about the Alpha alone. Here, for anyone to see, was the history of our building. The feeling was a little like finding that somebody has been reading your diary.

On the night the men came to install the new equipment, I had asked Chas a question. 'I'm sorry to sound like an old fuddy-duddy,' I said, 'but this Internet. I'm dashed if I can quite … I mean – where *is* all this information? Who compiles it?'

Chas beamed at me.

'Everyone does,' he said. 'Anyone can put something on the net, and anyone else with a computer can read it. So it'll change all the time, it'll always be up to date.'

As I sat now under the new strip lights and screwed up my eyes to continue reading, I was still not sure I quite grasped how all this information had got there. But I understood enough. It was not the case, as I had once insisted to Ella and Lara, that a man's computer could only ever be as clever as he was himself. All the computers in the world were in league. Already they offered access to words and pictures and facts which had been out of reach for all history. Their interest reached even as far as our hotel. They knew about the fire, about the adoption of Chas.

What else did they know about us?

∞

The new and strange: that is how I thought of computers, mobile telephones and the like. But perhaps I was alone in finding them strange. They had invaded with such stealth that most people acted as if the invasion had never taken place: as if a computer were as familiar a design feature as a desk. The way computers colonized the smoking room had been dramatic, but with much less ceremony they had insinuated themselves in a dozen other parts of what used to be my haven.

There was a computer behind my reception desk these days: it competed for elbow space with the leaflets for Madame Tussauds and the zoo, and with the check-in ledger, like a bumptious dinner guest. It was operated by a lady called Suzie, the latest in a series of people to occupy what was once Agatha's place. She had long painted fingernails and dyed blonde hair and the habit of saying 'it's for you-hoo!' when passing me the telephone, or speaking in fragments of foreign languages: *ciao!* and *voila!* and so on. Armed with the computer, Suzie could accomplish a variety of tasks which were once exclusively mine. She could check guests in and allocate them a room without my having to write it in the ledger. She could encourage them to write on our 'website' what they thought of the Alpha, rather than going to the bother of telling us in person. Thanks to the website, they could even make a reservation without having to telephone us; and at the end of their stay, they could put a credit card into a new machine and pay for everything with barely a word exchanged between human beings.

'Breakfast is at seven o'clock,' I continued to say, 'because Mr York thinks no one should be ready for the day before then;

there is a games room, and a Wellness Suite, and we can make restaurant reservations …' but half the time these days, the spiel was interrupted halfway through. 'Yes, yes,' the guest would say, barely meeting my eye: 'I looked all this up. Speaking of which—' and here they turned invariably to Suzie – 'is there Internet in the rooms, and what is the password?'

Once more, I had to admit that check-ins were more efficient without all the conversations Agatha and I used to have over them. But then, it was more efficient not to play the check-in game than to play it. It would probably be most efficient of all for people to stop speaking altogether, to spend their time at the Alpha carrying out tasks in a preprogrammed manner like robots. Did that mean that it would be better?

I was unable to hold back Suzie's new ways of doing things, but nor did I mean to succumb to them. And so she kept on putting people's names on the computer, and I kept writing them in the book. She kept accepting reservations by 'email', and I kept acting as if there were no such system. We rubbed along like two people in a comedy of manners, each convinced the other is mad but happy enough to humour them.

And so the machines' infiltration of the Alpha had not ruined the place I loved; only filled me with a certain nostalgia for the simple past. It was a rather different matter, though, when Pattie decided to purchase a computer for the house. She had come to the Alpha for dinner one night, and JD had given her a demonstration of the so-called IT Suite's marvels. By the time I got away from my desk and came to join her, she seemed to be hooked.

'Look at this, Graham! See this?' She gestured at the screen. 'This is a page for the shop where we get your driving gloves.'

'I see it,' I mumbled. 'Very nice.'

'And if we click with this – this is called the mouse, look – if we click here, we can actually buy a pair of gloves and have them delivered straight to the house! Isn't that clever!'

'Ingenious,' I said. 'Probably the second-best method I can think of, after visiting the shop.'

'Oh, you old fusspot.' She patted me on the sleeve with what almost felt like a condescension to the elderly, as if we were not exactly the same age. 'Imagine being able to chat to all our friends in America!'

'Such a miracle already exists,' I said, 'in the form of the telephone …'

'And failing that, there's always telegrams, eh, Graham?' butted in Howard, who was never far away when some feature of the hotel was being shown off. 'Or smoke signals?' He elbowed Pattie. 'You should get yourself one of these. Perfect for when the old man's away from home banged up in here. You wouldn't believe how easy it is to set up. JD could come round …'

And there it was. In February 2001, only a few weeks after Pattie had touched a computer's keys for the first time in her life, we were the proud owners of a 'PC'.

I made its acquaintance for the first time after a rugby afternoon at Twickenham. Ed and I had been going to matches for years, since he was a boy: two or three chilly afternoons every spring, with tickets which were normally arranged by Howard's string-pulling. Today, though, the party was bigger: my grandson Christopher, escorted by his mother Caroline, was making his debut as a spectator, at the age of nine. From the way he galloped ahead like a goat as we went through the turnstiles, you might have thought he was in the team himself. Before the match began – and while Caroline fiddled with her mobile telephone – he squealed in glee at each sighting of a referee, a programme-seller, a policeman. 'Good heavens!' he shouted, when a try was scored; and 'Bad form!' when a penalty was conceded. It was not clear how he had acquired the antique vocabulary he had, but the finger was generally pointed at me. Christopher and I had a lot in common. At half-time I took him for refreshments, lifting him up with a creak of my old joints so that he could read the items chalked on the board.

'How has work been?' I asked Ed, who was standing in the queue with us, hands in the pockets of his anorak.

'It's all right,' said Ed. 'Ten years. Ten years.' He rubbed his face as if he were going to add something, but did not. Perhaps sensing a duty to his mother, I ventured: 'And how is life, in general?'

'Yes,' Ed remarked, gazing out across the milling crowds, 'it's all right.'

That was as much as I could get out of him: life was all right, work was all right. I could not really ask for more. Part of the reason we enjoyed trips to the rugby was that it had always provided an outing with minimal conversation. It came complete with its own circumscribed topics: the turnout, the standard of refereeing, the decision to buy or not buy Bovril. Those had always been enough. Perhaps it was a little late in the day now to start quizzing him.

We took the train afterwards from St Margarets to Waterloo under one of London's best autumn skies, a collaboration of pink and purple with wispy grey clouds. From Waterloo we decided to walk the considerable distance back to the Alpha, showing Christopher St Martin-in-the-Fields, Charing Cross Road with the tourist melee around Leicester Square, the bookshops with their ancient bound volumes in windows. The further we walked, the more relish I felt in the anticipation of the Alpha, as if it were a loved one waiting at the end of a great journey. How ridiculous it was, after three and a half decades, that I still caught my breath at the sight of the brickwork partly shielded by the rustling cedars, the magnificence of the atrium as one looked all the way up to the skylight. Perhaps, I thought, nothing had changed with the world after all.

Yet when I came home that night, Pattie was tap-tapping patiently at the keyboard, her back to me. I began to tell her about the game, but she had already looked up the result. I ate my ham and chips at the table, rustling through the newspaper. It had clouded over outside and begun to rain. There was the tapping of drops on the pane, and the tapping of Pattie's keys from along the hall. And it occurred to me that if someone were to ask me at this moment, I would say the same as Ed. Life is fine, I suppose; work is more or less fine. But it was rather unlikely anyone was going to ask me.

∞

If I rather resented computers' sudden influence, I was glad of one thing at least: they had come at a perfect time for Chas as his twenties approached. Yes, he could use a computer, all right. One afternoon in September he was sitting next to the reception desk, his hands dancing across the keys with the astonishing fluency they had, so that strangers were never able to believe he could not see what he was doing. He continued to hunch his shoulders and mutter, whereas JD carted his significant weight about the place with a proprietorial swagger; but all the same he gave the impression, as he sat with the laptop, of something like complete contentment. The computer – the same one Ella had given him, though souped-up over the years and repaired numerous times – had been the key to the life he had now. It had been the reason he got his job.

That job was for Lara Krohl and her 'PR' firm. He wrote, as far as I could make out, advertising materials and statements for the press and so on. Today, as on many days, Krohl was using the Alpha as a 'mobile office', which meant pacing incessantly from atrium to bar and back again, telephone pressed to her ear, a stream of barely comprehensible instructions issuing from her mouth. 'OK, whack that over to me.' 'Hack into my s--- and find the file, can you, the password's oh-five-oh-six.' 'Tell him if he doesn't get his a--- in gear, I'll have his b------s for breakfast.'

'It sounds like your boss may be in for an unusual breakfast,' I remarked as she went by, looking the same as she did every day: dark hair scraped back from her forehead, white shirt and black trousers, laptop under her arm and a paper coffee cup in the non-telephone hand.

Chas grinned. 'She's a bit stressed.' His fingers traced their rapid paths across the keyboard, never letting up. 'We've got this relaunch tomorrow.'

'What are you actually ... working on?'

'This is a release for a chain of gyms. Lara's client has, literally, fifty. Take a look.'

'Fitness World is proud to announce the unveiling of another ten state-of-the-art integrated fitness centres, offering an innovative design concept ... '

I looked back from the letters neatly lined up on the screen to Chas's face, still in its aspect of pleasurable concentration.

'Are there any mistakes in it?' he asked. 'The computer doesn't pick up everything, frustratingly. Not even this new software is perfect. I'm waiting for a patch.'

I thought of the patches on Mike Swan's old sports jacket. 'A ... ?'

'A patch is a computer program which corrects problems with a previous program, basically.'

'Ah. Well, there aren't any spelling mistakes,' I assured him, 'but I would find it hard to say if there are mistakes in general, because although I understand all the words individually ... '

'They're gibberish.' Chas laughed. 'Yeah, sorry about that. You'll have to forgive all the industry-speak.'

How inevitable it was, and yet how peculiar, this turn-around. This boy who used to hang on our words, groping for meaning in the nothingness in front of him, was so much more fluent than us in the language of the times. I looked at him with a combination of emotions. There was the bemused pride one feels as a father being outstripped by a son; only as an after-thought came the reflection that he was not really my son after all. We had lived together for so long that it was sometimes hard to remember that.

'We're doing a relaunch,' Chas elaborated, 'because there's been stuff written on the net about the gyms – bad reviews posted by some rival or something.'

'Isn't there a way of monitoring that sort of thing? Other-wise, what's to stop any Tom, Dick or Harry writing whatever they like?'

'Nothing's stopping them,' Chas agreed with a laugh. 'That's what the Internet is for.'

'You see, I find that a bit troubling. The idea that any opinion is as good as any other. Mike Swan, for example – you know, the hotel reviewer – well, he was telling me that there are … web-sites now which allow people to post their own reviews, even if they can't tell a good hotel from a pair of long johns.' I had seen Swan less often of late; when he did appear, there were dark patches under his eyes and his manner was distracted. 'He's struggling, I think, to sell as many guides as he used to. Don't you think … '

The conversation, along with many other conversations under the Alpha's roof at that moment, went no further. Ray, the red-headed barman we had appointed a few years back, came bustling into the atrium.

'Something terrible's happened.'

Even now, nearly two decades after the fire, these words could rouse me instantly into readiness. I walked round the desk. Chas got to his feet; he stood almost as tall as me now, and that – as much as his cleverness – continued to surprise me, no matter how used to it I ought to be.

'What? In the bar?'

'No, no. In New York.'

Already a good number of people had collected around the television, which was mounted in a corner. Before you knew it every one of them seemed to be talking on a mobile phone.

'They're saying a hijack,' someone reported over my shoulder. 'They're saying loads of planes were hijacked.'

'They're saying four, but nobody knows what's going on,'

said somebody else. An American woman was shouting into her own phone: 'What the hell is this? What the f---ing hell is this?'

Then the television showed an aeroplane flying into a tower. Now there was pandemonium: forty or fifty people in the bar. Sentences criss-crossed, syllables collected in the air like rubbish on a breeze.

'They're saying four planes.'

'What are they saying about Washington?'

'It has to be a bomb.'

'Can you hear me?'

The telephoners began to walk in circles, exchanging frowns as they got in each other's way, all of them with their eyes still pointed up at the little screen. Above us, newsreaders went on describing the scene; but all we could hear were each other's voices.

'This is going to screw the launch completely,' Lara Krohl was saying behind me. 'This is going to be headlines. Trust me. We need to act fast on this.'

This was very much as I would have expected her to react, but then came something less expected. She put a hand on my sleeve. I turned round. Her eyes were small and dark, marble-like, and quite unreadable.

'Is Chas OK?' she asked.

I followed her stare. Chas was sitting very still, his face pointing down at the floor. Howard's arm was round his shoulders.

'Perhaps he's thinking about Ella, his tutor from years back,' I explained. 'She left very suddenly; she and Agatha – you remember Agatha, my colleague – both of them did.'

'Yah,' said Lara, 'right.'

'And both of them said they were going to America, you see. So naturally, although it was years ago – well, at a time like this, one imagines ... '

'Yah, yah, right, I get it,' snapped Lara Krohl. I glanced up, thinking this was rude even by her standards; but then I saw the look on her face. It was a look which only lingered for half a moment. The mention of Agatha, or of Ella, had stirred something in her which she did not want to be stirred.

Half a moment: then she shoved the computer onto the edge of a table and was tapping away like everybody else. The look had been taken back like a word typed and deleted off a screen. But I had heard Chas say that a file erased from a computer could often still be found there, if you knew how to look. It was a similar situation here. She had deleted that twist of her mouth, that twitch of the eyelids, but they would be remembered, nonetheless. They would be remembered by me, all right.

෨ 6 ෩

CHAS

Graham and I never discussed the departures of Agatha and Ella, not in the several years that saw me develop from pining adolescent to where I was now. The conversation just never happened. We didn't seem to have the tools for it. Howard wasn't keen on the subject, either: he'd made that clear from the beginning. And in the end, maybe it was better for me not to bring it up. As I couldn't go to New York, I had to regard anyone who did as gone altogether. Although Ella and I carried on writing letters for a while, I was the one who let it lapse in the end, and not just because it was hard work dictating to Howard and awkward having him read her replies. The time we spent together was now a chunk of a past I felt increasingly disconnected from. I was hell-bent on the present.

What that present consisted of, as I went into my twenties, made me feel reasonably optimistic. I was gauche and timid, a full-blown agoraphobic in all but official diagnosis, with a continued dependence upon others to read out the headlines, point out the toilet, tell me what colour clothes I was wearing. All the same, I was making a more credible stab at a life than I'd once thought was possible. I had my own little studio in the York household, a bedroom with an en suite which Howard and Sarah-Jane had created around the time of my eighteenth. And, of course, I had a job.

On my old laptop, now kitted out with all sorts of smart keys that allowed it to speak to me, I wrote press releases for the army, a new fragrance supposedly created by a supermodel, a dozen films, the 2001 London Marathon. Lara looked after the biggest stuff. Important people with affairs to cover up, or unimportant people with affairs to publicize, went straight to her, but gushing to the media about a sensational new product or event: those jobs were shared between a team of six or so, some working from home and some in an office in Canary Wharf. Most of that team – I gathered from the nights they spent drinking at the Alpha – found it grim, unrewarding work. They wanted to be at the launch nights, fetching production-tab cocktails for actors. Or they'd set out on an artistic path and ended up here in the suburbs of creativity. I on the other hand had soared beyond any realistic expectations. Not only was I working, but I was good at it.

'PR is insincere, obviously,' Lara told me when I began my job, which she had offered me after three weeks' temp work which I tackled so fanatically that she was left with little option.

'But you need to be sincere about the insincerity. In other words, you have to believe what you're saying, even if it's crap. People can smell it otherwise.' This wasn't a problem for me. We did press for a new hospital wing which was apparently an eyesore, and a designer's London Fashion Week output which JD said looked like the result of a factory accident, and since I couldn't see them I was happy to write that they were breathtaking or innovative. I was the closest thing that existed to Lara's dream: a machine that expressed human emotions and opinions without needing to connect to them myself.

When I wasn't on a computer for work, I was using one for leisure. These years were both exhilarating and maddening. The Internet posed the most dramatic version yet of the problem that had shaped my life: everything was out there, but someone had to show me where it was. Although I could sometimes get Graham or Suzie to read me an Internet page, the way I used to hear the headlines, it wasn't till Howard finished his meetings and conferences and drinking sessions for the day that I had a light to navigate the web's million tunnels. As always, you could hear him a long way off: the half tuneful whistling of 'Satisfaction', the heavy tread on the floorboards. The sweet smoke-cloud muscled in alongside me and the computer whined and whirred its way online.

After the terror attacks, we spent a lot of time looking up the new words which were suddenly everywhere, like a song everyone was singing. Al-Qaeda; suicide bombing; Islamic fundamentalism. We began at the BBC webpage and cata-pulted from one link to another. Howard read to me and sipped whisky; Sarah-Jane brought cups of tea and told us not to stay up too late. There were frequent detours from the 'war on terror', as it was being called, because Howard kept finding things more interesting than the destruction of the Western world. It might be an explanation of a magic trick, or a picture of a new electric car someone was working on. 'Listen to this! This will blow your mind!' The net was a great new toy for Howard as well as a price-less tool for me. At one time he had chosen knowledge for me: now we were discovering things together. That at least was what it felt like.

One night I was trying to find out something about the ori-gins of 'jihad'. Months after 9/11 Lara was still getting almost daily enquiries from airlines, companies with Arabic owners, anyone with a connection to the Islamic world who wanted us to convince their clients they were perfectly safe to do business with. New ad copy had to be written; mentions of Islam had to be toned down; someone asked Lara if a website could be made to look 'a little bit less Muslim'.

'Jihad means literally "struggle", Howard read in a booze-thickened voice, 'and it can refer either to a Muslim's attempt to live by the Koran, or the more general struggle to defend Islam, by whatever means possible, including violence.' I was typing as fast as I could, making a note of useful phrases. My newest software could read chunks of text aloud, allowing me to cut-and-paste them straight into my own work. Howard made a disapproving noise by clicking his tongue. 'Including violence, indeed. I thought we'd seen the end of all this. The IRA with their fucking bombs in hotels. Used to have a special phone number if someone checked in sounding Irish and we weren't sure about them. Never got a bomb, of course. Got the fire instead.'

My fingers stopped on the keyboard. He had never really mentioned it before: at least not unprompted like this. I found myself full of questions, not all of which had a clear shape.

'Do you remember – I mean – did you see my mother much before it happened?' I asked. 'Do you remember what she was like at all?'

'I only saw her two or three times,' Howard said. 'It was Graham who checked her in. She was – well, the two of you didn't have anywhere to go. The dad ... your dad had cleared off somewhere. No, I only saw her once in the lobby with you, playing with a ball. And then once ... you know. On the night.' He cleared this throat. 'On that night.'

'What was it like? Did you try to save her as well?'

'Why are you asking about this all of a sudden, mate?' said Howard, not angrily but at a diminished volume which made me aware of a prickliness in the air.

'No reason. I don't know. It's just a big thing in my life, but I don't remember it at all.'

'Of course it is,' Howard agreed in an easier tone. 'Of course it is. Well, yeah. There was no time. You were screaming for her. That was the hardest thing – you were begging to go back to her. But she was out cold. Graham tried to get in and drag her out, but he couldn't.'

He let a long silence go by.

'Graham and I never talk about it,' he said.

With each moment of quiet that passed, I could feel the topic – which had landed so unexpectedly in the conversation – floating away once more. Howard must have drained off his whisky; he set the glass down on the desk. It was hard to know if he was upset or irritated by the discussion, even though he was the one who'd started it. I asked him to look up something else. The computer hummed in thought, and the moment passed.

The hotel was hosting a singles night which would show, in Lara's words, that 'the Alpha is fun, it's modern, it's sexy'. I could almost hear Graham snorting across the desk as I parsed this into a press release. It would be, apparently, 'a night of love in one of the capital's coolest spots'. By the time a DJ hauled his decks and speakers into the bar and the first hopefuls were drawn in on the wash of frothy pop, I'd taken up residence in the IT Suite: secluded from all the fuss, but without the feeling of hermitism that sometimes settled on me if I retreated to my rooms too early in the evening.

The synthetic quiet was bolstered rather than broken by the hum of machines. It seemed a long time since this was the smoking room adults occasionally smuggled me into. I had been working for a couple of hours on a piece for our gym client – '*get away from the stress and strain of today's uncertain world …*' – when I registered with slight irritation the presence of a new-comer. There was a female cough, then some fiddling with keys or personal effects and a Howard-like tapping. I made a show of typing extra-fast to avoid being interrupted by small talk, and waited for the modem's screech.

'For the love of Christ!' the person burst out.

There was no ignoring that. I asked if I could help.

'Do you know anything about computers?'

'I'm not bad.'

'This laptop was working half an hour ago. Now I can't … it won't turn on.'

'Are you trying to connect to the net?' I asked.

'No,' said the woman, 'I'm just trying to get the computer on so I can type something up quite urgently.' Her voice was posh and precise. It sounded like she was secretly furious at the way things were unfolding, but containing the fury with a decorous effort. There was something interesting about her smell: it pro-voked a thought which I could not quite access.

'Is it the battery?'

'Fully charged. I always have it charged. Maybe the hard drive's packed up or something. Oh, shitty hell.'

The expression made me want to laugh, but it was hard to tell quite how much force was behind it.

'What exactly is the thing you need to write up?'

'It's a piece,' she said. 'I'm a journalist. But there's two thousand words of stuff already on that machine. I'll have to use one of these computers and try to remember what I wrote before. Christ, it's going to take me all night. Do you work here?'

I told her I did; it was easier than explaining. Her swivel chair squeaked as she moved closer to me and I suddenly got a much clearer impression of her. Her breaths were audible; she clicked or tutted while thinking. Like Howard, I gathered, she was a noise-maker, she commanded space. As to her smell: it was salty and shiny, somehow elemental, like the sheer smell of flesh, the stuff of a person. That must be it, I realized: no perfume. It was almost like a feeling, a touch, rather than being a smell at all.

'Feel free to ignore me,' I said, 'but if you want some help typing it up, I can do two thousand words from dictation in, I would think, well under an hour.'

'Are you busting my balls?'

'Sorry?'

'Why would you want to help me?'

'Well, just if you need a hand.'

'It's pretty boring stuff,' she said. 'It's about Iraq.'

'I don't call that boring. I'm writing about cross-trainers.'

'About what?'

'Exactly. I'm Chas, by the way. Who do you write for?'

'Kathleen. I'm freelance, but this will go in the *Independent*.'

Should we shake hands? I hoped not. It didn't seem to have occurred to her, anyhow. She cleared her throat.

'Are you sure about this?'

By way of an answer I flexed my typing fingers. My head was low over the keys, my shoulders hunched, as they had been since she arrived. I hoped she hadn't had a chance yet to get a proper look at my face, wanting to defer the moment as long as possible.

'*It's daybreak in Basra, in Southern Iraq near the border with Kuwait.* Basra is B-A-S...'

'I know it. Don't worry.'

For half an hour we worked together. Her subject was the likely invasion of Iraq which – in her view – would spuriously follow on from the current Afghanistan situation. I pretended not to be agog at the idea that I was spying on an opinion piece by a journalist whose words Howard had undoubtedly read out at some point. It was as if a chunk of the Internet had come alive and was talking to me in person. The spell was only broken when Kathleen hesitated in the middle of a paragraph. 'I'm going to have to look this up, actually,' she said, 'or Kirsty will have my balls on a plate.' Among all the surprise swearing, I particularly liked the way she kept referring to her fictitious testicles. 'Can you put into the search engine ...'

'I'll let you do it,' I said, passing the laptop towards her.

'Work has been saved,' it announced.

'Gosh,' said Kathleen, 'my computer doesn't talk to me like that.'

The game was up. 'It's because I'm blind.'

'You can't be,' she said.

'I think I'd know by now if I wasn't.'

'You're ... actually blind?'

'One hundred per cent.'

'Pissing Christ!' Kathleen exclaimed.

'That's one way of putting it.' I squirmed in my swivel chair, aware of her eyes scouring my warm face.

'But then how the hell can you type like that?' she asked. 'And how did I not notice?'

'You didn't notice because I quite deliberately never moved my face from the screen,' I said. 'And I can type like this because, since I first got a computer, I've basically done little else. But there'll be spelling mistakes, I warn you. I have a program which spell-checks out loud, but ... '

'Hang on,' Kathleen interrupted, 'are you Chas York, then?'

'How could you know that?'

'What, you don't think people have heard about you?' she said. 'I have got this right, haven't I? Howard York rescued you from the fire? And you've always lived here and now, now you work for that frightening lady?'

'Lara Krohl. Yes, that's me.'

'Has anyone ever done a profile piece on you?' she asked.

'I haven't exactly sought the limelight. I've only been out of this building about ten times in my life.'

'Seriously?'

'All right, four. I was trying to sound cool.'

'Fuck a *duck*.' She paused, and then: 'I was just going to ask if you fancied getting a drink once this nonsense is over.'

I almost thought I'd misheard her, and there was a pause as I tried hastily to chart the currents of excitement and confusion which were swimming around me. She misread my hesitation and began to backtrack.

'But, no big deal, I ... '

'No, that would be ... that's a good idea,' I said. 'There's a bar here.'

I could hardly believe it even as I held the door open for her a little while later and felt the swish of her skin as she passed me. I had come to this room to avoid meeting people, but the opposite had happened: somebody had entered my life from the great unseen beyond, and – although I tried to hold back the idea – it felt already as if she might stay.

❦

'I still don't understand how you can manage so well if you literally can't see a thing.'

Around us, the end-of-evening noise could have been from almost any night in the bar: words fired at departing companions, lacklustre witticisms, the feeling of life and excitement draining from the place like bathwater. Within half an hour Ray would be starting to shoo the final clingers-on from the premises.

'I manage the same way as you,' I said, 'repetition. I know this place like the back of my hand. Better than the back of my hand, in fact. And I pretty much don't go anywhere else, as I've said, so ... '

'But you must *want* to. You're obviously interested in the world around you. Don't you want to travel?'

I could sense, from the vibration, her legs jiggling back and forth. 'Well, the universe is kind of theoretical to me. Whether I was in here or in Egypt, it would still be the same thing.'

'Not really. If you went to Egypt, you'd smell the spices in the market, the quality of the air. You'd experience it as a new country just like a sighted person does. You'd hear them shouting from the minarets. You'd smell the sewage in the river.'

'You're really selling it.'

She laughed. I didn't want her to sense how scared I was of everything outside the Alpha; how little appetite I had for it. I took a third large swig of the Prosecco that Kathleen had ordered. There was the brash shock of it in my mouth, and a nearly instant sense of being taken away. I kept a firm hand clasped round the champagne flute: there'd be no mishaps or spillages, no reminder for her that I wasn't normally in this situation.

'How did you get into journalism?' It sounded, as I asked it, a hopelessly banal question.

'I went to hack school. I worked for local news, was hoping to be one of those glamorous war correspondents. But I don't look right for TV.'

'What *do* you look like?'

She snorted a laugh. 'This must be what it's like meeting someone on the Internet. Er – dirty blonde hair. Dirty as in colour, not literally. It's hard to describe yourself, isn't it? I've got a big long nose which is a bit of an obstacle, looks-wise. Normal height. Normal-ish weight; I wouldn't mind being a bit thinner, but it's not terminal. I look like a normal twenty-nine-year-old woman, essentially. You can tell I have a gift for describing things.'

Twenty-nine! Women loved younger men, JD had told me recently, as the preamble to an anecdote which involved him having sex in an aircraft toilet on the way to Los Angeles. At the time I was hardly listening – these stories were ten a penny – but now I wished I had him beside me for guidance. I had no idea what I was doing; whether there was a danger of overplaying my hand or underplaying it, whether I should talk more or just keep taking her in. She told me about places where she'd seen snakes swimming in the drains as she crossed the road; places where they fired guns into the air to celebrate a football result and she thought she was being shot at. There were also places she had been shot at. She'd been to Uzbekistan, Biafra, Greenland; even places I struggled to recall the capitals of. We chatted on into the small pocket of night when the Alpha was truly becalmed, when you could stand in the middle of the atrium and hear only rumours of noise from the balconies above: a cough, the creak of a door.

'It's gone two,' she said at last. 'I'm going to be home at fuck-o'clock.'

'You don't live around here?'

'Nobody but you lives around here. I'm a writer. I live in Zone one hundred.'

'Why don't you stay here?' I hazarded. 'I could get you a key to a room.'

'For free?'

'Of course for free.'

Boldness had sprung my natural defences and was now running me like a different person altogether. The momentum of this long strange night felt implacable.

'Will they even have a room available?' asked Kathleen.

'There's one that will be empty.'

One of the night team gave me the key to Room 25 without any questions: they were used to the strange hours I kept when sleeplessness came, and used to helping me, as everyone was around here. As Kathleen unlocked the door we were met by a strange coolness. The bedsprings cried out in surprise as she flung herself down and sprang back up again.

'This is amazing. Thank you so much.'

'This room's always here,' I said, 'if you want it.'

'Well, next time I'm nearby ... '

'I hope it'll be really soon,' I blurted out, still annoyed by my previous remark: of course the room was always there, where else could it be?

'I've got a feeling it might be soon,' she said. I touched her arm vaguely in response, and we traded goodnights. As soon as I had closed the door behind me and heard the automatic click of the lock, I wondered whether I'd been too formal. Another man would surely have ended up staying in the room with her. Another man would have said smoother things, known how to behave.

Although the events of the night had barely finished, my brain was already replaying and dissecting them in the jittery manner of a rolling news channel. Soon each replay would be a copy of a copy, and the reality would be a little more elusive. I paused outside the door for a while, gripped by the knowledge that she was in that room, would be undressing.

I went down in the lift, trying the old trick of foxing my brain with a nearly impossible sum. Kathleen kept swimming into my head, in something closer to a visual form than anyone ever had.

Kathleen visited three times in the fortnight that followed, and each time I ended up borrowing the key to Room 25 and sitting there as she typed.

The wall between not knowing somebody and knowing them quite intimately turned out to be startlingly thin. It all became commonplace so fast: the smell of her breath, the thinking-noises she made with tongue and teeth, her muttered curses as she mis-hit a key, the upward curl of her laugh. I was only now starting to realize how much I'd feared the mass of invisible people out there: now that one of them had appeared from the nothingness and was borrowing my laptop, eating my crisps. Each time she left, I wondered – as on the first occasion – if I ought to have pushed my luck a little further.

After the third visit she told me she was going to Dubai for nine days. It was surprising how long that sounded, and what a superstitious fear welled up inside me. 'You will look after yourself, won't you?'

'It's Dubai,' she said, signing off with a cheek-kiss. 'I'll be in a hotel with other journalists and yuppies on holiday. I'm not going to Mecca to shit on the Koran.' I ushered her down to the atrium and wished her good luck as we parted; she seemed surprised, even amused. To her, a flight to Dubai was little different to nipping to the shops; to me, going to the shops would feel like a trip to Dubai.

The first night of the nine I felt a curious combination of boredom and fear. I tried to focus on six different tasks. At ten, around the time her plane should be landing, I found myself back in the atrium mustering the courage to ask Graham for a favour.

'Something for Kathleen?' There was a certain twinkle in his voice.

'Yes. She's just a friend.'

'I didn't say anything to the contrary.'

'She's been using Room 25 – a few times, now. I just wondered whether I could, sort of, requisition it for her. I mean, just on an occasional basis.'

My discomfort brought a low chuckle out of Graham. 'On an occasional basis! Are you going to submit a written request?'

'I'm sorry. I didn't really know how you felt about … about Room 25, generally.'

Graham cleared his throat. 'Well, the fact is it's not been used, really, for a long time. Hardly at all, since Ella and … and Agatha.'

The mention of the two of them, after all this time, made it feel almost inevitable I would ask the question that had never found its opening before.

'Was it coincidence that she and Ella left just like that? So quickly?'

As soon as it was asked, the question felt as if it had been unavoidable. Yet we had avoided it for a very long time, and while waiting for an answer I half lost my nerve and began to apologize. Graham swept in with his response before I finished. 'I honestly do not know,' he said.

What was behind the flinty emphasis he put on the adverb, and the even greater than usual fullness of his enunciation? Had he disliked my asking the question, or just the mental route it sent him along? With Kathleen, recently, I had felt – like never before – the frustration of having no face to navigate by, of having only tones of voice, and at a moment like this it was even worse. I pictured Graham, his long stooping shoulders, the last person to see my mother alive, perhaps the last person to see Agatha in this building. All this made me want to scuttle away from the conversation, but uncorked curiosity was driving me forward.

'Did Agatha ever leave an address, or … ?'

'She did not,' Graham said. 'She said she would probably go to Florida, where she had family; I think I told you that. She did mention getting in touch when things had settled down. But that did not, in the end, happen.'

'I miss her, sometimes. I know it was years ago. It's just I never had a chance to say goodbye even.'

'Yes,' said Graham. 'It was a long time ago.'

It sounded like he was talking to himself as much as to me; the voice was coming from a new direction – he had turned his back. I heard the row of keys jangling on their fobs like wind chimes as his hand swept through them. 'I shall give you both keys to 25, and Howard – well, once again, Howard need not know. Not, I'm sure, that he would mind. But he can be a little wary of journalists.'

'She's not a gossip columnist or anything,' I said. 'She's a foreign correspondent really.'

'I have seen her suitcase,' Graham assured me. 'It is battered almost beyond recognition as a suitcase. She is a very charming lady, by the way.'

When I got back to my room, there was a new email. 'From: Kathleen,' the computer said, eliding the h and l so the name came out in an unnatural squelch. 'Message: Landed alive.'

That was it: just the two words, but a very different feeling from none. I smiled in the dark, imagining her in Room 25 beside me.

∞

Howard arranged a separate modem for the room, and without saying much about it we gradually made it an arrangement that Kathleen worked at the hotel whenever she was in the centre of town. This might happen on two consecutive days, or not at all for ten. At any time she could be round the corner or thousands of miles away cowering from grenades. Howard was zealous as usual in getting the most up-to-date technology we could, but there was no gadget which could predict when she might be in touch. There were no rules, there was nothing official. There were only these moments when she appeared from blackness and folded away into it again. I didn't even voice her name to Howard or Sarah-Jane until just before the May Bank Holiday, when Howard was planning one of his now traditional dinners in the atrium. Kathleen was keen to come; in fact she claimed she would give her left breast for the opportunity. Howard told me he would put her straight on the top-table list.

'Are you sure? You've not even met her.'

'Oh, I've heard things.' Howard ruffled my hair like he used to when I was younger. 'And it's great. It's great for you to meet people. I want you to have that.' I squirmed in part-pleasure, part-mortification. Was I really such a case, a person whose achievement in recruiting a friend was to be celebrated like a baby's first steps?

Kathleen was delighted. 'I will have your children for this.'

'I won't take you up on that immediately.'

Was I too keen or too remote? If I could see her face, would I know how to proceed? It was a ridiculous question to ask, but it clawed at me all the same. I tried once to explain it to Graham. 'I don't know, if I could see her face, whether I would know what to do. Or whether I'm so far away from understanding the idea of human expressions that it would be like ... like looking at a page of hieroglyphics. Do you see what I mean?'

'I think so, Chas.'

'It's crazy; I've *seen* faces, but I've got no memory of them. In a lot of ways I hardly even know what a face *is*.'

'It's a bit like a foot,' said Graham, 'but higher up.'

On Bank Holiday Monday I met Kathleen in the noise and throb of the atrium. She took me decisively by the arm. JD had brought someone called Holly from his extensive girl-friend roster. Lara included herself in the introductions. I heard the four-way dialogue of assessing and sizing up, all the silent exchanges, the instant judgements acknowledged by nothing more than a wavering note in the voice.

'Nice to meet you!'

'You, too!'

There was the scrape of a chair, then another a moment later.

'Right here,' said Kathleen, a piloting hand on my arm. JD began to say something. 'Oh ... ' Kathleen began to apologize.

'Don't worry,' JD muttered.

I gathered they'd both moved a chair for me at the same moment, and I had chosen hers. Holly giggled nervously. Silk slunk beneath my hand as I set it down.

'I've got a dress on,' Kathleen explained. 'It's sort of fawn. Matches my eyes roughly.'

'Well, that's useful for Chas, isn't it.' JD's voice was pepped up, full of challenge. Lara made an amused, faintly admon-ishing noise. Holly and Kathleen cradled the conversation until it breathed more easily, but it was only a temporary reprieve. During the main course, Afghanistan came up: JD had a couple of Sandhurst friends who, he said, were excited to be 'seeing some combat'. I heard a whisper of fabric and a little sigh of the chair as Kathleen readjusted herself. Lara was on to it like a sniffer dog.

MARK WATSON

'You don't look like you agree over there, Kath,' she remarked with a trace of malice.

'I don't, personally, agree with the war.' Kathleen swallowed; the printed page was where she preferred to argue.

'You don't think we have a responsibility to fight against people who've killed thousands of innocents?' Lara asked, as neutrally as if she were getting Kathleen to pass the salt.

With fortunate timing a gong struck: Howard was shushing everyone to attention for one of his auctions. He was going to perform a trick, he said, and the winning bidder would be told how the trick worked. 'Once-in-a-lifetime opportunity,' he hectored the guests. 'You will never again meet a magician who will tell you how to do this. They threatened to kick me out of the Magic Circle for this. But I pointed out I wasn't in the Magic Circle.'

Kathleen laughed beside me, and I felt as if I'd won the laugh myself. Howard continued with his nonsense, bringing out a papier-mâché elephant which Graham complained was 'very nearly the size of the real thing', and making it disappear from a wardrobe in a manner which by all accounts was pretty miraculous if you could see it. I allowed my indignation at JD and Lara to break up in a tide of white wine, from a glass which had been topped up each time it was out of my hand. The afternoon began to sag and ooze, and now Howard was giving a speech, telling the well-worn story of the day he first stood right here and dreamed of a hotel, and they were naked in front of the police, and he said 'we've got music on'.

'I think I've heard that before,' said Holly.

'Howard's famous for this. For passing stories off as his own,' Kathleen told her.

'How do you know?' JD came in as quickly as an actor at a rehearsed cue; he seemed to have been waiting for another chance to fight. 'You've never been to one of these before.'

'I've … I've just heard about it,' said Kathleen.

'You seem quite an expert on things you've heard about,' Lara observed. I felt the glow from Kathleen's face as if my hand were there.

'Do you realize that Dad organizes this every year, some-times twice a year, and feeds all these people, and everyone's got an opinion, but no one could do half of what he's achieved?' JD's mouth was half a pace ahead of him; his words tripped out like unruly children. 'That's what he's "famous" for, mate.'

'Oh, stop making trouble!' Holly scolded him, and soon the argument had fizzled out again, but it had left me with that heat at the back of my neck which I associated with a younger, more helpless version of myself, and with a fury at JD. After dinner Kathleen touched my elbow and said she was going up to Room 25 to work. JD melted away into the atrium's ruckus. I was about to flop into self-pity when a familiar hand landed on my shoulder.

'What's up?'

Howard's smell was festively enhanced: it had booze and sweat in it, and the glow of a man well sunned in the limelight. Sarah-Jane's cosy essence came piping in from the side. I pointed my face towards the whole comforting package of them.

'JD and Kathleen didn't get on.'

'Oh, he's being a real arsehole today, is J,' said Sarah-Jane. 'Kathleen seems lovely.' I was so cheered up by this that I didn't reflect how odd it was – yet another person having an opinion of Kathleen. 'Let me talk to her, love,' Sarah-Jane went on. 'Where is she?'

I explained she was upset, had gone off to the room. Howard and Sarah-Jane scoffed in unison as if this were a laughably thin bluff. 'Take a drink up to her!' said Sarah-Jane. 'What's she drink?'

Before I had finished the word 'Prosecco', Howard was badgering a bellboy to bring the best bottle we had. 'On the best tray we have. And the best glasses, as well, to be on the safe side,' he shouted after him. 'This is what it's all about,' he said, and I imagined the expansive arm gestures, the hand round Sarah-Jane's waist. 'A bit of class. This is how I wooed S-J.'

'I seem to remember you put your hand down my knickers in the stockroom.'

'She's got no sense of romance, your mum.' Howard laughed.

The bellboy arrived next to me with the stacked tray. Their laughter carried me into the lift, out onto the second floor. I wanted to be like them, effortlessly in love, wisecracking, a rosy past with the promise of a rosy future. I asked the boy to put the tray down outside Room 25. From the atrium below, faint noise floated up over the balcony, like the voices of guests long gone. My stomach was fizzing.

'Room service.'

I heard her voice from inside, a little wary. 'Oh, I didn't order ...'

'Hurry up, will you,' I said, 'I'm fucking blind.'

Kathleen's laughter melted into a croon of joy as she pushed open the door.

'Would have been awkward,' I said, 'if it turned out I *did* have the wrong room.'

'You're a miracle-worker.'

I took two steps into the room and launched immediately into my speech. 'I'm really sorry about JD. I think he was just drunk. Or, well, I don't know. I don't ... we're not as close as we used to be.'

There was a pop-and-plonk as she poured out the drinks. Her glass touched against mine like a hand brushing another. We sat next to each other on the bed. I felt her foot swing out and nudge against mine; felt the plush contour of her thigh against my trouser leg.

'I guess the main thing is, I'm an outsider,' she said. 'Any outsider is going to be looked at with a bit of suspicion. You and the

Yorks have been a self-enclosed thing for so long. And then the Alpha is a bit of a world all to itself anyway.'

My instinct was to say she was wrong. The hotel was famous for welcoming strangers: that was how I had originally come to be here. How could the Alpha be a closed world when it flung its doors wide open every day? How could she say that outsiders were unwelcome when everybody came here as an outsider and felt straight away like a regular? But then I had never approached the place as a visitor. I kept quiet.

'Plus I'm a hack. Lara tells them which journalists to like and which ones to dislike. I suspect I'm on the dislike list. And, you know, Howard was never wild about journalists, was he, and I suppose that's trickled down to JD.'

I was wrestling with the strangeness of it: having these people whom I knew so well spoken about with a detachment I could never feel towards them. 'What do you mean? About him and journalists?'

'You didn't hear about the Mike Swan thing?'

Swan had approached Howard, she said, a couple of months ago for an interview. He wanted to do a piece for one of the papers to promote the *Swan Guide*, whose sales had been falling away. 'He wanted to ask him about the fire, twenty years on, that sort of thing. Howard was really aggressive, apparently. Said why would anyone give a fuck about the fire in this day and age. That Swan was living in the past. Swan was crying, someone said, round the back of the hotel.'

The story landed sourly in the room, which was silent around us; it had nothing to add, for all its experience of humans and their dramas. There was the image of this horrible thing, of a middle-aged man weeping, and behind it there was something else that disturbed me – the idea of Howard's being cruel, perhaps – which my mind did not want to alight on. I told myself she had heard an exaggerated version of the story; or that it never happened at all. It was a relief when she spoke again.

'Also, on a shallower note ... ' Kathleen took a gulp of fizz. 'Not to sound paranoid, but JD's girlfriend is stunning. She's got her come-to-bed eyes and her fuck-me hair and whatever, and she's on him like a jacket, so he can dismiss a woman like me.'

'A woman like you. What does that even mean?' I crossed and uncrossed my legs; I could feel a pressure inside me like explosive matter waiting to detonate.

'It doesn't matter.' Her voice was clipped and terse, as it had been that first time we met. 'Why are we discussing this?'

'Because I am really ... I feel very strongly about you,' I said, wincing at the silly, costume-drama sound of the words, 'and your appearance has, quite obviously, got nothing to do with that.'

'That is very sweet of you.'

'Don't patronize me. It's not as if, because I can't see, you don't exist physically for me. I can see you in ways you can't even comprehend.'

'So what do you "see" now?'

'Your smell,' I said. 'Smelling you is like ... is like touching you, almost. I noticed that as soon as I was first in the room with you.'

'Why don't you do it, then? Why don't you do it now?'

As if in slow motion, Kathleen took my head in both her hands, turned it to face her and pressed it into her shoulder. I kept my head buried there, drinking in her tangy, shiny scent. Her hair fell around and teased my cheekbones.

'How is it?' she asked.

'It's wonderful,' I said, 'like I told you.'

'Feel just down from where you are. There's a little zip. Can you find it? It's fiddly.' My fingers grasped for the bite of metal, but hesitated there.

'Go on then.'

'Are you sure about this?'

'Yes. It will be so nice to get the sodding thing off. I hate dresses.'

'And is that the only reason?'

'No,' Kathleen conceded, 'that is not the only reason.'

My hand was trembling. At the third try she reached round and made the first inch with the zip. I began to apologize; she shushed me and slid off the bed. 'I'm stepping out of it,' she said. 'And the shoes.' She kicked them off against the wall as JD used to after school.

'You've got no chance with the bra,' she said. 'But you can probably help with the rest.'

My hands found the elastic of her tights and peeled them down until she freed her feet. The grip of blindness had never been so loose. It played no part in my experience. My whole body felt like one tensed, throbbing muscle. I took hold of the even slighter material of her underwear and eased it down.

'So, there you go,' said Kathleen, her voice losing a notch of volume. 'Completely naked now.'

'Are you sure you … '

'If you ask again whether I'm sure,' she said, 'I will kick you in the cock.'

Kneeling in front of her, I pressed my face against her shin, up to her calf, onto the softness of her thigh, wanting to be swallowed up by the flesh. There was a strange urgent sound of which I was only half-aware: I realized she was breathing at an almost panicky pace. As I eased my face into her stomach, she took a step back.

'Sorry. Sorry.'

'No, it's fine, it's me.' She came out with a fearful sort of laugh. 'I'm not entirely sure I … I thought this through.'

'We can stop.'

'I didn't say to stop. I just mean, well. I didn't entirely pre-pare to be inhaled. I could have had a shower, used some of those little bottles you have in the bathrooms here.'

'This is the whole point. I don't want you to hide anything. I want everything.'

'Take everything, then.'

I breathed in her stomach, moved upwards to the long curve of her breasts, into her armpits, and back down until my mouth was nestling against the fuzz of hair where her legs began. She was sighing loudly now. I shuffled forward on my knees, so I was behind her, and plunged my face between her buttocks. When I surfaced she was down at my waist, grappling with my belt. I felt as if my eyes opened, only to close again as I drifted away with her.

꩜ 7 ꩜

GRAHAM

I had seen a great many odd sights in the Alpha. That man who broke the door of Room 25, and his wife who hurled her wedding ring up into the balconies; a demonstration of a chemical mixture which, injected into the body of a dead person, could preserve their organs for hundreds of years; the American astronaut who was first to walk on the Moon. There was a lady who seemed able to predict the future with almost chilling accuracy, a bird called a cassowary which was capable of killing a man, and a reputed intellectual who swore that he had been visited in his room by a ghost. And four dead bodies, all except Roz Tanner wheeled out of the front doors in the early hours of the morning when as few guests as possible would be around. I had, as they say, seen it all. But in its own way, nothing was quite so queer – and wonderful – as the spectacle of Chas, only months after meeting Kathleen, simply walking out of the Alpha's doors as if he had not spent most of his life steadfastly refusing to do any such thing.

Here he was, all of a sudden, early on a cool September evening, standing in front of the reception desk in a running singlet, a pair of plimsolls, and a giant sickly grin.

'We'll just have a quick trot in Regent's Park,' said Kathleen. 'I'm going to hold Chas's arm at first, like you hold the back of a bike, and I reckon he'll get into it.'

'And you … you are all in favour of this?' I asked Chas.

'About time I got some exercise,' he said.

'You've had *some* exercise,' Kathleen murmured, and the two of them fell into snickering. I was reminded against my will of Agatha, the risqué remarks she occasionally brought out of me.

Chas fairly skipped along with Kathleen, and the doors swung behind them with a joyous energy. I rubbed my eyes and pictured the scene in the park: Chas jogging along beside Kathleen in her T-shirt and leggings, the two of them hooting at some joke between their snatched breaths.

Not a few weeks into their relationship, Chas had been outside more than in all his previous life. She had lured him to the cinema, and to restaurants, and now the running became a weekly thing. Kathleen seemed to do it a lot; she had a timing gadget which I always teased her about because it seemed unnecessarily complicated. 'Have you heard,' I once asked, 'of this marvellous new invention called a stopwatch?'

'That's enough of your cheek, Graham,' she said, and laughed; but the moment, like many an atrium moment, was snapped off at the end by Lara Krohl. Emerging from the bar, computer under her arm, she offered one of her blunt unsolicited remarks. 'Getting into shape, Kath, yah?'

'I run a couple of times a week,' said Kathleen, colouring a little. Lara Krohl continued on her way, having done what sometimes seemed to be her job: remarking, observing, stocking up on the details of others' lives and making them aware of it.

That night was a hot one, and Pattie shuffled and sighed and plugged in a fan which made such a racket that sleeping became even more difficult. 'I really feel,' I said, as we lay on our backs in the semi-dark, 'certain people think Chas is theirs, and they're hostile to Kathleen out of some sort of rivalry. Jonathan David, for instance, and Lara Krohl ... '

'Who's Lara Krohl?' Pattie shifted onto her side again.

'I've told you about her. South African lady. Chas works for her, and Howard ... well, he's advised by her.'

'Do you think Howard's got a thing going on with her?' And before I knew it, we had boarded – as it were – another train altogether. 'Do you know, Margaret sent me a story from America to look at, something she found on the Internet. It was about a man who's having an affair with his secretary. Quite a famous man, I think. So, they go on like that for a few months.'

And Pattie herself went on for what felt like a few months. The description of this Internet flim-flam tired her out at last, and I was left to think about Kathleen and Chas and their courtship.

Courtship: not a word anyone used nowadays, I supposed, yet it sounded appropriate. Chas was always skittish and chatty before she arrived, forlorn if something detained her, goofy as a drunkard when they exchanged a final kiss in the atrium. It reminded me a little of when I was wooing Pattie and had to hang around on the corner of the road in order to meet when she finished work at the swimming pool. Nobody now leaned on a lamp post in case a 'certain little lady came by': they carried telephones, they could change their plans by the second. Chas and Kathleen, though, always met and parted in the same place. Theirs was an old-fashioned affair.

'I didn't think we'd ever get him to go out,' Howard said, watching fondly as our boy strode off on another expedition to the Tate gallery, Kathleen swinging his arm energetically. 'Turned out he just needed to be going out *with* someone.'

A strange business, love. I ought to have known that. Hadn't I seen enough, in this very building, of the bother it caused? Yet right in the middle of this blooming romance, midway through a patch of gloomy July days which had disappointed tourists scuttling like mice through the atrium, its workings caught me quite unawares.

A grey day had turned into a wet night. As I walked up the hill towards home, my mind was on this new war we had got ourselves involved in. It was terrible to think that more mothers, now, would have to pick up the telephone and hear what Agatha had once had to. I was certain that Kathleen was right – we were better off out of it. Howard felt differently, but all that meant, I sensed, was that Lara had persuaded him differently.

At the turn of the key in the lock I heard a youthful voice raised, and thoughts of politics went clean out of my head. Christopher was here! In surprise I almost galloped into the living room, wanting to lift him and spin him round. It was only after arriving in the room and calling out his name delightedly that I troubled to assess the scene.

Christopher had been crying. Caroline was dishevelled in a cardigan and jeans, her hair unwashed and scraped roughly back, looking close to tears herself and almost as old as her mother. Patricia was wearing her blue M&S dressing gown and a frumpy expression, arms folded.

'Can we play a game, Gramps?' asked Christopher, his little pink nose twitching hopefully.

'It's past midnight, young Topher,' I said.

'Actually, Dad, if you could … ' Caroline appealed to me. 'We've got … we're in the middle of talking about some stuff here.'

'Well, I don't see the harm in dominoes,' I said obligingly, not at all sure what was afoot. 'Let's go up to your room, Topher.'

'Or what about Hungry Hippos?' he haggled.

'Very well,' I said with a comical sigh, 'or Hungry Hippos.'

I quickly threw together some jam sandwiches and took

him up to our spare room – once Ed's room, and still boasting his old map of the world, some of whose national borders and names were now obsolete. Christopher climbed into bed and the two of us played without talking: there was just the rumble as the balls rolled onto the board, and the fast clack-clack of the hippopotamuses' heads as Christopher bashed zealously away. Before long he seemed to droop, his eyelids sliding half down. He looked near sleep when suddenly the original problem, the problem under discussion downstairs, stole back onto his face.

'Oh, Gramps,' he said, 'everything is jolly awful.'

'What exactly is happening, Christopher?' I put my hand on his shoulder, marvelling as usual at how big he had grown, and how little he still was.

'Mum's taking me away,' said Christopher. 'She doesn't want to live with Dad any more. She wants to live with someone else instead, in Inverness.'

'Inverness? In Scotland?'

His lip curled and his large, long-lashed eyes surged with fresh tears. 'Yes. It's very far indeed. I won't be able to see Dad.'

'Now, then,' I said, switching off his bedside light. 'I'm sure you've got it confused somewhere. I'm sure that's all it is.'

But my gut was full of misgivings as I went down the stairs. Patricia and Caroline were sitting in a washed-out silence.

'Is it true?' I asked.

Caroline looked out of the window.

'I can't live with him,' she said. 'I can't do it. He's never there.

He only cares about work. He doesn't ... our relationship isn't a real relationship. I can't do it,' she said, again.

'But another man?'

'He's a good man.' Caroline's tone was flat and functional; she had had this conversation too many times already. 'He'll look after us. He will.'

'You are seriously proposing,' I asked, 'to move to ... to Inverness, and take Christopher with you?'

'Tell her, Graham,' Pattie appealed, 'tell her it's madness.'

'How on earth did you meet a man in Inverness?'

'Over the web,' she said. 'I got chatting to him. He's been in a failed relationship too. And one thing led to another, we texted. We met up one time when Brian was away. *One* of the times he was away.' She snorted. 'Anyway, I realized Neil is who I should have been with all along.'

'Tell her, Graham,' Pattie begged again, as if there were some password I needed only to utter and all this would be solved: we would be back in an Indian summer for their wedding day, back at the joyous announcement of a grandchild.

'Please, Dad,' Caroline countered, 'please understand I wouldn't do this unless I knew it was right. He can see Brian every couple of weeks, every ... we'll sort something out.'

And me? I wanted to ask. What chance did I have of seeing Christopher if even his father was to be an occasional player now, if truly she was going to take him to the other end of the British Isles? I pictured his baffled, sleepy eyes and imagined him in a new bedroom, in the house of a man he did not know. It was cold in Inverness, too. I could not quite think about it all.

'You have to support me,' said Caroline. 'I mean – I'm asking you, please, to support me.'

I cleared my throat, which felt sandpaper-dry, but managed to say nothing. Pattie got up and went to the kitchen. I heard her fill the kettle. I reached out and held Caroline's arm. After a short while she got up and went up the creaky old stairs to check on Christopher.

I stared at the curtains, the ones that had hung there when we played charades that Christmas; it was impossible to believe it was the same room. My wife and daughter came back into the room simultaneously, moving round one another in the doorway like complete strangers.

∞

That was a hard night. First there was Pattie's bedtime address to get through, as long as the Queen's Speech and with as few surprises. I did not blame her: these were exceptional circumstances. Did it seem reasonable? Pattie enquired again and again. To meet someone on a computer and go off with them? It seemed like madness, didn't it? She was not really looking for an answer. I let her talk until she ran out of steam and drifted off, leaving me and the gloomy grey-orange night outside. I went quietly down to the kitchen and mustered up some ham;

the effort of putting chips in the oven seemed somehow to be beyond me, so I ate it on its own and thought about what had happened tonight.

It was not as if I thought love affairs were all as neat and predictable as the marriage we ourselves were in. I had not stood behind the reception desk all this time with my ears closed to arguments, coded conversations and anguished phone calls, no matter how much the people involved might have thought their situation unique and undetectable. And I had seen first-hand the consequences of this sort of thing a long time ago.

It was a couple of years before JD was born, and a long time before Chas came into our lives. Sarah-Jane stormed into the atrium one night, a slammed door echoing behind her. She was wearing what they call a kimono jacket, as they were meant to be going to a Japanese-themed ball. But there would be no ball – you could see that, all right. She was in tears. I took her by the arm to the privacy of the smoking room. Howard had cheated on her, said Sarah-Jane. There was a guest who came often. They went to a room. He went to meet her in Bloomsbury. She had left a message on the answerphone and Sarah-Jane had found it.

Worse, this apparently was not even the first time. I had thought the nickname Howard-you-like referred solely to his inexhaustible appetite for high jinks; not that it was also meant to reflect his persuasive abilities in a very specific arena. I was rather dumbfounded.

'So,' I asked, 'what are you going to … do about it?'

'Do?' echoed Sarah-Jane. 'I'll do what I always do. I'll forgive him. Because I haven't got anywhere else to go. And because I love him. That's the stupid thing, Graham. I still love him.'

Where my own reaction was concerned, I had two options: to regard my hero in a new and rather unpleasant light, or to go on exactly as I always had. You are familiar by now with the sort of decisions I generally make.

People's love for one another could outlast the misery caused by betrayal or disloyalty: that was one thing that episode taught me. Another, obverse, lesson was that loving somebody – even for a lifetime – did not exclude you from having strong feelings for somebody else. Howard had learned this fairly early in life. As ever, he was ahead of me.

There was the dancing with Agatha: well, that was nothing to worry about. There were all the jokes and the games and the fact that looking forward to tomorrow's workday, and looking forward to seeing her, had become difficult emotions to separate. I began to take her into my confidence; I told her about Howard's past misdemeanours, and about certain other matters of the hotel's history which had weighed on my mind longer than I admitted to myself. And finally there came the afternoon in February when I visited Room 25 with a tray of fish and chips, her favourite. Come in! she shouted, and I walked in to find her trailing water across the light-coloured carpet, wearing only a towel, and barely wearing that. I set the tray down with a crash.

'Hey, you trying to demolish Mr York's nice hotel?' she said, cackling, turning away from me. I could not take my eyes away from her body. She seemed to catch sight of herself in the mirror and understand the situation. She turned to face me again. Drops of shower-water fled her wetted hair, raced down her shoulders towards her great cleavage. She let the towel fall gently away. I looked at her, all of her, and did not know what to do. Then there was noise in the corridor; Mrs Davey, perhaps, or a bellboy delivering an order. Agatha seemed not to panic but to consider coolly that we had made a mistake.

'Go, go,' she said, moving with sudden, alarming swiftness towards clothes, throwing something on. 'You need to go, Graham.'

I went. I went down in the lift and walked to reception and gave someone directions to Covent Garden, called Ed about rugby tickets, tidied my pile of leaflets, went on a rapid circuit of the hotel to see what else could be done. Agatha was back at the desk late that night, after the final housekeeping rounds, and we did not discuss what had happened. Nor did we the next day, nor the next. We played the check-in guessing game. We swatted flies. After a week or so of this, it became another of those things that you left undiscussed so long they disappeared. I went back to Pattie every night; Agatha back to her one-room apartment with the picture of her son. But one day, barely two months after the incident, she looked up from her Bible.

'Graham, I'm going to leave next week.'

'Leave … ?'

'Going to depart from the hotel.'

As I caught up with her meaning, my first feeling was a violent twist in the stomach as if I were about to be sick.

'Why?'

'Another job,' she said, 'found a different job.'

'Really?'

'Yes. Good job. Got to go, Graham.'

But she would not meet my eye and she would not talk about it much more than that. The more I thought about it, the more convinced I was: it must be my fault. Either Howard suspected us of wrongdoing, or he had found out I'd told her something about him and was getting rid of her; or she had simply decided to leave because of what happened in Room 25. Anyhow, it was my fault, all right. That was why she could not tell me any more about it; why she continued to hold her tongue over the hollow days that followed.

Her last day is not one I look back on with affection. We made our usual amusing conversation. The clock raced round and round, perfectly indifferent. At eight, we had drinks in the bar. Howard was away, but Sarah-Jane toasted her with champagne. As I walked Agatha to the doors, everything felt flat and thin, as if the Alpha were a film set used years ago and left to moulder.

'What are we going to do without you!' I said, trying to make it sound like a joke.

'Now, it will be all right, Graham,' she told me, 'because these thing, they always are.'

I drove her to Hornchurch that last night. She would write when she could. She was thinking about travelling; she had a sister in America. She said a few things like this. She might, though, have been whistling 'Auld Lang Syne' for all I could take in. I had the strong impression, as I embraced her, that the goodbye was likely to be a permanent one.

'Good luck,' I said.

She was wrapped in the same enormous coat as the day I first met her. It made me feel as if the whole thing were beginning all over again, instead of ending. She put down her heavy bag and struggled with the front door for what seemed a long time; somehow I wanted her to disappear properly before I went anywhere. At last, as the door yielded, I tore my eyes away and started the engine.

When, not long after, it emerged that Ella was also leaving, I did wonder if something more complicated might be going on. But Howard and Sarah-Jane were disinclined to talk about it; and after a certain point, as the months went by, it no longer really mattered why Agatha had left. Only that she had, and that it was quiet without her, and that every time I heard a raucous female laugh, or the tread of big boots on the marble floor,

I looked up in case she had decided to come back, knowing already that it would be someone else.

⚬⚬

It was years now since I had thought properly about all this. It served no purpose to think about it, but tonight everything was peculiar. I could hear Christopher cry out in his sleep; Caroline creaking over the floorboards to his room. Once I went out to see her, making her jump, and asked if she were all right. 'No,' she said, with a sorry smile, 'but thank you, Dad.' The wind whined outside; a cat, or something wilder, gave a wail from time to time.

As I finally took myself back upstairs, I passed the computer, off-duty on its big ugly table in the living room. I thought about Caroline sitting at another computer, tapping messages to this man in Inverness, planning to whisk Christopher far away from me. I thought of Lara Krohl and the look that had come over her face at the mention of Agatha and Ella; it was impossible to picture Krohl without also seeing the laptop computer that always sat six inches in front of her. I pictured the PCs humming their way through the night in the smoking room where Agatha and I used to dance. It was clearer and clearer that I had dismissed these machines too easily. They were living among us like a new species, and the world was theirs as much as mine.

8

CHAS

Kathleen had a journalist's ruthlessness. She could skim for five minutes through the whole daily stack of papers and absorb what mattered, like the body breaking down food into nutrients. She knew all the columnists' names, their particular agendas. She could speed-read to me from a webpage faster than Howard, faster than anyone I could have hoped to meet. She knew about food, famous people, musicians, architecture, all kinds of things which had never found their way into what now seemed the arbitrary spectrum of my knowledge. Sometimes she was astounded by the things I hadn't come across.

'I refuse to accept you don't know the Rolling Stones.'

'I know "Satisfaction". Howard sings it.'

'Bowie? Dylan?'

'Is Dylan the one with the funny voice?'

'Christ in Hong Kong!' she marvelled.

'Well, what was I meant to do? Search the net for "what music is good"?'

'I'll do you some playlists. I am your Internet now.'

It was as if I'd only ever seen the universe through the Alpha's skylight, and now I was up on the roof with a sky full of stars above me. 'That's a nice way of looking at it,' said Kathleen when I shared this with her. 'But it'd be even nicer if we actually got you going outside.'

'It's not really my thing.'

'I had noticed. But you'd be surprised. Some of it is actually quite nice.'

We went to lunchtime recitals at St Martin's. We saw films in the early afternoon in a perennially empty one-screen place where the foyer's air tasted of cigarette smoke. Kathleen provided audio commentary. 'Guy comes into the room. He's got a big nose like mine. He watches the two of them kissing. Is pretty pissed off.' Once, there was a man slumped in a seat several rows in front of us: it was only when we got up to leave that Kathleen noticed him. 'I'm so sorry,' she said, 'I was wittering on all the way through.'

'Actually, it was very helpful,' he said, 'I couldn't really follow it.'

He told me I was a lucky man to have Kathleen. 'Not so lucky to be blind,' I pointed out.

'Ah, fair point. That must make it difficult, eh?'

'His dick isn't blind,' Kathleen assured him.

We went on our way through a London whose frantic noise and action no longer frightened me. The more I moved through it, in fact, the harder it was to get back in touch with that fear: it was like someone whose name I couldn't quite remember. People lived their lives, nothing more or less. The non-blind life was the same as mine. Some days I never even had the thought that I couldn't see. I tried to explain this, not very successfully, to JD.

'What you're saying is, things are a lot better when you're banging someone.'

Moving through the atrium, these days, I felt as if a suit of armour had been lifted off me. Even so, when Kathleen first suggested a run, I thought she was out of her mind.

'What am I going to run in, exactly? You think I have a sponsorship deal with Nike?'

'I took the liberty of picking up some kit for you.' She put it into my hands, a plastic-feeling top, a pair of shorts. 'I hope you're joking about Nike, by the way. Their record is appalling. What are you waiting for? Do I have to help you get undressed again?'

It was one of the first evenings of September, which had put a soggy summer out of its misery. There were memorial concerts planned for London and New York; my computer was reading me 'one year on' articles. We walked along arm-in-arm. I no longer worried which direction was which, or how far anything was: I would have walked to Land's End as long as she kept hold of me.

I trusted her even when, at the park gates, she made me do a series of loosening exercises, standing on one leg, swivelling my ankle and stretching my calf.

'Are you sure this doesn't look stupid?'

'Listen to you, all interested in what things look like suddenly.'

At first it was barely more than walking, then she coaxed me into a sort of walk-trot, then a trot-jog. 'Just keep going. We're not going to hit anything. You're not going to fall over. It's the same principle as walking.'

The first fallen leaves were already dying at the bases of trees, she said. You could smell the damp of them, and bonfire smoke in the air, and the shock of a clear sky losing its light. They were seasonal smells, I supposed, but I'd never noticed seasons before. I could hear Kathleen's breaths and the squeaking of her shoes, and my senses conjured up the rest: her muscled backside tensed in Lycra, an expression of studious concentration. I allowed my breathing to slip into time with hers. Others trotted by harmlessly, like trains on parallel rails. I was a tiny speck in the universe.

The atrium was warm and homelike as we walked arm in arm across the echoing floor. Of course, it had always been like that. Howard, returning, never failed to take exaggerated breaths in and out as if newly arrived in a restorative mountain retreat; Mike Swan, in his guide, had written about the way all your problems seemed to be shut out when those big doors closed behind you. It was part of what people came to the Alpha for: the impression it gave of being another country from the cold, tough one they might have found outside.

But it was only now that I was really starting to understand how cosy it was to return to the hotel: now that I'd mastered the task of leaving it. The atrium murmured with its usual good-spirited soundtrack, glasses clinking and intimate voices hatching plans. Howard, from the area of the bar, called out a jokey welcome: here comes Seb Coe. I threw back some remark about his smoking. In Room 25, Kathleen set the shower running.

'Going to stand there watching me take my clothes off, pervert?'

I peeled off my things and followed her into the sound of the water, pressing myself into her shiny scent before it was all washed away. I grew hard against her as the water pelted us and she covered us both in sweet-smelling gels. I liked showering together, but the best bit was always the moment before, when I could smell her day all over her, all the bodily exertions.

There was nothing better than breathing her in, all the secrets of her skin. I smelled her when she arrived sticky from the Underground, I stood by as she peed with aggressive force in the echoing bathroom, I let her throw me suddenly onto the bed only to flip me over and ask me to take charge. When she was on the phone to editors or interviewing subjects in strange parts of the globe, I let my impatience boil deliciously into excitement. I was the only one who could win. None of these people with whom I was forced to share Kathleen could know what she whispered in my ear and what her body told me as I held her in her sleep.

But there was always something or someone waiting to steal her. Though we might fall asleep together, she always seemed to have woken up before me. There was an anti-war march somewhere, she was booked onto a lunchtime flight, she had to go – 'I'll be back tomorrow or the day after,' she'd say, kissing me on the forehead, slipping out of the door. If she left in the evening, the routine would be drawn-out and painful. She'd take a long shower, brush her teeth vigorously, zip up her overnight bag, and the innocuous sounds would plunge me one note at a time into sadness. The airport car would be waiting, booked by Graham with his postcode joke. I always tried to kiss her a final time, but she liked to keep the partings brief.

'Don't. Or I won't go. I'll just end up coming back to the room and getting back into bed with you.'

'Well, yes. That's what I'm aiming for.'

After she'd gone, her absence was huge in the room. It stood between me and my keyboard; it lay in the cold bed. I would pace the corridors, hearing from behind identical doors the whispers of strangers' nights: low voices, drinks poured out, TV chatter, anguished monologues. I tried unsuccessfully to immerse myself in my work, writing copy for an army recruitment campaign. Nothing was as important as wanting Kathleen back. 'Tomorrow or the day after.' As if there were no difference, which for her there barely was. Her days were brief units of time, eating themselves up as she raced to squeeze out of them what she wanted. Mine, without her, were edgeless again.

How had I come to need her so much, so quickly? Probably the need had always been there. Only now did it have a name and a shape and a smell.

I dreamed about her moving through strange landscapes, calling me to come after her, and when I woke I would have to check my talk-out-loud phone and email and then ask someone to look up flight arrivals on the Internet to be absolutely sure she still existed.

Late September threw us a surprise series of sweltering afternoons, and Kathleen marched me out to do some shopping for winter clothes.

'But it's baking hot.'

'Yes, but as the year goes on it will get colder, you see. I thought you were blind, not an idiot. Oops.' Our joined arms, swinging back and forth, clipped a passer-by.

'Hey, watch where you're going!'

'He's blind,' Kathleen shouted after him. 'Did you say you hated the blind?'

We went spluttering with laughter down the escalator to the Tube. This was the second time, for me. The train hammered its way into the station with a rush of air in our faces, and Kathleen waited for the bleep-bleep of the doors' sensors, the thud as they came open, and helped me inside. I liked the feeling that everyone was as blind as me here, with nothing but dark outside.

She talked to me in pictures back up to ground level. 'There are ads all along the side of the escalator. Just a massive jumble of crap. West End shows, very thin women in shoes. Speaking of West End shows, we're now behind about two thousand old ladies who've been to a matinee. Oh! And there's another blind guy. Being helped along by an Underground man in a blue cap.'

Kathleen steered me into a shop. Noises lay in wait like caged animals: throbbing music, the whine of an alarm, the hiss of a security guard's radio. Nothing made me flinch. 'A few minutes actually on a train or in a shop,' I said, 'is better than a lifetime of theory.'

Her kisses were surprise attacks, swooping out of nowhere and hitting like a stun-gun, putting my brain out of the fight so that I was just a body. She clattered me along Regent Street towards Piccadilly and we stood with people piling past us like sound waves.

'What can we see?'

'We're right beneath the famous screens, the adverts. Pigeons everywhere. Buses and cabs keep looking like they're going to crush them all, then the pigeons fly away at the last second. The buses are incredibly red when the sun hits them. Red like in a tourist brochure. Actually, the whole place looks like a tourist brochure today. The sky's a fantastic blue. The ... is this weird for you?'

'Is what weird?'

'Is it unhelpful for me to talk about red and blue?'

'No. I feel like I know what red and blue are, with you. I feel like I know what everything is.'

Her hands climbed, in their unapologetic way, across my waist and gave an almost vicious squeeze to my crotch.

'Presumably lots of people saw that.'

'Oh, yes.' She laughed. 'This is one of the most public places in the United Kingdom.' A kiss stung my lips. 'It's such a shame we can't have full sex. But there are policemen and so forth. Any more tourist guide stuff I can help with?'

'What do I look like?'

'You have a lovely, handsome face.'

'Despite the funny bits around my eyes?'

'Including those bits. Which, in fact, are hardly visible. Your mouth curls in a wicked way when you make a joke. You are a perfect height, now that I've cured your appalling posture. Your penis is aesthetically pleasing ... '

'Aesthetically pleasing. Yes, I thought that's what you were saying last night.'

' ... as is your bottom.'

'Well, I sound absolutely delightful.'

That night, as we made love in Room 25, we pretended it was still Piccadilly Circus and people were walking by, watching us or affecting not to notice. It was a fantasy, but it was also reality. Reality was what we said it was.

We lay on the rumpled sheets afterwards, her breathing fierce on my chest. A trolley rattled by outside; there was a loud knock and an answering cry and we listened as the bellboy took the tray inside. He would ask for a signature and leave the tray on the desk, or maybe the bed, and the guest would eat the meal and look out over Fitzrovia and the BT Tower. Kathleen and I could lie here and everything else could go on without us.

'Do you know who Agatha Richards is?' she asked.

It was as unexpected as her kisses, as the way she sometimes disappeared in the morning.

'Yes. She used to work here. She left. Ages ago.'

'Why'd she leave?'

I experienced a trace of discomfort almost too fine to be detected. 'I don't know. Another job or something.' My tongue came out and touched my bottom lip. 'Why?'

'It's just the couple of times I've been on the net in the IT room, there's a lot of searches for her.'

A pause played itself out.

'She left at the same time as Ella,' I said, 'my old tutor, who was, apart from you, the only person who ... Anyway.'

'And you never asked why either of them left?'

'People were never that keen to talk about it.'

'You can't *not* talk about stuff,' said Kathleen, 'because

people aren't keen to.' She slid off the bed and began to walk around as if working up to something. The mood in the room had shifted rapidly into something spiky and brittle. 'Did you ever see – I mean, you know … '

'You can say "see". See what?'

'Did they ever show you the medical records on you? Like, after the fire, the surgery you had? Or anything about your father, any of the paperwork … '

'No. None of it. Why?' The post-sex warmth was intruded upon by a deeper, unpleasant blush. 'Why would I want to see all that shit? Why would it matter to me?'

'Well, don't you wonder about your dad from time to time?'

'What is there to wonder about?' I felt a vein in my neck pulse with sudden anger. JD told me that normal people sometimes saw faint shapes in front of their eyes, or spots of light, when they shouted. There was something similar happening to me now: a hazing and shifting of the dark, only just perceptible, perhaps imaginary. 'He's gone. He's dead, or he's nowhere around. And it doesn't matter. Howard is my dad. Why would I think about someone who never came to see me – '

'You wouldn't. I'm sorry.'

' – when there's someone who's been here nearly every day of my life? Who has done everything for me?'

There was a silence. She came softly back to the bed and touched my face. 'Chas? I'm sorry.'

'It's fine.'

There was a pause, and she went into the bathroom. The water bellowed from the metal jets and I heard her exhale as it hit her skin. The dissonant moment had passed quickly for her, like all her moments did. Kathleen was a journalist, she was bound to seek out intrigues, she was accustomed to firing off questions.

I thought about the fact that someone had been looking up Agatha online. It had to be Howard or Graham. I wasn't sure I wanted to ask myself why, or to think about how angry Howard would be if he'd heard Kathleen's questioning. Kathleen stayed in the shower for a long time. When she came out, it was as if this first little argument between us had never happened. But the tension lingered, all the same, in the effort we made not to acknowledge it.

∝

A nightclub in Bali was attacked that October. Kathleen had written a piece just weeks before about the risk of more terror attacks in the wake of 9/11. A Melbourne paper now took up her article. It began to get hits on her site as others linked to it. We went to dinner and there were a thousand; when we came back, it was four thousand. 'Shit in my *hat*!' shouted Kathleen, grabbing my hand in excitement. 'Three thousand hits in an hour! Fuck me twice!'

'I'd be delighted,' I said. But she was already on the phone to someone; she'd already begun another conversation. I would be lucky if we did it once. And that was how it was, at the moment. She went to Madrid and Berlin in the space of a single week. There were going to be demonstrations everywhere, she said. She had also become obsessed with the Olympics being planned in China for 2008. They were frantically whitewashing their civil rights record, she gabbled at me. They were bombarding us with propaganda. The Olympics was a filthy business, she told me, flying off to Beijing on a November night.

'Four days. Four or five days. That's all.'

The Olympic Committee was corrupt, according to Kathleen, but Howard and Lara were entertaining their members every other week in the Alpha Bar, planning London's bid. Kathleen said the war in Afghanistan was a terrible idea and an Iraq invasion would be worse still, but many of its architects and supporters were welcome in our bar; they were Howard's friends, they engaged in calculated flirting with Lara. Come the new year, I was on the recipient list for a government email detailing ways we could play down the importance of the coming Iraq protest. Ten hand-spans away from me was somebody who would play up its importance as much as she could.

For a long while we acted as if the clash didn't exist. I listened to my headphones and we talked about which songs I liked best and ate in restaurants where she read out the menu with ironic commentary. I kept tapping away at my press releases, she at her articles. When she talked on the phone to other anti-war writers, I turned the music up and sat at the keys like one of the pianists they hired to play romantic tunes in other hotels: fingers moving mechanically, droning out a message that had nothing to do with them.

None of this would work forever. I'd come a long way with the notion that the world was now virtual and could be experienced from my room in the Alpha. World events, though, were not virtual; the world was still real, this war was real. The problem it created for us was also real.

By now I could trot along behind her in the park, as long as she never speeded up unexpectedly or went so far ahead that I couldn't reach out and touch her. I was still less like a training partner and more like a skittish animal, but then, not many track athletes were people who'd been unable to leave their house for twenty years. Afterwards she always told me how brave I was, and how proud she was of me, and in the shower she would generally do things to me which didn't happen every day even to a gold-medal winner.

One February afternoon, when we went out at three, the grass was already slippery and the air carried the threat of chill. We had been running for about twenty minutes, and Kathleen's breathing had ramped up gradually in speed and intensity so I could follow her now like a drumbeat. Conversation, by this stage of a run, had to be conducted in snatched sound bites. I chose this as my moment.

'Hey ... '

'What?'

'This protest. The march.'

There were a few breaths, a few seconds' worth of padding footfall in front of me. 'Yes?'

'Are you going?'

'Of course.'

My own heart was thudding away. I took a gulp of air. 'I won't. Be able to.'

'I know.'

'Because of Lara.'

For what could have been a whole minute, it was just my breathing and her breathing, and the thin air, and the park's silence.

'Lara would never ... let me ... do something in public. Which would ... compromise the agency,' I managed to get out.

'I know,' she said again.

'But.' I ran on a little way. Squelch went my shoes over the muddy turf. A dog yapped an order to its owner somewhere out on the breeze. 'But you don't approve.'

'Of course I don't approve.'

I ran on. She ran on. Her words jogged between us.

'I think the principle involved ... ' she said. We ran a few steps more. ' ... is more important than any job.' The rest of her verdict arrived in a single rush. 'It's an illegal war. That's being proposed. By our own government.'

I had one card I'd been saving up. 'It's the day after our anniversary. The day we first met.'

'I've already … ' she panted. We were both panting. I craved the slowdown that normally came around now. 'I've already booked. A restaurant. The march is the next morning.'

When we finished our circuit and stopped at the gates, all either of us could do was rope our respective breaths back in. I reached towards her voice and my hand landed on her arm, singing with sweat in the way which zipped through me as always like an electric current. I yanked the arm towards me and, without resisting outright, she stiffened and inched backwards. I felt her touch fall away from me.

'It's cold,' she said, and we began to walk back to the Alpha.

⁂

For a couple of hours on Valentine's afternoon, Howard made the Wellness Suite unavailable to the public and we had it to ourselves. Kathleen took me into the female changing room, which smelled of wood and spice, and undressed me to a soundtrack of whimpering pan pipes. Below the hot tub's waterline she touched every part of me, breathing hard in my ear. We showered together and I dressed in a new shirt she had bought me. Graham drove us across town to the restaurant.

'*Carpaccio of long-line-caught yellowfin tuna flavoured with a lemon and dill garnish*. Right, "carpaccio of tuna" means "bit of tuna". "Long-line-caught" means they didn't scoop it out of the Pacific with their bare hands. "Flavoured with" means "with".'

'Well, it all sounds pretty nice now you've explained it.'

'Oh, you're not having it. It's endangered.'

We were onto a second bottle before too long. The wine slipping down my throat was like a series of kisses, and the sensation reminded me of drinking with her in the Alpha Bar a year ago. Words galloped out of me.

'I don't know if you can imagine how much difference you've made. How many things I can do now which wouldn't have seemed possible.'

'Well, it's the same for me,' she said. 'I would never have believed, a year ago, how much time I could occupy a hotel room without paying a single … '

'Oh, don't make a joke out of it,' I found myself pleading. 'Say something real.'

'You complete dick-bag. Do you think I would have walked around in a spa, a year ago, all confident like I am now? Or walk into a restaurant full of pretty people and feel good about myself?'

'I don't know,' I said. 'I didn't know you, did I?'

'All right: well, I'm telling you. I wouldn't have. All that is you.'

We held hands across the table and I thought about all the people who would love to be living my life at this moment.

'I want you to come,' she said.

'Come ... ?'

'On the march. It would mean a lot to me.'

'What, it would mean a lot to you if it was a million and one people, not a million?'

'To have you there on a big day. Something I've put a lot of work into publicizing and drumming up interest for. You know. Just to have you by my side.'

I heard myself agree to it, and as her hand tightened round mine, it felt as if it had been the right thing to say.

The second annual singles' night was meandering to its end in the Alpha. A mawkish ballad floated out of the bar. Howard and Lara were standing at the entrance, said Kathleen.

'Your boss is giving out leaflets for something or other ...'

'Oh, yeah. We do PR for all these singles nights. There's one for Christians soon. And one for naturists, which Howard has said they can do here.'

'There's a crowd round Howard,' Kathleen said. I could feel the weight of bodies and hear ragged, tipsy cheering. 'He's ... what's he doing? Some sort of trick. Oh, he's juggling.'

'He does do that.'

I felt as if I'd seen his face a million times: turned eagerly to his makeshift audience, grinning in a way that was assured of their love, yet winningly asking for more of it.

'Now he's balancing ... what the fuck?'

'Balancing a chair on his face. Yeah. It's one of his party pieces.'

Again I could all but picture it: his face turned up towards the skylight like a performing seal's, the chair's back legs miraculously supported by his forehead. Whoops and whistles echoed. Kathleen took my arm, but Howard had seen us.

'Say hello, everyone,' he said in a voice so loud and assured he might indeed be addressing everyone in the building. 'This is my son, Chas.'

The applause now swivelled around like a sprinkler.

'Been out tonight?' asked Lara.

'Our restaurant not good enough for you, mate?' Howard teased. The tug on my arm was almost violent this time, and we were in the lift almost before I had tossed a reply back over my shoulder. Kathleen was stiff and hot in the airspace next to mine.

'What's the matter?'

'*I'm* not good enough for you,' she said, 'that's what he meant. Always the same thing.'

'He was only joking.'

'You didn't see his face.'

'Well,' I said, 'I do apologize for that.'

'Oh, for fuck's sake.'

When the lift doors opened, she went out a few paces ahead of me, and as I followed down the corridor I didn't know precisely where she was. It was, just for a moment, as if she had been claimed back by the darkness which had given her up to me on this night a year ago.

∞

The cries of the housekeeping staff, as they went knocking on doors, landed heavily on my ears. My head felt wrapped in a layer of grease. Kathleen came from the bathroom and kissed me, showering me in a film of droplets and laughing as I cried out in surprise.

'Get up!'

'I don't feel too good.'

'You feel hungover. Surprise. Come on. Up! Big day!'

I rolled out of bed; in the shower, putting my feet in the puddles she had left, I flashed back to the nasty exchange in the lift and tried to put it out of my brain.

Downstairs, the atrium was busy, and outside a couple of dozen protesters were using the forecourt as their meeting point. Each time the main doors opened, the breeze brought in strange reports. Music blared from speakers. Someone was leading chants through a loudhailer. I sat in the bar trying to eat breakfast, wondering who was here, whether someone would tell Lara about my involvement, and what would happen if they did. Kathleen went in and out with her mobile phone, as excited and impatient as a kid. When we got outside, the noise of the protesters was ten times what it had seemed from inside.

'Tony Blair is a war criminal!' yelled someone inches from my face. There was the cloying sweet smell of weed. Half a dozen people were between me and the doors already, and I didn't know where Kathleen was.

'No war for oil!' chanted a group of voices somewhere over my left shoulder. 'Not-in-my-name!' they chorused. The voices sounded jubilant rather than angry, as if the point had already been won and this was a celebration. There was a feverish quality to things. *This is stupid*, I snapped at myself. *We're past the time when big groups of people are frightening.* It should have been true, but I didn't believe it.

'Kathleen? Where—'

'I'm here. What is it?'

'I don't think I can do this.'

'You can.'

I was angry with myself for having gone along with this in the grip of drunken adoration, and with her for being so zealous, and with myself all over again for being unequal to the situation. For not knowing how many people were here, how many more of them there would be, how long the march would go on. My stomach squelched and gurgled. The noise dropped suddenly and my heart swam towards Howard's raised voice.

'I would appreciate it,' he boomed, 'if you could clear the path so people can get into my hotel.'

'You should be coming with us!'

'Much as I'd like to "stop the war",' Howard shouted back, 'I have a hotel to run.'

'Lara Krohl and the Hotel Alpha support the murder of civilians!' cried a woman in a voice as high and piping as a bird's. 'The Hotel Alpha has blood on its hands!'

'Fuck off,' I blurted out, 'what do you know about the Alpha?'

There were gasps and shocked laughter.

'Jesus,' said Kathleen, 'do you realize who you're talking to?'

'Does *she* realize who she's talking to?' I retorted. 'Does she think she can just call Howard—'

'You need to get over this Howard thing,' Kathleen hissed. 'Are you coming, or are you going back to him?'

'Chas, mate,' Howard called at almost exactly the same time from the hotel doors.

My bowels were overfull, my face felt red. I hated all the well-intentioned people, their chants, banners I couldn't read, their sense of unquestionable rightness and the things they were saying and thinking about Howard. I began to blunder through the crowd. Bodies parted. Kathleen shouted out my name, but she sounded a mile away already. I half-tripped over a leg, began to stumble; then the hand was on my arm.

'I will thank you all,' Howard said, nimble and as pumped-up as the protesters around us, 'to get the fuck out of the way of my boy.'

The big doors shut behind us and the atrium was warm, humming with activity, clinking glasses and calls, footsteps and wheeled trolleys and telephones ringing. The nest of noise and anger vanished as if at the press of a button.

'Stupid bastards,' said Howard. 'Are you all right?'

I muttered that I was. The toilets in the atrium were the closest at hand. The door felt heavy; from the background gurgle and trickle, I couldn't tell if anyone was there. I slammed the door of a cubicle and sat with my head in my hands.

Kathleen would be on her way to Hyde Park already, and I'd let her down; her anger at me would be all churned up with her anger at the war, the whole mixture like fuel, propelling her further and further away. I was here in the Alpha where I had always been, locked away from the world. She was on one side of things; Howard, Lara, everyone else in my life was on the other.

9

GRAHAM

London's bid to host the Olympic Games was the new thing around the Hotel Alpha. Lara was one of the people in charge of publicizing the campaign; Chas was one of her 'key men' on the project. And Howard was contributing in his usual way. He entertained members of the committee; he shook hands, badgered, claimed long-owed favours. A couple of months after the war protest – a protest which had proved fruitless – he welcomed two dozen members of London's 'bid team' to the hotel. They would receive one of Howard's addresses to pep them up, which was probably necessary since Paris was ahead in the running and the whole business might easily prove a stupendous waste of money. Then they would have dinner, and then ...

'Then you, and they, will get drunk?'

'That's not part of the official schedule, Madman.' Howard produced his naughty-schoolboy grin.

'I was not, as they say, born yesterday.'

'Suzie can cover it,' he said, his features softening now into that mollifying expression nobody was able to resist. 'You should never feel you have to be here every minute of every day, mate.'

He knew that my duty to the hotel was only part of the equation. Duty to myself had more to do with it. It was a point of pride to stay behind the desk: and all the more so now that it felt less like my own territory than it ever had before.

Suzie was beside me as the Olympic people checked in. Her hair was newly restyled and smelled powerfully of what she called 'salon products', which she ordered via the computer and whose effects on her hair she described in jargon that meant no more to me than Japanese. As the big group collected round the desk in their sweatshirts with the words 'London 2012' emblazoned on the front, Suzie got briskly to work. She took a computer-generated code from each person. She rattled away on her PC, allocating a room to each and dispatching a dozen guests to the lifts before I had finished checking in my second. He – a good-looking fellow about Ed's age, sporting a patently unnecessary pair of sunglasses – stopped me in the middle of 'breakfast is served between ... '

'I need to get to Heathrow in the morning, for nine,' he said. 'Could you find out times for me?'

'I can very likely arrange a car for you, or take you myself,' I replied. 'Leave it with me, and—'

'No,' the young man explained patiently, 'I'll go on the train. I just need times.'

'Ah.' There was the Heathrow Express these days, of course. Guests could go down the road to Paddington and be on their way to the airport in a jiffy. I had not quite got used to it yet. 'Well, I don't know the times for that train off the top of my head,' I apologized, 'but I shall telephone the National Rail line for you, and then call up to your room with—'

'I've got it here,' said Suzie, peering at the computer. 'Every fifteen minutes. Ten past, twenty-five past, twenty to and so on.'

The man slung his bag over his shoulder, snatched the key I had been about to hand to him, and thanked Suzie as if I were not there. And watching him stride across the atrium, with the far-off-sounding *LONDON 2012* announced by logos on his clothing, I felt for a minute as if I were not.

That evening, during a coffee break scarcely merited by the amount of work I had found for myself that day, I slunk in at the back of our main conference room and watched Howard deliver his inspirational address to the Olympic people, who sat with their heads bowed over laptops and electronic notebooks. If any of them found time to look up at the speaker, they would have seen a man who was as comfortable with this time of life as he had been in his twenties. 'A magician, I like to say ... '

Here he goes, I thought, with that mingled weariness and love his speeches generally conjured up. 'A magician is nothing more than an actor impersonating a magician. What do I mean by that? I mean that a lot of life is about confidence and presentation. The best way to reach your goal is to convince as many people as possible that you've reached it already.' There was a stirring of laughter at this observation, and some of the lowered heads bobbed in gentle recognition. 'Now, when I founded this hotel ... ' he went on in his well-trodden groove, and I retired to make sure the restaurant was ready for them.

The meal spilled over into a long Alpha night of drinking and shouting and mutual impressing, just as it had been bound to. I dropped in to check on things just after midnight and saw Howard with his arm round Lara Krohl at the bar. Chas was between them, eagerly chipping into the conversation. My spirits rose as usual at the sight of him – at his new ease with people – but they were dashed again as a secondary survey revealed a number of people who were not so happy. There was Mike Swan, the reviewer: he sat alone with a little array of empty glasses in front of him, making his way through gin and tonics, most likely without much of the tonic. This was a common sight, these days; he was always in the corner, looking thinner each time, the patched green sports jacket flapping ever more desultorily around his frame. And there at the bar – a little way removed from all the jollity, and with a strained expression that was also more common of late – I saw Kathleen. With a little effort I could make out the conversation that was riling her.

'There's been a lot of scaremongering,' Lara Krohl was saying. She looked, at this late hour, exactly the same as she always did when breakfasting in the atrium: the scraped-back hair, plain white blouse, the high-heeled shoes and the laptop computer tucked under an arm. She was drinking mineral water. 'Tony knew this was going to happen.' She meant the Prime Minister; even after six years, I found it odd for her and even Chas to be on these terms with him. 'But you ride it out, and sure enough, the backlash, it never really happened.'

'He knows what he's doing, old Blair,' Howard agreed. I cast back my mind to when he had been a Conservative supporter; or at least, so it had seemed. He just liked to cheer for the winning team. 'They've nailed it pretty well, the whole thing. Just need to catch the bugger now.'

'They'll smoke Saddam out,' Chas put in. 'He's not got enough support to hide forever.'

'Yah, and that will be that, pretty much,' said Lara, sipping her water, 'unless we're meant to believe the lefties and Iraq is going to invade us back ... '

The laugh around the bar had a nastily triumphalist quality to it. Kathleen touched Chas's arm and pointed to the door. There was a brief exchange during which he tried and failed to change her mind. Then she brushed past me, managing a wink, and walked out of the bar and across the black and white tiles of the floor.

'She seems tense, that one,' said Suzie. 'She should think about t'ai chi.'

I told Suzie she could go home. She blinked and smiled with a sort of indulgent kindness as if, really, it ought to be her dismissing me. '*Ciao, bella!*' she remarked, trotting out of the place.

I waved and said something feeble in reply. Then I stood looking at the telephone on my desk, willing it to ring with a request from a guest upstairs, anywhere on the silent balconies around and above me. The telephone was a replica of the Bakelite one from the sixties, but it had push-buttons instead of a dial, because these days you generally had to get through about ten questions from a recorded voice before hearing a real one. Pattie had bought me the phone from an Internet site which specialized in 'the favourites of yesteryear'. It was a while since we had been to the market.

Suzie was away the next day, and I hoped that meant I would be kept busy; but the telephone was mute once more as afternoon turned into evening. The hotel was almost at capacity, I believed, though it was hard to be certain as my colleague had checked most people in. I did not keep up the ledger as thoroughly nowadays: in truth I had begun to feel a bit silly doing it in front of her. A song by the Rolling Stones thumped out of the bar; Howard had either requested it from Ray, or was (as he liked to say) 'on the stereo' himself.

I thought about the early years of the hotel, when the telephone never stopped ringing. Where is this restaurant? When is my coach in the morning? Can you arrange a vegan meal to be cooked for a special guest, find an emergency dentist, accomplish this or that miracle in the next five minutes? For a second, the gap between those days and these yawned so painfully in my chest that I had half a mind to go up in the lift and wander door-to-door seeing if anyone needed something done.

There had been a few nights like this in the past couple of months; I could not dismiss them, any more, as aberrations. The fact was that my job had diminished. For the first thirty-five years of my time here, I had piqued myself upon being a concierge, if not without equal, then at least with few superiors. Who could work harder than I did, or be more devoted to the task? I had failed to understand that my greatest rival in the end would not be another human in a suit and tie, but a coalition of machines. Every guest now had a concierge in his or her own room: one that never slept, knew everything, and was not troubled by the problems of being alive.

The tradition of keeping a whisky bottle for emergencies had outlived the smoking room: these days it was buried in a drawer of old leaflets and timetables which Suzie never had recourse to. I unstopped it and poured a very small measure into a teacup, glancing about in case anyone was interested: no one was. The bar was quiet tonight, and so was the restaurant. In the process of lifting the cup to my mouth, I inspected the back of my hand: there was a smattering of small liver spots like the ones I used to see on my father's hand before it clipped me about the temple.

I was getting old, all right; I had got into a rut from which I could see the past with ebbing clarity and the present only with trepidation. Nothing was going to change. But the Hotel Alpha

– like its owner – never stopped playing tricks, good and bad. Within an hour it had dealt me a card that took my breath away.

It was late, and I had almost decided to let the desk stand empty for what ought to have been my final hour until the arrival of the pair of alarmingly young coffee-drinking chaps who wisecracked their way through the night. Then footsteps sounded in the quiet. I somehow knew straight away that it was Kathleen; there was that urgency in the tread, the silent intensity she communicated. She was wearing a shapeless sweater over blue pyjamas, as if she had already been to bed and failed to sleep. I was about to attempt a witticism on this subject, but the look on her face stopped me.

'I need to talk to you,' she said.

Her eyes were moist, and I thought at first there must have been some fight with Chas. On closer inspection, it was a sort of fierce excitement which had got into them. I felt a shamed, but inescapable, pleasure to be called upon like this.

'Of course.'

'It can't be here,' she said. 'Somewhere private.'

The light in the former smoking room was as sickly as ever, the screens' glares in uneasy harmony with the wan bulbs overhead. What had happened to the lamps we used to have here? I wondered. Kathleen brought a plain brown envelope from the pocket of the sweater and handed it over without a word.

It had been opened before; the flap came away easily. I

brought out a single sheet of paper. A shiver ripped through me as I recognized Agatha's erratic handwriting.

> *To Whoever Reads this!*
> *I did not Want to Leave.*
> *Howard York is a Bad Man.*
> *Howard York has lied to Everyone.*
> *Howard York Will go To Hell.*
>
> *Agatha Richards.*

I read each of the five lines five times.

'Where is she?' I asked. 'Where—?'

'I don't know,' said Kathleen, and my heart thudded back to ground. 'I found this in the room.'

'That's impossible.' I thought about the number of times I had been in Room 25 since Agatha left and the servicing it had received from housekeeping staff. 'It can't have been there all this time or …'

'It was in the Bible. In the drawer. I was looking something up for a piece. You know what it's about, don't you?'

I was shaking a little.

'You have to tell me.'

'No,' I said. 'I do not have to tell you; I have never had to tell anyone.'

After a silence, she cleared her throat and then touched my hand so softly that I had to glance down to make sure I had not imagined it.

'Please tell me,' she said. 'Please.'

'I need to think about this.'

'Jesus Christ,' she said, 'I'm in my f---ing pyjamas here and I'm wondering what the hell Chas should know about Howard which has presumably been kept from him, and in the morning I'm going to have to see him and—'

'Half an hour.' I was almost pleading, I realized with embarrassment. I sounded like what I was, a man who had kept a secret for an unconscionably long time. 'Just let me collect my thoughts, Kathy.'

I had not meant to abbreviate her name, and it sounded very peculiar. She crossed one leg over another, swallowed, and looked into my eyes. There was a silent understanding; I thought – I hoped – that we were on the same side.

'I'll wait,' she said.

I took the note and left her sitting there. It was clumsy of me to handle it like this, but the stakes were higher than Kathleen could possibly know. I walked unsteadily across the atrium like one of the drunken guests I would nod to on an ordinary night. I made for the lift, and then – without really knowing why – went up to the top floor and stood outside Room 77. Since the rebuild, it had functioned as a normal guest room; there was no trace of what had happened there. Still, it had its memories for me, and it felt like the right place to take stock. There was a stockroom a little way along the corridor; I would duck in there if anybody came. The note in my hand felt like a bomb which would be detonated if anyone so much as saw it, and which would destroy everything around us.

But nobody came. I looked at the handwriting. I pictured, as clearly as if it were happening in front of me now, Agatha writing the note, sealing it in the envelope, placing it in the Bible and walking heavily out of the Alpha. It was harder – but vital – to imagine what had been in her head as she did it. Did she hope that somebody would find it and that the situation could be reversed? That I could save her from going, or bring her back?

I did not want to leave.

Each of the words was like an electric shock, even now. I could hear her voice rupturing the silence of the hotel, and the crestfallen way she put down her bag and struggled with the door the last time I ever saw her. Not everything about the note was clear to me; but it was clear enough what Agatha would want me to do, what she was willing me to do from wherever she was now.

I walked slowly down the back stairs, passing the spot where I met Howard on the night everything changed. I crossed the atrium, relieved now rather than dispirited by the absolute quiet which filled all the space from the marble floor to the skylight. Kathleen was sitting at one of the computers but did not seem to have turned it on. As I pushed open the door, she lifted her head and the hair fell around her shoulders. I sat down next to her and spoke so quietly that she had to lean in to hear me.

∞

When Howard had croaked the number 77 and gestured desperately at me, I came to realize that he was begging me to go up there alone: to save the day, without him. There was no time to wonder why. There was little enough time to do what I had to do.

The door of Room 77 was ajar. Roz Tanner lay naked, passed out upon the bed. Next to her on the bedside table was a mess of empty bottles and smoking paraphernalia. The boy was lying on the floor, pleading for his mother to wake. In the time it took me to perceive all these things, flames had licked further into the room and were shooting along the carpet with appalling speed, and a wall of smoke meant it was already impossible to make out the way I had come in. The boy was keening in pain as tongues of fire began to lick at his face. His cries turned to chokes and I realized I, too, was choking. When I opened my mouth to shout at Roz Tanner, smoke charged into my throat and I coughed and retched.

My God, I thought: we shall die here, all three of us. I saw the faces of Caroline and Ed. This vision can only have taken a quarter of a second, but it stirred me into the fastest motion of my life. I gathered up the howling boy and ran, head down, through the smoke. Outside the room was only more heat, the ashy murk of the air, and I could not see. But I had been in this hotel so long that I did not need to. I ran towards the staircase. I was not thinking about the screaming boy in my arms, or the violent red scarring I could see upon his face, let alone the woman I had left behind to die. I simply wanted to live.

'Graham!' a voice was yelling, and Howard took the little bundle from me and steered me towards the staircase. That is the last thing I remember.

When I came to, I was in one of the ground-floor guest rooms: Room 7, as it turned out. I had been taken out of my clothes and was lying in a bed. A doctor had hold of my wrist and was examining my pulse. I tried to say something and coughed up soot and ash and bile.

'Good man,' said the doctor. 'You're going to be right as rain.'

I had only been out for a few minutes, as it seemed. People floated indistinctly around the room. I was given information. The fire had been overcome. The boy's face had been badly burned, and he might lose his sight; but he would live. His mother had not been saved, but I should not blame myself.

I stayed a long time as I was, my head on the cool pillow. But after an hour or so I felt better; I sat up and began to have conversations. In the course of these, a rather different story unfolded from the one I thought I remembered.

Howard had been first on the scene. He had gone up and rescued the boy just in time. I had arrived afterwards and tried to get the mother out, but the flames and smoke had driven me back. By the time Pattie arrived, this version of events was so well established that she had heard it already. She stroked my forehead as I lay with my eyes closed.

Everyone was saying how brave I had been, Pattie told me. And indeed I had. But something, I thought, was not right here.

It was some time in the early hours of the morning that Howard came and sat in the chair next to the bed. I had been left alone to sleep, and when I opened my eyes I cried out in surprise to see him. In his face I saw such utter abjection that I had to turn my eyes down to the blankets in front of me.

'I'm sorry,' he said in a voice nothing like his own. 'They jumped to conclusions and I let them do it. I couldn't tell them the truth. I couldn't tell them I was with her when it started. But you can tell them, Graham.'

I wanted to get it straight, all this, though to someone a little less addled it would have been straight enough already.

'Why were you with her?'

'You know why, Graham.' Howard began to sob. 'Oh God. I just wanted her. If someone comes along … I'm a weak man. I can't seem to resist when someone wants me. When someone falls for it. I can't seem to do the right thing. I don't know what you must think, Graham. You're such a good person.'

I let Howard weep and bleat through a few variations on the

theme, quite at a loss. He was as unstoppable in his new mode of defeat as he had always been in triumph.

'This is it now,' he said. 'I did know this would happen. It had to fall apart.'

'What do you mean?'

'Well, imagine when it gets out what really happened,' Howard said. His voice began to lose that pitiful, wallowing note, taking on a quality which – oddly, in the circumstances – was almost noble. It was like a man reading the announcement of his own death. 'That I got off my face with her and as soon as I woke and smelled smoke, I bolted. And then had to pretend I'd only gone up there to save the kid. That I was the hero. The hero, not a total, total …'

And the word he now used to describe himself I hesitate even to write with spaces.

Even accounting for a bit of Howard-exaggeration, it was true that his situation was a terrible one. If the story he described were to get out, he would be, as they say, finished. His reputation as a playboy conjuror, naughty on occasion but impossible not to love, would disappear. Instead people would see a criminal and a liar. Sarah-Jane would leave him, this time. And Howard himself would go, he would have to. He would either close the hotel outright or sell it to somebody new who would waste little time in starting from scratch. In either outcome, it was clear enough what would happen to me.

'Who, other than you and me,' I asked Howard, 'knows about this?'

'No one,' he said.

'The police will ask questions, I suppose.'

'It's not them I'm worried about, Graham. I'd *rather* go to prison than what is going to happen when this gets out. When it gets out I was responsible.'

'What is going to happen if I tell anybody, you mean,' I corrected him.

'Yes.'

'Well then,' I said, and shrugged.

A silence followed, the duration of which I would put somewhere between three and five minutes. I was thinking about what it would mean to promise what I was about to. I would be weighed down by a secret until the end of my life, and a terrible one: I would be obscuring the real reasons for the death of a guest. Moreover, I would miss out on the credit I deserved for saving the boy. But if I did not? Well, the Yorks' lives would probably begin the very same day to fall apart, and with them the hotel that had given me my main reason to get up each day for the last twenty years.

Howard must also have been running through these calculations, but he still hardly dared believe I had decided to protect him. He looked up at me, and then slightly over my head, as if this last hope were a beam of light on the wall behind me. He opened his mouth halfway.

'Are you sure?'

'Quite sure,' I said, 'and I propose we do not discuss it ever again.'

He began trying to say that I was the greatest friend he could have – or that anyone could have – and that he would always have to live with it, what he had done, and this was the start of a new him, and a great many more things until I put a stop to it.

'I meant,' I said, 'we do not discuss it ever again, with immediate effect.'

Howard grabbed my arm and looked very hard at me for a moment, and then his eyes began to overflow. I felt immobilized by fatigue, as if a concrete block had been lowered onto me. I was abandoning myself happily to unconsciousness when a final thought snapped my eyes open.

'What will happen to the boy?'

'The boy?'

'To her child.'

'They said he'll probably be blind,' said Howard, the final word seeming to disappear back into his throat. 'But he will live.'

'Yes, but where will he go?'

'Leave that with me,' said Howard.

∞

I offered to make tea. Kathleen nodded, seeming barely to have heard. A few drops spilled as I carried the mugs back from reception. Never mind, I thought. Somebody else, for once, could worry about it.

'So you told Agatha all this?' Kathleen said.

'I did, eventually. We had become close, and I needed… I felt I could not last forever without telling a soul. But she left soon afterwards.'

'Because Howard found out you'd told her?'

'I assumed either it was that, or there were other reasons, possibly. I never knew.'

Kathleen was holding her tea in front of her without any apparent intention of taking a sip. 'And Chas … '

'Has never known. No.'

'You don't think he deserves to know that his life has been founded on a lie?'

'I have had this to live with for more than twenty years,' I hissed, 'and you for twenty minutes. So I hardly think that you ought to be telling me how to proceed.'

'I'm sorry,' she said; immediately I apologized myself for speaking so harshly.

'Why did you tell me?'

'Because it was what Agatha intended by leaving that note. Because I owe it to her memory, as it were. And perhaps because I feel that you deserve better, too, than to be in the dark. And,' I added pointedly, 'I decided I could trust you never to let it go further.'

She nodded, her eyes cast down into her lap. 'Thank you. But ... '

I saw the weight of the secret, a weight very familiar to me, settle upon her shoulders. She leaned forward and took a long breath, and then shivered and took hold of her own forearms as if embracing herself for warmth.

'S----y f---,' she muttered to herself.

'Indeed,' I said, with feeling. 'Would you like a taxi home?'

'Would you mind?'

I squeezed her shoulder in response, noting how hard and unyielding it was. She went up to get dressed, and we walked in silence out to the front of the Alpha. A couple of cars hummed past on the Euston Road. The night air was cold, like a building where nobody lived. I hailed a taxi and gave the driver Kathleen's address. As she got into the back seat, she reached her hand out and I held it for a moment.

The note was still lying in the computer room. I picked it up and looked at the writing. For a moment I thought about keeping it, hiding it, so that I would have something of her. It was a ridiculous thought. Before it could take root, I had folded the paper carefully, torn it eight ways, and walked to the Gents, where I disposed of it. Its work was done.

My hands, when I looked down at them, had barely regained their steadiness. I pressed the button on the hand dryer and allowed it to blast them for a little while as I attempted to collect myself.

It was difficult to ascertain exactly what my emotions were. I was frightened in part, certainly. The bomb was part-exploded, and the rest of the explosion was a prospect which would hang over us. Kathleen might easily tell Chas, in spite of my entreaties. Her loyalty to him might trump her respect for my wishes. And so, for all I knew, might her journalistic instincts. She might not be able to resist writing about it: what a story it was, after all! Yes, there were a dozen ways in which she might in some way let everything slip. If she did, it would be very dangerous for her, for me, for all of us.

But other things kept bobbing up in the froth of these thoughts. There was a longing for Agatha, which I did my best to force back under the water. And something else which was close – strange as it might be – to the thrill which my hardier army comrades had felt as they went into battle.

Things, I felt, were going to change now that this secret was out, unearthed by a note left in a book all that time ago. Change was not something I had ever embraced, yet I could not mistake a certain faint excitement, or at least intrigue, at the prospect. In any case, it did not matter what I thought of it; it was as if the events had simply set their course in this direction, and I was caught up in them. Change happened, in the end, whatever you did: this much I had learned. It was coming to the Hotel Alpha now, whether we liked it or not.

PART THREE

ↄ10ↄ

GRAHAM

'Drive on, Madman,' commanded Howard in a giddy slur, 'drive us back to the Hotel Alpha, and don't spare the horses.'

'Don't spare the *what*?' Sarah-Jane giggled; behind me, the seats squeaked as the two of them grappled with one another, erupting into further laughter. I opened the glove compartment and got out my driving gloves, the sixth pair, purchased in a fit of stubbornness from the shop on Savile Row rather than 'online', even though it had meant going there on a very wet day and getting into a foul mood. I turned the key in the ignition and the machine started up, as smooth and even-tempered as ever. Howard was unscrewing the lid from a little bottle he had smuggled out of the theatre. They had been to see *Les Misérables*, not for the first time; and they seemed to have got so drunk that they barely knew whether they were in France themselves. It had been Sarah-Jane's sixty-fourth birthday last week. Howard hid sixty-four roses around the Alpha and had Paul McCartney call with a birthday message.

Stuck behind a succession of minicabs whose drivers honked at one another and drove in unpredictable bursts of speed, we crawled eventually onto the Euston Road. There had been no point really in my coming in the car to drive such a short way when they could have got the Tube. There was no real need for the driving gloves, either – the steering wheel, whose ivory they were meant to protect, had been reupholstered a few years ago. But it was a performance, and for Howard everything was about performance, after all. I was certainly not complaining. The Mercedes was the place for me, now. It had become the part of the Alpha where I felt most at home.

The hotel itself was slipping from my grasp a day at a time. The old guest ledgers, forty books in total, had been moved from the cabinet behind the reception desk into storage in the cellar, which was to say that they would never be seen again. Suzie talked brightly about 'archiving' the information on a computer, but it was not as if the names of long-gone guests were any use: I had simply liked having them there. All the same, when the move came, I put up very little resistance. I considered salvaging the three books on whose back pages I had kept score in the check-in game with Agatha, but the sight of my past self's handwriting, the naivety in the joyfully scribbled characters, deflated me. Behind the desk there was now a second computer, which I occasionally used – when nobody was about – to search for Agatha, as I had done before. Pattie had bought me a book called *The Internet for Dummies*.

Soon, perhaps, I would need *Hotels for Dummies*. Howard's taste for modernization was as sharp as it always had been; but the improvements were more and more alien to me. There was talk of replacing all the lovely keys on their wooden fobs with plastic cards which would unlock doors by means of an electronic chip. There was talk of improving our Internet service to 'broadband', so that it could do its work more quickly.

In the forecourt Howard flung open the car door, in the way he had which always made me wince, as if it were an old banger ready for the junkyard. He and Sarah-Jane made a tipsy fuss of getting out, her dress becoming stuck in the door as he slammed it again. I stayed in my seat, watching through the driver's window as the two of them returned to their castle, his arm round her back. His hair was thinning very slightly now, and hers was cut short and coloured. Each of them was a little thicker-set than forty years ago. But they still moved with the urgency, the thirst for what was ahead, that they always had; Howard still held open the mahogany door, and Sarah-Jane still stepped inside with a nimble excitement as if they were twenty-four and had taken ownership of the place that afternoon. They were a perfect couple, as if from some romantic story. And a story, you might say, is exactly what it was: a story that, all this time, Howard had managed to tell the world.

Until recently, it had been easier than I had imagined to keep the pact: to listen to Howard's chatter, raise an eyebrow at his petting of the Captain, pick a card – any card – and not tell him what it was. It had not really been a matter of sacrifice. I had gone along with the rewriting of history to protect him, it was true: he was my friend and my mentor. But I was also protecting the hotel, and that meant protecting myself and the future I wanted, which was a future in which the Alpha's reputation continued to sparkle and I was able to stand behind this desk until I could not stand at all.

The hardest part had been getting through the first days and weeks while Howard tried to avoid all the publicity caused by the fire and his supposed heroics and Sarah-Jane nursed Chas in the evenings. During that time the secret felt gigantic, like a pimple pulsing on the forehead which one feels must be visible to all. But each day after that, it had shrunk a little. In the course of this, my brain – and Howard's, I supposed – had changed shape, the secret being incorporated so fully that it was no longer even recognized as such. And so we carried on, outwardly the same as ever.

This process, however, had required energy. It was not for nothing that Howard kept himself on the move, would travel a thousand miles just to get someone's signature on a donation cheque, would erect Christmas decorations at ten soup kitchens in one morning. It was not an accident that he thrust so relentlessly into the future. If you were Howard, you too would be getting as far away from the past as you could.

Not that his past twenty years of good deeds had been mere penance. It was in Howard's nature to help people and to make the grand gesture; he would have given thousands of pounds away whatever had happened, and would unquestionably have raised any orphan fate cast into his path. He was always minded to gallop around the world collecting his thrills, just as I was always happy staying in Muswell Hill and dining on ham and chips. But in the twenty-year aftermath of the fire, those energies had been more specifically directed. It was no longer only about maintaining the legend of the Hotel Alpha, the great fiction he had willed into life. It was now about maintaining a myth of a different kind: a tall story even by Howard's standards.

To do that, he had to keep moving further and faster from the real events. I had never felt the same compulsion. The daily hum of Alpha business had been enough to drown out everything else. Each time I took my place at reception in the morning, or settled into the driving seat, I had been able to wipe the slate clean: to pretend that Agatha had never been next to me, and Howard had never lied to his wife, to Chas, to the whole of London.

But now that daily hum had dropped somewhat. It had been replaced with the tapping of computer keys, with the silence of the once-vocal telephones. Less time spent helping guests meant more time to think, and thinking was dangerous. And that was probably why I had taken to getting into the car at the slightest excuse, ferrying guests to this end of London or that. Each time I turned the key in the Mercedes and heard the old thoroughbred report for duty, I was running away, as Howard had been doing for years. By telling Kathleen the secret, I wondered if I had condemned her to run the same race.

∞

Almost a year had passed since the night of the note, and Kathleen had been back and forth more times than I could count: to the front in Afghanistan, and to talk to widows in Iraq, and several times to China. There were still the tearful goodbyes in the atrium, the fierce farewell kissing at Heathrow. All the same, there was no mistaking her appetite not just for the trips but for the experience of getting away.

Her latest trip was a particularly ambitious one: first to Athens where the Olympics were being staged in the summer, and then on to Beijing to meet some of the people protesting against the games to come. Already, some of the evidence of corruption she had uncovered was being used in a *Panorama* programme to be broadcast while she was away. This would make her exceedingly unpopular with Lara, and I supposed with Howard, but Kathleen was not the sort to be put off by that idea. This morning she had been in the atrium well before the time we arranged, whistling, the battered and dust-chalked travel suitcase by her side as ever.

'I don't suppose a couple of packages have come for me, Graham? Amazon?'

'Packages from the Amazon?'

'From Amazon the website.' Kathleen shook her head in exasperated fondness.

Suzie went into the backroom and emerged with a couple of cardboard parcels. '*Voilà*,' she said. I took Kathleen's suitcase out to the car and waited until she emerged, Chas following.

Now we were on the Westway, stationary in a queue, the still heat of the road coming through the windows and coating us like dirt; yet I felt happier than I would at reception.

'Jesus on the toilet,' Kathleen said, 'stop pawing me, will you; it's hot as hell in here.'

I met her eyes in my mirror. 'Perhaps it will be cooler in Athens?'

She laughed. 'F--- off, Graham.'

'I tell you where it *will* be cooler,' Chas was now saying, his hand moving obligingly away from her; 'the Business lounge. It's meant to be lovely.'

'Yes,' said Kathleen, looking out of the window, 'that's good.'

'And Business Class itself,' Chas persisted. 'I bet you're glad you're in there, not rammed in with everyone else.'

'It'll be nice, yes.'

'What's up?' he asked.

'I just … I'd be perfectly fine in Economy.'

'But Howard wants you to have a good time,' said Chas. 'He loves doing stuff like this. You know, he once—'

'I would rather not feel beholden to Howard.' Kathleen had taken the bait. Chas pursed his lips.

'You don't think we're both slightly in his debt?' he asked.

My eyes and hers came together in the mirror again as she swallowed what must have been a mouthful of impossible replies; we met eyes once more at Departures as I hauled the suitcase out of the boot. I patted her on the shoulder and wished her a good trip. When Chas returned, guided out by an airport official, he was carrying a Starbucks coffee cup and his face was slick with tears. I clapped him on the shoulder.

'She'll be back before you know it.'

'Don't suppose she's still in the car after all,' he said, 'and you two are winding me up?'

I always felt a curious mixture of things when Chas cracked a joke relating to his blindness: relief, affection, but also a kind of indignation that he had had to suffer this and always would have to. It made me realize with a shock, as if for the first time, that he was blind: and that every single moment since I last had the same thought, he had simply been getting on with it. He was quiet a while, sipping his coffee: I dearly hoped he would not spill any of it on the seats, but I never liked to tell him to be careful as he'd had more than enough of that in his time.

Near the gates of Fuller's Brewery – like so many before him – he began to speak.

'She loves going there so much.' It was precisely what I had been thinking earlier, but I was not sure it would be helpful to say so. 'And she's incredible at her job. There aren't many journos who can speak the language and everything. It's just … you know. I've never even been on a plane.'

'Well, not so long ago you had never been to the park.'

'I worry I'm holding her back. She gets much more frustrated with me than she used to.'

This might be true: but there was more to it, so much more, than he dreamed. Kathleen's biggest reason for being uncomfortable in Chas's presence – the secret that she carried – was quite impossible for him to guess, yet it was now known to three of us. I watched him in the mirror as the Mercedes sliced through the city, easing instinctively past the Trellick Tower, a dense, vertical block of hemmed-in humans; past a gigantic billboard asking Londoners to 'Back the Bid' and another half-dozen all designed by Lara and Chas's team. From the Westway there was a view of trains in sidings, a cemetery, a park where young people sloped about on skateboards, and then the traffic was fed in quarrelling lines onto Baker Street, where the Planetarium's domed green head pointed the way to the Alpha. I had seen it all so many times, Chas not once: he could not even see the great big poster with his own work on it. I experienced a powerful twist of guilt in my guts.

SEE PROFILE

' … made so much progress,' he said, 'but at some point, obviously, someone like me is going to hit a glass ceiling. And Kathleen – she isn't exactly a fan of glass ceilings.'

I had drifted out of his speech as I sometimes did with Pattie's rambles, and it took me a few moments to realize he was not talking about a real ceiling. I mumbled some comforting gibberish about the course of true love and led Chas from the forecourt into the Alpha, where Howard was waiting to take him like a baton. He began talking twenty to the dozen about some idea to do with the Olympics. 'I need to pick your brains, mate,' he said, and Chas's face lit up – as it always did, as everyone's always did – with the glow of Howard's attention. They went into the bar, howling with laughter at some joke. Still feeling uneasy, I stepped back through the doors, joining the huddled band of smokers who had tended to gather out here since the hotel went non-smoking. If only we had such a thing as a smoking room, I had quipped to Suzie once; but she was too young to know what I was on about.

I watched as the smokers carried out their solemn business in the shadow of the hotel, lighting one cigarette from another, faces close as if hatching some conspiracy. As one of them went back into the Alpha, the big doors swung open and I was sure, even from this range, I heard Howard's irresistible laugh ring out.

It was so perfect – it made so much sense – the story of his having rescued Chas: just as it felt absolutely right when he told the story about opening the door naked and winning the day with the Marilyn Monroe line, though it had not been him who did that either. Chas had lived a long time in a theatre set designed by Howard, and I had never thought of tearing the scenery down.

What Chas did not know, I had believed, could not hurt him: at least, not as much as the truth. But now I suspected it was hurting Kathleen. Perhaps the weight of secrecy had been hurting the lot of us all along, in fact, in ways we had never been aware of.

∞

In Howard's words, the *Panorama* programme 'went down like a rat sandwich'. Lara Krohl had got hold of a copy and there was a private screening on the morning before it went on the air; she emerged from the function room with her eyes low over her telephone and marched up and down the atrium conducting a string of her jargon-ridden conversations. Amid the lunchtime clatter, the low, ill-intentioned tone of her voice rumbled like thunder in the distance. She remained in the Alpha Bar till after midnight, sitting and typing and taking her tiny sips of water. At one point I ambled in to speak to Ray about a room-service request for bourbon; before I had got within ten paces of her, Krohl reached for the screen and snapped it down over the computer keyboard, glancing up at me as if I were a spy narrowly thwarted.

Whether or not because of the fandango caused by the programme, Kathleen stayed in China a week longer than expected. Chas, as always when she was away, made strenuous attempts to fill the time. One afternoon he turned up at reception in his gym kit.

'This is my white top and blue shorts, right? Kathleen left them out for me.'

'You can't be planning to go for a jog?' I glanced over at the doors. Outside, the breeze was a knife slashing at the few green scraps still clinging to trees; the cedars stood as proud as ever.

'Not outside. On the machines. I need someone to regulate the pace for me and someone just to check I'm not going to fall off. Just while I get started.'

Howard and I escorted him down to the subterranean Wellness Suite, where I scarcely ever set foot; it was run and looked after by its own staff, manicured and white-toothed ladies who thought me as old as their great-grandfathers.

Chas jumped up onto one of the treadmills, recently vacated by a powerfully built fellow I had seen about the atrium before. He mopped perspiration from the machine's armrests as he left. Chas asked us to position ourselves at opposite sides of the machine. My job was to watch that his feet were safely positioned on the conveyor belt; Howard's was to increase the speed. 'OK, bit faster,' Chas commanded, graduating from a stroll up to a trot. 'Faster,' he said again. The machine's previous occupant came past, nodded approvingly at Chas's exertions and sat astride the almost floor-low saddle of another toy. After a moment he began to zip back and forth in what seemed to me a ridiculous parody of a man rowing a boat. 'Faster!' shouted Chas. Howard raised an eyebrow.

'Sure, mate? You're going along pretty nicely there.'

'How fast?'

Howard glanced at the electronic display. '9.2. Whatever that means.'

'Bit faster,' Chas insisted. Howard, with a wry look at me, pressed the button again. The machine gave an incredulous whine.

'You're really bombing along,' said Howard, admiration and concern mingled in his voice.

'Need to get up to this pace regularly.' Chas's breaths were shortening. 'Kathleen is getting quicker and it's annoying for her.'

'You don't have to do everything Kathleen wants, old mate,' Howard said in a tone that was almost perfectly neutral.

'I know she can be a bit … ' Chas began. There was another short interval of hammering feet and moaning machinery. 'She's just doing a job,' he said, 'doing what she believes in, and—'

'There's a time and a place,' said Howard.

'I don't think she feels it's ever wrong,' Chas said, inserting chunks of sentence into the gaps between his jagged inhalations and exhalations, 'to say … to say what's true.'

'No, well.' Howard's mouth was a firm line. 'I'm suggesting that it isn't always right, either.'

I looked at Howard's big, solid profile, so powerful and yet in its way so vulnerable. Then Chas half cried out as his momentum took him to the edge of the running belt and his shoe caught for a moment. I put out my arm and steadied him, and Howard plunged down the button to slow the thing. After striding a few paces to recover, Chas asked for it to be speeded up again, and on he went as we stood vigil: running to keep pace with someone who was thousands of miles away.

The telephone rang late at night. 'It's for you-hoo,' said Suzie. How was I to stop her, I wondered, from doing that? I thought it must be a telephone booking from some old-fashioned soul like myself, but the voice was far away and criss-crossed by background noise as if our line were tangled up with some strangers'.

'Madman?'

She was coming back very early tomorrow, she said. Might I come and collect her?

'I would love to, Kathleen. Chas and I will be waiting at—'

'Ah – Graham.' Her voice tightened a notch. 'Chas doesn't know. I want to surprise him. Is that all right?'

I said that it was, of course, but I could not help wondering what was behind this. Kathleen was not a natural liar, and the notion of the 'surprise' for Chas had rung unconvincingly. I could not say whether or not I was looking forward, as I usually would, to picking her up.

The Mercedes' interior next morning was stale with cold. I coaxed its heater into life and ground the old chariot slowly westwards in thin early-morning traffic. The sky was heavy and dark as the car approached the gateway to Heathrow with its large model aeroplane and lit-up advertising boards. Kathleen was quickly out of Arrivals; she avoided my eye as I took the aged suitcase.

'How was the trip? Did you sleep on the plane?'

'Not very well.'

'Despite the comforts of Business?'

'Even despite that.' She came up with a strained smile. 'Despite the free pyjamas.'

There was a little more conversational circling of whatever was really at issue. We were some way past the brewery when she cleared her throat.

'In answer to your first question,' said Kathleen, 'it went well, very well. I've been offered a post out there.'

'A post?'

'A correspondent job.'

'You would be living in China?'

'Pretty much.'

Click-clock, went my indicator in the pause. Click-clock.

'Jesus at a barbecue!' I eventually managed. Kathleen cackled in surprise.

'Did you say that specially for me? As a homage?'

'It was an attempt at that, yes. I wish I had made it more Chinese-specific, thinking about it.'

Her eyes twinkled as they met mine. 'Oh, Graham. You're lovely.'

'Never mind that.' I glanced back fondly at her. 'Are you going to take it?'

The indicator ticked away again. I heard Kathleen take a breath, saw her lick her lips and shift her position on the back seat, and it was suddenly clear why she had brought me alone to the airport: it was for the opportunity of a private conversation. I could feel her eyes on the back of my neck.

'Graham, we have to tell Chas.'

I let her continue. 'He needs to know what happened,' she said, in a manner which made me think she had rehearsed this speech half the way home. 'He needs to know the truth about the fire.'

'I explained before,' I said, 'we always felt he needed *not* to know.'

'*Howard* needs him not to know.'

'Imagine if everyone found out … '

'Not everyone. I'm not saying we tell everyone. I'm saying Chas deserves to know.'

'All right. Imagine that Chas found out this man, Howard, whom he has idolized, trusted – the person he has trusted most – was responsible for his mother's death.'

'But I should be the person he trusts most.' Kathleen's voice threatened to crackle into fury. 'I deserve that now. And what about you?'

As we stopped at lights, she leaned across the partition so that her face was almost next to mine. I could smell toothpaste and just about make out the tiniest of light-coloured freckles on her cheekbones.

'Don't you ever think,' Kathleen said, 'that you should be the one Chas thinks of as his ... as his de facto father, if it's going to be anyone? You saved his life! You saved his life, Graham!'

'Twenty-odd years ago. It's the past.'

'It's still part of who he is. He's thankful – he thanks God every day that he's alive at all. Except it's not God, it's Howard. And it should be you.'

'I don't need to be thanked,' I said. 'I don't want any special attention. I put the hotel first, always. And I want to honour the promise I made to Howard. I believe it's better this way, Kathleen.'

I reached for the switch; the windscreen wipers began their shuffle back and forth.

'I'm not sure you really do,' she said quietly.

Our eyes met in the mirror with a sort of qualified hostility:

neither of us wanted this conflict, but neither of us could move from our position. Kathleen, however, had one card left to play.

'If we don't tell him, Graham,' she said – not in a calculating tone, but with an air of considered impartiality – 'I'm going to take the job in China. I'm going to have to. I just can't do this. Keep something so big from him.'

I began several replies, none of them substantial enough to finish. Kathleen wound down the window and let the drizzle blow in onto her face; she stared out at the road and the dim scenery. The wipers scraped a path through the fuzzy screen in front of me, and I looked out over flat familiar sights: the eye hospital, the squares of Georgian houses. Chas was waiting, less than a mile away, in the dark.

∞

The next time I was to drive the Mercedes was to pick up Howard, Lara and Chas from a travel 'expo' at a newly refurbished place in East London. Lara and Chas were there in the interests of an Internet site they numbered among their clients, Howard in the interests of drinking and shaking hands. Ever since they had gone off, loudly trading witticisms, I had felt an ill mood descending on the Alpha. It was there in Mrs Davey's curse as the wheel of her trolley caught the edge of my desk and a pile of sheets went flying; it was there in a lovers' argument, the man pursuing the lady into the lift, she pushing him out and leaving him to hammer on the doors; there was even a tension in the *'ciao, bello'* Suzie simpered at me as she clocked off.

Were all these things really connected, though? Were they even real, or was I merely projecting onto the hotel what I was feeling myself? Since collecting Kathleen from the airport I had experienced several nights of brittle sleep. The consequences of doing what Kathleen asked and finding some way to tell Chas the truth ran round and round my head like a tune one cannot stop hearing.

Even if it went no further, the story would devastate him – not to mention Sarah-Jane and JD, who would, of course, also have to be told. The obliteration of the York family and their fortress, which I had done so much to protect, would finally come to pass. Chas, whom I had rescued, whom I had secretly thought of as my own son many times, would go somewhere far away, just as Christopher had. But not telling Chas would do a different kind of harm: it would drive Kathleen away from him and from the hotel. One night I had awoken with the phrase 'rat sandwich' in my head and had to go downstairs and open the door for some fresh air. Another night I had cried out in my sleep and frightened Pattie so much she put the light on and we both lay there wide awake.

I had almost decided that I would go home tonight and tell Pattie everything, if I could prise her away from the computer: tell her about the long pact of deception between Howard and me, the way things were coming to a head, and the fact that I did not know what to do. It would take a lot of explaining and I was not sure I had the stomach for it, but the secret had been eating away at me these past few days, more than it had for years at a time when it was safely locked away.

Pattie would be asleep, though, by the time I got home. Howard had said he would call me when I was required; as usual this proved to be at a late hour. I ground my way through some time by tidying and retidying my leaflets, which felt rather an empty occupation these days: it was rare that a guest picked one up. Eventually I decided to ring Ed.

It had been a little while since I'd seen my son, and I had good news for him. With Howard's help I had gained a pair of much-coveted tickets for the coming autumn's match between Australia and England, who had won last year's rugby World Cup – an event Howard marked by inviting the whole squad to the Alpha and posing for photographs with people he would not have recognized the week before. It took a couple of attempts before Ed replied, and when he did come to the phone his tone was rather odd, as if he had just woken from sleep.

'I don't think I'll make it, Dad,' he said.

'Bother,' I said, 'does the date clash with one of your trips?'

'No, it's not that, it's … ' He coughed. 'It's … it's … Money is a little tight,' he said in the end. 'It's all a little tight.'

It pained me to hear him speak like this. 'I will of course buy the tickets,' I said. 'In fact, I'm not sure that Howard even wants us to pay for them.'

'Well,' said Ed, 'maybe, then. I'll have to, I'll have to see.'

It was one of those nights, all right: nothing was as it should be. By the time I collected my well-oiled passengers from the event near the proposed Olympic site, a confused gloom had descended upon me. I almost considered asking Howard if he wouldn't mind taking a taxi back; but if I ceased to be useful as a chauffeur on top of everything else, I might as well hand in my notice, paint myself silver and start busking in Covent Garden.

When I reached the exhibition hall, people were streaming out already. Howard bundled himself and Chas into the back. He was pink and loud, his tie knotted halfway down his shirt; he and Chas reviewed the event in excitable exchanges, while Lara talked on her telephone. 'Yah, just get a car and put it on the tab,' she said. 'Oh-five-oh-six.'

'How was the event?' I enquired.

'Went pretty well,' said Chas. 'The site's hits are up a thousand per cent on this time last year.'

'I would have thought,' I said, stepping on the accelerator with a little more force than necessary, 'that more than a hundred per cent was impossible.'

'Howard got busy schmoozing with some of the guys from Travelocity,' Chas volunteered.

'I'm going to need more proper words than that.'

Howard laughed, clapping his hands as he sometimes did,

like a king to a court jester. 'You kill me, Madman. It's a web-site that plans out holidays for people. They work hand in hand with Lara's client. So I made sure they'd, how shall I put it, look favourably on the Alpha from now on. Website recommenda-tions are the reviews you want to get, these days. They're the ones that count.'

I thought about Mike Swan labouring over his typewriter. Lara Krohl lit a cigarette and smoked out of the window. Her other hand kept the telephone pressed to the side of her head, and the ever-present laptop computer was across her knees. 'Just tell them, they get it done or they lose the business,' she commanded some person somewhere.

We stopped at lights; somebody hesitated in front of us, and since I did not like to honk my horn without a very good reason, we were soon caught up in two merged lanes of traffic. 'This is slow,' said Lara Krohl; it took me a moment to realize she was addressing me and not somebody on the phone.

'Yes,' I said, 'it's because—'

'Are we sure this is the quickest way?' she asked without looking up from the computer. I doubted that she noticed any of the seedy landscape lit up around us: the colourful squalor of the high streets, the now incongruous tile mosaics at Under-ground station entrances, the warehouses reborn as artists' studios, the gangly youths gawping at the Mercedes when we came to zebra crossings. The landscape of her computer screen, the invisible people down invisible phone lines, were more real to her than the physical environments she shuttled between. But that did not stop her from having an opinion, from assuming she knew my business better than I did.

'This is certainly the best way,' I said. 'The traffic's just unusually heavy at the moment, and—'

'There's a little gadget you can get,' Lara interrupted – confound it, I thought to myself, did nobody ever tell her it was rude to do that? 'You put it in the front of your car and it tells you which way to go.'

'It sounds clever enough, if you don't know the roads already ...'

'Well, even if you do.' Lara Krohl's voice took on that note of polite, as-if-accidental challenge which she did so well. The upward inflection was so slight, the ice so lightly sprinkled onto the words. 'I mean, anyone can make a mistake.'

'Not Madman,' said Howard. 'They'll never make a gizmo that's better than this man's brain. Honestly. Bloody miracle-worker. Did I ever tell you about the time we had about thirty cops combing the hotel looking for one of the Stones, and Graham hid him in a wardrobe ... '

It had been three policemen, not thirty, and the musician had hidden himself while I merely stood guard. There were many other embellishments; and yet as he went on, I began to feel that perhaps I was misremembering things. Heat crept into my cheeks, that pleasantly uncomfortable flush one felt when, for a minute or two, Howard made it feel as if you were the only thing worth being enthusiastic about. It was as hard as ever to resist it, that feeling, and as hard as ever to imagine destroying the world he had created. It might not be the real world, but it was the one we lived in.

11

CHAS

'What is it? Jesus, Chas.'

'Are we crashing?'

My mind was punch-drunk from the stream of new experience.

'You want something, sir?'

Kathleen interceded, her voice low and scratchy. 'He's just worried the plane is going to fall out of the sky.'

The stewardess laughed. 'No, no. Plane has just had little turbulence. But will remain in sky.'

'It's all right for you,' I said, 'you're on a plane twice a week, but I—'

Kathleen shushed me. 'You'll wake everyone up. Go back to sleep.'

The plane ground on with its steady drone. I pressed my watch button for the time, but the time made no sense; there wasn't a time here, we weren't in a place. I remembered the feeling of lying below JD, hearing him snoring, drifting through an uncharted night.

❧

Two months ago we'd been on the London Eye as a sort of rehearsal for the flight. The November air on the South Bank had been full of language and noise; a quartet played on electric violins. Kathleen pressed my hand against her thigh. I felt filled up by the closeness of her and the music and the pinpoint cold of the night. I raised my face and imagined the giant wheel peering down on us.

'Now, concentrate, hang on to my arm. They don't actually stop the wheel, so we need to get in nice and quick or one of us will fall through the gap into the Thames. And then we'll feel less upbeat.'

The ascent began. Kathleen let out a short excited squeak. I could feel the uncramped dimensions of the capsule. I reached out and ran my hands up the shield that separated us from thin air.

'Oh, it's beautiful already,' she said. 'The river is all dark and sort of … stately. We can see – I think that's MI5, and Charing Cross station, looks a bit like a giant photocopier. And lights, lights. So many lights.'

'Keep going.'

'When you come to China with me – well, the lights of a city from the air are an incredible sight. You're just in awe at how humans have made all this. All the millions of lives in little grids, building up into one super-grid. It makes you feel small in the best possible way. I could talk you through it all.'

'What about now? What's down there now?'

'Everything. We're the highest people in London right now. Seriously. There's not even anyone in the pod below us.'

My hand crept under her skirt and made its way up her leg. She breathed out sharply, grabbed my hand and moved it inside her. We staggered together across the capsule and she groped for my belt. It was all over quickly; we were already beginning the invisible slope back down to land. We stood, a little out of breath, and waited for the rest of the city to catch up with us.

Howard had bought me a set of CDs to learn Mandarin from and Kathleen had corrected my erratic first efforts. Howard had read me Wikipedia entries on Chinese history and Kathleen had corrected those too.

January arrived, and I had grasped the armrests as the plane barrelled along the runway and took off, a series of worrying noises giving way to the continuous hum of the past few hours. Now we must be within a couple of hours of our descent. We had bulleted through vast empty fields of airspace over strange lands. I was going to make it to what I used to call Peking. It had been unimaginably distant then; or even three months ago. For me this was going to be like landing on the Moon.

Yet all these huge steps had been merely to get to the point I should have begun at. I'd started the race a hundred miles behind the rest. Kathleen loved me in spite of the blindness, the hundred-mile gap; or at best she loved the way I lived through it. She didn't love the blindness itself – I didn't want her to. It was the enemy; I was not interested in getting extra credit for overcoming it. But without that extra credit I wondered if I would always be in arrears.

❧

It was a little after midnight, apparently. I produced my passport when Kathleen prompted me. We got into a taxi and Kathleen uttered a number of phrases which I could not even pick apart into individual words. Then we were driving and I thought of Graham, now many miles away. It was bitterly cold as we got out of the car. Strange music breathed through the hotel lobby like a draught: it was a version of 'Satisfaction' by the Stones, sung by a woman at half the tempo of the original.

In our room something rattled and buzzed. The mattress was thin to the touch. I'd been in hotels other than the Alpha a few times now, for events with Lara, but never stayed the night in one. This didn't feel as if it would be a good place to start. I wished Kathleen hadn't chosen a budget hotel when Howard could probably have got us a room anywhere in Beijing.

Recently, her principles had seemed to converge on a point of antagonism towards him.

'What's that noise?'

'What?'

'The buzzing.'

'It's the heating thing.' She sounded exasperated. 'It's normal. I'm going to have a shower, all right?'

As she was getting undressed, I tried to take her in my arms, but she writhed away. 'It's not the time.'

'I've got no idea what time it is. I just want to smell you.'

'We've been travelling for twelve hours. That's the main thing you need to know.'

'Does that mean I'm not allowed to want you?'

'No. But it does mean I'm allowed to tell you to go away.'

In the morning she was businesslike.

'I've got to meet someone a fair way across town. We'll get the underground.' For a moment I thought she meant the Tube; then I remembered where we were. I groped my way groggily around a new, formless room. Getting ready took longer than usual. The air in the bathroom was claggy and Kathleen had to help me in and out of the shower. I knelt naked on the floor and began to rummage through my case. Kathleen, sighing, got down to help me.

'There you are. Pants. Jeans. Shirt. Let's go.'

'Are we going to have breakfast?'

'Christ and his dog, come *on*. We'll get some breakfast on the way or something.'

We ate gooey pastries, unevenly packed with some sort of meat, on the way down to the subway. Kathleen led me off the train, up onto the street where we were blasted with cold. She was meeting someone to talk about the way the Internet was censored here, someone who worked for an NGO. The details were too fast and numerous, the context too intricate. I waddled along beside her impatient stride, feeling like a toddler. The wind kept rearing up and dealing us slaps in the face. Or dealing them to me, at least. I didn't feel as if we were having the same experience as one another. Kathleen pulled me into a small-feeling building and spoke to someone, and then we were in a room.

I had brought my laptop, but its battery was depleted and it felt as if asking someone about power sockets would lower my status here still further. I tapped away for a little while on the release I was writing for a credit card 'exclusively designed' for owners of a specific car. *This has never been a car for people who play it safe. But sometimes you don't want adventures. When you're trying to pay for things away from home, for example. And that's why we've come up with …*

It was stupid: what could I say about adventures when all I wanted was to go home? I began to delete it all from the screen. Fleetingly, and without knowing why, I had an urge to begin writing to my father.

Where are you? Are you alive? Why do I not even know your name? Why did you never come back? You must have heard about me. Why don't you want to see me?

Later on I persuaded her to take me to Tiananmen Square and we stood there in the chill. I wanted to hold her hand, but a brush-off, any little hint of impatience or cooling desire, would be too much to swallow. I remembered the two of us in Piccadilly Circus, seething with shared desire, and castigated the version of myself who had stood there and felt as if it would never fade.

'They're going to march in a minute,' said Kathleen, 'the soldiers. You can see them all gathering in their green uniforms. Sort of a dull green. Just dozens and dozens of men, all short hair. They march a couple of times a day.'

What was a dull green, what was any green? I felt physically cowed by this place, by its hordes of people and its unknowables. She described the small gangs of wandering tourists, the wintry sky, the chaotic frontispieces of the imperial buildings, the plumes of smog on the horizon. She was doing her best: it was just that for all these word-pictures, and despite the occasional strange smell and background chatter in a foreign tongue, I was still walking around in the same darkness as ever. I wanted something I could experience as a new and enriching sensation, something that would say, *You are in China, you are worldly-wise.* The massacre had happened here: Graham had read the report to me, and I had relayed it to Howard. I wanted to feel a clear line from that moment of my childhood to this one of maturity, but it was more as if I had simply exchanged one description of something for another.

The next day, I volunteered to stay in the hotel by myself. It wasn't so much that I wanted to; more that I could not stomach another day as an encumbrance. Kathleen had three meetings. I would stay here and work. She'd come back and we would be like any couple – the return from the office, absence making the heart fonder. We ate a breakfast which she picked out for me, gelatinous offerings that felt wobbly in the mouth. Then she chaperoned me back to the room.

'I'll be absolutely fine.'

'Just call down to reception if there's anything. I've told them to have an English speaker ready in case. You just press the big button. This one.' She took my hand and showed me. 'All right?'

'Yes. Go. It's fine.'

She brushed her teeth with those vigorous brushstrokes, spat, pecked me on the top of the head and then – as if deciding to increase her offer slightly – came back to kiss me on the mouth. I stiffened and reached for her, but she was out of the door. There was the harsh cheep of the lift as its doors juddered aside. Within the next hour she might be anywhere in this city of fifteen million people, this city which could swallow up the Alpha, the whole of London.

The heating unit clacked away. I should have asked her to

switch it off. She had laid out two cups of water for me; there were coffee granules in a mug and I could boil the kettle with a single button-press. She had set up my laptop to surf the net, and left me her own computer with a DVD ready to play. I could order room service from the Anglophone staff member. These various distractions sucked away the rest of the morning and the beginning of the afternoon. At least I thought so: in fact, when I checked the time, only two hours had gone by. I finished off the press release; I listened to a long series of BBC news clips online. The time oozed by, as sluggish as sewer water.

I didn't want to eat anything. I had drunk both my cups of water. The hall outside was narrow and the only sound was my own footsteps. When I re-entered our room, reaching out and counting the door handles as I did to navigate at the Alpha, I was gripped by a loneliness which made me resentful and ashamed. An insect was buzzing in a corner, its steady noise woven in and out of the mechanical breaths of the heating unit. I felt the skin on my arms prickling.

Kathleen called early in the afternoon. 'Everything OK?'

'Completely fine. How were your meetings?'

'It's going really well. I might need to see a couple more people this afternoon. I'll tell you about it later. Sure you're all right?'

'Of course.'

Afterwards, the sudden absence of her voice brought me to a complete standstill for a moment. My palms were damp on the desktop. Something felt alarmingly out of joint. The heater was clicking its invisible tongue. I felt hemmed in by the room, even by the air I was breathing, exhaling, rebreathing. I turned to the Internet, to my version of the world, and set the auto-read to pluck fruit at random from its billion branches.

A stampede at a temple in Mandhar Devi. 250 dead. I didn't know anything about this place, or a single thing about any of the two hundred and fifty people who had been wiped off the human register while I was doing something else. Click here for more about Mandhar Devi. The robotic almost-voice read out some particulars. It was a twenty-four-hour-long festival. Pilgrims sacrificed animals and offered curd rice to a goddess. I typed curd rice into Google. It was a yoghurt rice commonly eaten in Kerala. I typed in Kerala. There were thirty-three million fucking people in Kerala alone. And all these people in Beijing. I had started to sweat. It pooled at the base of my spine, misted my forehead. I could hear the insect again. What sort of insect was it? I could taste the memory of the blood that filled my mouth when I was stung by a wasp at the zoo.

I was clicking on links at random, letting the impassive cyber-voice wash over me. Later-in-the-15th-century-the-lucrative-spice-trade-attracted-Portuguese-traders-to-the-region, droned the computer. I was rudderless in a sea of facts not connected to one another, or connected only in the subtle, impossible ways that all the people out of the window were connected, all the way back to Howard in the Alpha. The connections were there but I could not see them. Kerala is the state with the lowest population growth rate, the highest life expectancy. The human sex ratio is of particular interest to anthropologists because. Anthropology is the study of humankind. Margaret Mead was frequently in the mass media during the 1970s.

I closed the browser. I walked again to the end of the corridor and back, reminding myself that the crucial facts were as clear-cut as they'd always been. I was Chas York, I was going to be twenty-four this year, the year being 2005. It was January. I was in Beijing, once Peking, the capital of China. Despite the fact that my girlfriend's precise whereabouts were unknown, she would be back before long and my skin would be against hers. Howard was only a plane ride away.

In closing the Internet down I had accidentally shut off my connection. I tried to reconnect, in vain. The shortcut keys led nowhere – my computer was beached. Kathleen's was a little further along, but the keys felt strange; the desktop was a mystery. I called downstairs. After a considerable wait, someone spoke to me in Mandarin.

'------,' said the voice.

'Hello,' I said. 'I'm in Room 82. There's someone who speaks English?'

'------------?' said the voice. I heard the words helplessly as if they were objects I was being invited to look at.

'English,' I said, and gave Kathleen's name.

'------,' the voice replied. I could hear the insect buzzing.

There was a click and I was put into a holding queue. The music was again a version of 'Satisfaction'. It finished and got halfway through a second playing before somebody picked up.

'Hello, sir?'

I explained the Internet problem. The man on the other end listened patiently and asked me to repeat myself. I re-explained.

'Yes, yes,' said the English-speaker, leaving another pause. 'We don't deal with Internets,' he said in the end. 'I give you another number. You call.'

'I ... could you do that for me, by any chance?' I asked reluctantly. 'I'm blind, you see, I can't see what I'm doing, and my girlfriend ... '

There was another click, a further short burst of music, and when a voice appeared again, it was with a new spurt of Mandarin which I recognized as being the same phrase we had begun the entire interaction with.

'------?'

I gave up and dropped the receiver. There would be no Internet till Kathleen got back, then. I began to listen to the DVD, which was ready to go. It froze after ten minutes or so. I drew back my fist to punch the machine, remembered it was Kathleen's, and brought it down hard on my own keyboard.

Before long my field of options had narrowed to two. Both of them felt like defeats. I had been alone for five and a half hours. It was a good effort for a blind, inexperienced person. But I didn't want to be a blind, inexperienced person. I didn't want to interrupt Kathleen with the news I hadn't quite made it. I pressed one on my speed-dial. The first letter of the alphabet, the first hotel in the list of London's five-stars.

'Hotel Alpha, good morning,' said Graham's voice, as crisply as if he were just behind me.

'Is Howard there?'

'Chas!' said Graham. 'How is China?'

'Lovely,' I said. 'It's been really, it's been really …'

That was as far as I got before my voice careered off and I was spluttering into the handset. Sarah-Jane came on; Graham must have transferred the call. 'Darling,' she said, 'it's all right. It's all right.'

'There's a wasp here, I think,' I managed to say.

Sarah-Jane talked to me for two or three minutes until my breathing had slowed down, and then Howard came to the phone.

'Think of a number between one and a hundred,' he commanded. I laughed out loud through a barrier of snot. The number was seventy-one. He got it right.

'I shouldn't stay on the phone long,' I said, 'it's expensive to—'

'We'll pay your fucking bill, for fuck's sake,' said Howard. 'You should never have to be out of your comfort zone, mate,' he said. My comfort zone was so tiny that leaving it was unavoidable, I started to say, but Howard was off. 'I've told you, you don't have anything to prove. It's enough that you've gone to

China, fucking hell, without being left on your own in the room as if this is some sort of *Big Brother* thing where we try to torture you ...'

'She's only gone for the day. I said she should go on her own. I don't want to be in the way.'

'Mate,' said Howard. He cleared his throat. 'This was my whole point, this was why I wanted to go with you. I—'

'What do you mean?'

'I offered to come,' said Howard. 'I would've stayed in a different hotel if necessary. In fact, looking at yours online, I *definitely* would have. But no, she wasn't having it.'

My mouth was dry. Howard resumed; a breath-long pause had always been enough for him. 'That's not the point. My point is just that I'm the person you should always turn to. Kathleen has her job to worry about.'

'So do you.'

'But none of it as important as you, mate. My whole mission in life is to make sure you have a decent time of it.'

'I'm not a kid.'

'You still need help, though, Chas.' Howard's tone had shed all its rhetorical bullishness, even its normal joshing quality. 'And I'm the one who helps you. I like being the one who helps you. It's a privilege.'

We talked for a few minutes more. I could hear the sound of Sarah-Jane singing, pots and pans being thrown about. I could construct, as a reflex of the senses, the atrium's web of voices, the whirring of the lift, the touch of Room 25's slightly mis-shapen door. There was a stab of pain like a stitch in my lower abdomen.

'Are you all right?' Howard asked, picking up on some change in my breath in the way he alone could.

'I just … I've got this stupid idea that I should never have left. That the hotel will never quite be the same when I go back.'

Howard laughed softly. 'Well, you've got that right. It *is* a stupid idea. This place never changes, mate. It'll all be waiting for you.'

His words made me feel as if I were an explorer pined for by those left at home, rather than a man who had left just over seventy-two hours ago. A strange pride took hold of my heart. By the time Howard said goodbye, the room was just a room. My being there was a neutral thing, a matter of indifference. When at last Kathleen's footsteps rang outside and the door let her in, I was in a state of quiescence like someone recovering from a violent vomiting fit. Everything was pleasantly out of focus.

There was the clanging of loose change onto the desk, and she filled my horizon, suddenly, kissing me on the forehead. 'Hello.'

'How was your day?'

She slipped away as I grasped for another kiss, and I heard her flinging herself onto the flimsy bed. 'Amazing. The woman I met just then basically all-but-said the correspondent job is mine. If I want it. Jesus juice,' she added, 'it's warm as hell in here, have you had the heating on all day?'

'So, obviously you *do* want it ...'

'It's kind of too good to turn down,' Kathleen said.

There was a pause in which I might have said congratulations, or she might have reassured me that the relationship could survive across continents, or either of us could have said something optimistic about my chances of relocating to China. None of these things happened. The heating unit came sighing to a silence of relief as she yanked the cord.

'Have you been OK?'

'I've been great.'

'But really?'

She took off her coat and slung it somewhere, and I caught the scent of her, the real flesh and blood of her as she moved closer again. 'Really, no. I panicked a bit. There was ... I had trouble with the Internet and there was an insect. It was fine.'

Kathleen's hand toyed with the sleeve of my jumper. 'You could have called me.'

'I called Howard.'

We stumbled over his name, as we always seemed to now. She drew back her arm.

'He told me he was going to come, but you didn't want him to.'

'Fucking hell,' said Kathleen. 'He's bloody good at telling you things when it suits him, isn't he!'

'What's that supposed to mean?'

'Forget it,' she said. 'Nothing.'

We were slipping into a pattern which I thought I recognized, as if we'd spoken these exact words before. I realized with sorrow that it wasn't about the words but the rhythm. I'd heard many strangers' iterations of this dance: the quickstep through grievance, anger, resignation, the rise and fall of voices, the sudden lurches of volume. Early in our romance we would laugh at them, warring couples in the bar. And now here it was, here we were.

'What do you mean, nothing? What were you going to say?'

'It doesn't matter.'

'Obviously it matters, because now you're being defensive.'

'I'm always going to be defensive,' said Kathleen, 'if you go running to Howard at every sign of a—'

'I didn't *go running* to him. I'm on the other side of the fucking world from him.'

'All right,' she said, 'great, but I wanted this trip to be about you and me. If Howard is here, the trip ends up being about him. Everything is always about him.'

'I don't know why you have to be so antagonistic towards him the whole time. Literally the whole time.'

'There are a lot of things you don't know,' she spat back.

'What's that supposed to mean?'

The silence was so biting, I almost wished for the insect-buzz or the heater noise again. Kathleen sighed. 'Listen. I wanted you to feel independent. Feel like you can get away from that place, from the hotel.'

'It's my home. I've never known anywhere else.'

'Precisely,' she said, 'and that's the problem.'

'Just be upfront with me. What have you got against him? Against the Alpha?'

Kathleen hesitated. 'Against the Alpha, nothing.'

'Against Howard?'

She let a moment go by. 'I think he dominates you, and you're a bit too dependent on him, that's all.'

'Could you not at least have told me he'd suggested coming so we could have had a conversation like adults?'

'Thanks for letting me know how adults behave,' Kathleen snapped. She walked right past me, so that our bodies touched for a moment, and on into the bathroom. She slammed the door and the shower began to gush.

I'd got through the day's trials as if Kathleen's return was the answer, but it had only brought new unhappiness. I headed for the door and down the corridor, not bothering to count the handles, and stood with my back against the wall. All the day's inactivity bore down on my muscles. My head throbbed. Some time went by before the door was flung open at the other end of the hall.

'Chas!'

She sounded shaken. 'Christ. I thought for a second maybe you'd just upped and gone.'

'How exactly would I do that?'

'Look, I'm sorry.' She took my arm. 'I didn't shower. I didn't get in.'

'What?'

'I wanted you to smell it all. All the day I've had. The fumes – fuck, it's smoggy out there – the sweat, everything.'

My heart was galloping. 'Are you naked now? Out here?'

We drove each other back into the room and staggered to the bed, my palms' sweaty grip on her sides, and I crash-landed on her and pressed my head into her midriff and came in moments. We lay there, Kathleen talking filth until it was time to start again. We ordered food to the room. When she finally did shower, I made her get dressed for the pleasure of undressing her again, and we lay on the uncomfortable bed, her head on my chest.

'I'm proud of you,' I said, 'with the job and everything. I really am.'

'We don't need to talk about that,' she murmured. 'Just enjoy this. This moment.'

My body was as heavy as iron; I let sleep shove me under. When I woke up, Kathleen had shuffled away from me. I could hear her breathing.

Things she had said, or tried not to say, began to force themselves into my mind. What did she mean about Howard? Memory fragments fluttered in and out of view. The back of my neck felt hot.

Trying to track away from this avenue of thought, my brain

detoured towards a place it was even more afraid of and kept baulking until I forced it to go in. Kathleen had got the job. It was happening.

Kathleen would move to China. It was obvious that I couldn't move here with her. I belonged in the Alpha. I could not move to China any more than Kathleen could stay at my side. She knew it as well as I did, and what she had said before falling asleep was a way of acknowledging it. It was a way of beginning the goodbyes.

෧12෧

GRAHAM

Back the Bid! The phrase, coined by Lara and Chas at a meeting in our hotel, now seemed embroidered into the air of the city itself. It sang out from the backs of buses; it was even uttered by Mr Blair. It was accompanied by spectacular images of athletes hurdling over Tower Bridge, leaping over the London Eye, and so forth. 'Back the Bid' appeared on a banner which hung in the spot we normally reserved for festive wreaths, along with a set of graphite Olympic rings which would undoubtedly shatter a guest's skull if they ever fell down. In a matter of weeks the games would be awarded either to Paris, or to us.

Yes, us! I was getting caught up in all the enthusiasm in spite of myself. But the curious thing about all this was that it did not really matter a dicky bird whether I, or anybody else in London, 'backed' the bid. It had been conducted on our behalf and was probably confirmed by now as a success or failure. That result would not be affected by the goodwill which was being so elaborately solicited.

'It's about being *seen* to do all this stuff,' Chas explained. 'It's like Coke. Why does Coke spend a fortune every year on advertising? There's no one alive who hasn't had a can of Coke, but …'

'There is, actually.'

Chas grinned. 'All right, apart from you. But by spending all that money, they're showing that they have that status. And this is the same. Even though people might complain about the cost of the bid, they like to feel it's being done properly. Which means a campaign. Simple as that.'

Jargon like this still struck me as far from simple, and far from desirable, but perhaps it was only what Howard had said all along: it was not enough to do something, you had to do it with a splash. In any case, I was pleased that Chas had something to occupy him.

To avoid the dramatic farewell neither of them had the stomach for, Chas and Kathleen had gone out for dinner at a French place where Howard had an account that was never called in. I turned up in the Mercedes at midnight and waited outside the restaurant until the two figures emerged. They embraced on the pavement at some length; then Chas got into the back of the car, a brave smile on his face, and Kathleen stood watching us drive away. Chas babbled all the way home, his voice clambering over an unnatural range. At the Alpha, Howard was waiting with a bottle of gin.

Howard's company and work. Those were the two main narcotics with which Chas kept the thought of Kathleen from his door. Whether this meant that he was 'moving on', or merely moving back to where he was before he met her, I did not like to speculate. With Mr Blair's re-election in May and this Olympic bid to finish in July, he'd had two substantial projects to take his mind off Kathleen.

It was four months now since she had left. There had recently been an all-night bash at the Alpha for the election, and I had stayed until four o'clock or so, by which time it was clear that Labour would win, though by less of a margin than anticipated. Pattie and I did not discuss the outcome until a couple of mornings later.

'I didn't really follow it,' she admitted. 'I was chatting to Pam – you remember I told you about Pam?' She was someone's sister-in-law. 'Now, Pam has had a shocking time of it over there. Her husband – apparently this is quite common in America – her husband just gets drunk and goes bowling all the time.'

She gave a history of the indiscretions of this man I did not know, the spouse of a woman whose relevance I could not quite place, while I buttered a piece of toast and read the front of *The Times*, in case Chas needed any extra information today.

'I suppose Tony Blair won again, did he?' asked Pattie.

'He did, although … '

'He seems like a nice man,' she adjudicated, 'although the wife strikes me as a bit of a busybody.'

Digesting these political observations as I got onto the bus, it struck me that I could not even say with certainty whether Pattie had voted, though I supposed not. There were a great many things we could not say with certainty about one another.

You should be careful what you wish for, though, as everyone knows. Within a few weeks, we did have an item of shared interest to discuss.

It was evening. I had just used the reception phone to call Caroline in Inverness. There was no answer. Pattie had had more luck with emails. But I did not want an email from Christopher; I wanted to hear his voice. I slung the receiver back into its cradle and looked up to see Ed shuffling across the marble floor towards me. At first, given that I had just been thinking about my family, it almost seemed I could be imagining him. As he neared, I rather wished that I was. Ed was wearing a heavy raincoat quite at odds with the season. His eyes would not look into mine.

'Ed!'

'I've lost my job, Dad.'

'What?'

'I've lost my job,' he said again.

'They have sacked you?'

His face twisted. 'That's not how they put it, funnily, funnily, er, funnily enough. They said they had to make some cutbacks. Difficult time for the industry. Online bookings, you see. People like your boss,' he added with a bitter smile.

'Howard?'

'Always goes, goes online now,' said Ed. 'Always goes online. Too many people like that, you see. Humans, er. Humans not required in the office. Just computers.'

'But you are one of the senior agents,' I protested.

'Not so good with the old spreadsheets, though,' Ed muttered.

'Well,' I said. There was a happy cry on one of the balconies, a playful exchange between friends; we both glanced up towards the skylight, and I could see Ed's eyes bulging. I hoped to high heaven he would not cry.

'Well,' I began again, 'I'm sure something will … these situations often end up being a blessing in … That is … '

There was a story about a horse which Howard used to tell – it broke its leg, but it turned out well, or something of the kind – but I was damned if I could remember it. Ed, in any case, was past reassurance. He loomed suddenly into my light, clutching the edge of the walnut desk like a drunkard. 'Is there anything for me here, Dad?'

He looked pleadingly at me. This was ghastly: a grown man in his mid-thirties begging his father for work. I reached out and put my hands on his shoulders and we stood there, the desk between us, as if we were making a bridge over it. I cast a glance around. This was not what guests wanted to see; or what I wanted them to see.

'Look, old man,' I said, squeezing his shoulders. 'Why don't

271

you go to the bar and get a drink. Just ask Ray for what you want. Have a whisky, a double. And I'll get the desk closed up and join you in a jiffy.'

I was getting him out of the way, we both knew it, because I did not know how to make things look all right to him: I only knew how to make the atrium look all right.

Sarah-Jane was in the Alpha Bar ready for just this sort of situation. She gave Ed a drink and flirted with him with the finesse she undoubtedly possessed even now, and by the time I arrived he was beginning to grin and crack jokes with the warped cheeriness of a battlefield casualty. I drove him home; he went to bed in his boyhood room beneath the map of the world.

'What on earth is going to happen to him now?' asked Pattie.

I was as incapable as ever, I wanted to explain, of predicting the future. 'He will come back from this,' I mustered. 'Edward is a clever lad.'

'What sort of world is it,' asked Pattie, clutching suddenly at my hand as we lay in bed, 'that doesn't value a man who's been in a job for as long as he has?'

I had very little to say. What sort of world was it? An unfamiliar one. And yet, some of it was still so familiar. Pattie fell asleep on her left side, facing me. Her slender shoulders rose and fell; her face took on that aspect of childlike contentment. Outside, Muswell Hill was much as it had been for sixty years since the war. The occasional bus wheezed by; cats tightrope-walked along high fences, jumped down to disappear among under-growth; a milky moon gazed down on the odd young Romeo reeling home. A couple of miles south, back the way I had come earlier, the Hotel Alpha was in the grip of a hundred different sleeps.

It was the same world I had always known, all right. And yet it felt as if it had become an imitation of itself, somehow, like the Georgian house in Kensington we sometimes directed guests to, once a real home and now a simulacrum for the entertainment of visitors. It felt – and surely my mind would not run on so extravagantly when morning came – but it felt as if somebody had slipped in and removed the world and in its place erected something which looked and felt the same, like my imitation Bakelite telephone, yet was really only a prop.

Perhaps that 'somebody' was only time. But in the dreams that my brain finally stirred up – dreams which in some elusive way took up the theme again – the thief had a human face. This may account for the actions I found myself taking four days later.

∞

It was a hot night. The usual characters swarmed everywhere. In the bar, Howard gave a demonstration of sword-swallowing, which an overseas visitor had taught him the basics of. Chas talked to Olympic people. Midnight slipped away like a guest out of the doors. The scene in the Alpha Bar, when I wandered in from my desk, seemed much as usual. But then something curious caught my eye.

Lara Krohl was sitting on her own, her laptop computer pushed some distance away. She was for once not attached to Howard and his court: her vigilance had been substituted for an almost absent manner. By her elbow was a bottle of white wine which, as I watched, she emptied of its final dregs.

At about one o'clock, with febrile noise still coming in waves from the bar, Lara approached my desk with a speed her condition made her ill-equipped for. She folded her arms across her chest. Her appearance had an unusually haphazard character to it: her make-up had slipped and the normally crisp black jacket looked creased.

'Have you had a laptop handed in?' she asked.

'A laptop computer?'

'Yes, yes, a laptop computer, a Mac laptop,' said Lara Krohl. Her dark eyes danced with alarm over the items behind my desk: the blocky telephone, the rack of keys, all of it useless to her.

'Nothing like that, I'm afraid,' I said.

'F--- me,' she muttered. 'It's been f---ing nicked.'

'I don't think so. I would have seen ... '

'It's very urgent,' she cut in. I almost laughed. Did she think I had merely been waiting for her to pronounce the situation urgent? Did she think she could 'lean on me', 'chase me', all the other things I had heard her urge over the past few years? 'I need it back. It has classified information, which ... It has extremely sensitive information on it.'

Careless of you to leave it unattended, then, I nearly said. But I was still the head of this establishment, and nobody left dissatisfied with our service. 'We will move heaven and earth to find it, then, Ms Krohl,' I said.

She swallowed hard and said: 'Thank you, Graham.'

Then she muttered that she would stay in the building and I should tell her, please, if it showed up. The 'please', and the use of my first name, testified to her weakened state. I watched her walk back into the bar, where the voices would seem too loud, as they always did when one was alone with a misfortune. A certain sympathy brewed inside me. But another less worthy emotion was ahead of it in the queue. I was rather thrilled; that was the truth of it.

The news spread, and the hotel changed shape with it. The chatter in the atrium, the eyes of those passing the desk, all took on a character of suppressed excitement: the ordinary person's relish for the murder on the village green. Lara Krohl was scouring the bar, looking in places where the computer could not possibly be. Before long this lost its appeal for the casual observer, and the party began to break up at around two o'clock, people spilling in disorderly fashion out into the night. Lara, though, would not be going anywhere. To leave the building would be more or less to give the computer up for lost. As Ray locked up the bar and went wearily on his way, leaving me almost alone in the Alpha, I was not surprised to see her approach.

'I'm going to stay here the night,' she said. 'Can I have a room? Any room?'

Her hand, brushing against mine to take the A-shaped key, felt like a dead thing. Even as she walked across the floor towards the lifts, she seemed every few moments to glance back to the bar, or up towards the pitiless array of balconies, as if a solution were there.

But it had been in front of her nose all along, for I had the laptop computer. I had gone into the bar while she was strutting about on her phone and removed it calmly, and now it was safe and sound behind the desk. Would anyone in the whole place have credited this if they'd seen it? They would not. I scarcely credited it myself. But here it was, by my foot, in the bottom of a laundry bag which was firmly zipped up, and as Lara went miserably up to her room I emerged with the bag over my shoulder and stood in the empty atrium, my heart beating quickly. I, too, would spend the rest of the night in the Alpha.

For the first time in these forty years, I checked myself into a guest room. I walked up by the back staircase. It was years since I had trodden here; but it was the only way I could be sure of avoiding Lara.

Room 62 looked out backwards over the jostle of brickwork and pipes. Outside it was surprisingly light already, or perhaps it never really became dark at this time of year. The sky looked purplish, the upward swirl of the city lights seeming to shine right through it as if it were only a canopy put up until the real sky re-emerged. I unwrapped the computer with cold hands and worked out how to put it on, then relieved the room's fridge of a miniature whisky. The screen was asking for a 'passcode'. I had only one guess, but it was a good one. The passcode unlocked an invisible door, and I permitted myself a low laugh of satisfaction. The screen swirled and the internal engine chugged. I swigged the whisky. Here at my disposal, in all likelihood, was information enough to ruin half of Lara's illustrious contacts. Some of it might be protected by further codes; but by the way she had panicked, I suspected plenty of it was not. Here was a great vault of secrets, sensitive information by the gallon, if you knew how to get at it.

I, of course, did not. The computer seemed to have sensed this: it was amusing itself by drawing geometric shapes on its screen and wafting them around. I had no more idea of how to access its treasures than an ape let loose among the Crown Jewels. But there were people in this building who did know: that was the point. Lara could easily believe – would be thinking even now – that someone was about to get at everything on her PC. If I stood and listened, I almost believed I could hear her pacing the carpet of her room two floors below.

I got into bed, in the end, at around half-past four. My heart had barely slowed since I'd executed the theft – as I supposed it was. I still preferred not to regard it in those terms. I had taken the computer, it was true, but it was not as if I meant to keep or sell it. It was merely a case of setting a thief to catch a thief. I would give the laptop back as soon as Lara Krohl had given me what I wanted in return.

⤬

At half-past seven in the morning I used the room's phone to call Pattie. Nothing to worry about, I said: I had stayed at the Alpha overnight to deal with a crisis.

A crisis it is indeed, I thought, glancing wryly into the bath-room mirror. But not for me. All the same, as I reached again for the telephone my hands were trembling a little. I put this down partly to the muddling effects of sleeplessness and adrenalin, and partly to a chess-player's anticipation of victory. There was also the feeling that victory might not be what I hoped. That I was not going to like what I learned.

The telephone in 22 was answered after a single ring.

'Ms Krohl?' I said. 'We have your laptop computer.'

There was a long exhalation at the other end which was quickly dissembled into a clearing of the throat.

'At reception?' she said. 'I'll be there in—'

'Not at reception.' It was rather amusing to be interrupting her, for once, I had to admit. 'In Room 62.'

'What?'

'I have your computer and I am in Room 62.'

The phone clicked, the dialling tone hummed in my ear, and almost at once there was a series of sharp raps at my door. I swung it open. Lara Krohl was standing there with her arms folded over her jacket; her make-up had been reapplied, her hair washed. Without a word she advanced into the room and stopped, thunderstruck, at the sight of her computer sitting on the desk. I had worked out how to get it onto the Internet, and on the screen was a photograph which I had found by searching there. All this Lara Krohl took in with a narrowing of her already small eyes.

'What the f---,' she said, 'have you been doing with it? And how did you get into it?'

'Oh-five-oh-six. You have said it often enough when you supposed I was not listening.'

She virtually ran to the computer, though it was plainly too late. 'What is this f---ing picture on my machine,' she demanded, 'and what made you think you could just— ' In the middle of this sentence she seemed at last to grasp the full situation, and she swung round from the desk.

'Did *you* take it?'

'Lord above,' I said, 'I thought you would never ask.'

There was a pause.

'Are you out of your f---ing mind?' she asked. 'Are you completely out of your f---ing mind? Do you realize I could set the … the f---ing police onto you like *that*?' 'That' was a snap of the fingers. My heart was pounding, but I felt no fear: more a sort of exhilaration. Now the game was on. Now we were playing it, all right! Her final words had been at a volume close to a shout, and this unprecedented loss of control – along with the fearful way she now glanced at the computer – confirmed that I had the advantage.

'I don't think you will want to call the police,' I said, keeping my own voice low and calm. 'For one thing, I could very easily make it seem there had been some misunderstanding, and Howard would undoubtedly take my corner, rather than yours.'

'You think so, do you?' Lara Krohl's mouth curled upwards at the corner in a way I did not like. I had to steel myself against the implication in her words. Of course he would choose me over her, I told myself. I was the best friend he had. I was almost one hundred per cent certain. Besides, this was just a distraction. I had a stronger card still to play.

'More to the point,' I said, 'I think you should be trying to keep on my good side rather than threatening me, because I have had a good poke around in that machine – ' I nudged my head in the direction of the laptop – 'and learned quite a number of interesting things.'

The size of the bluff momentarily appalled me. Were she to call it by asking me to name something incriminating on her computer, I would be in difficulty. I saw her eyes sweep over my face like metal detectors and forced myself to concentrate on holding her gaze. There were a few thick seconds of tension.

I felt sure she would tell me that all those secrets were locked away; or perhaps there really *was* nothing damaging on her computer. She would screw my power into a little ball and toss it into the wastepaper basket.

Lara Krohl took a long slow breath out, however, and cast a helpless look at the computer. She looked back at me and shook her head, and I knew I had outmanoeuvred her. When she spoke again, her voice was hoarse and brittle, only just audible.

'What do you want? Money? How much f---ing money?'

As she uttered this, she continued to shake her head. It was preposterous, she must be thinking, that an old plodder like me should outpace an operator like her.

'Not money.' I gestured again at the computer. 'Firstly, I would like you to look at that picture on the screen and tell me if you know who it is.'

While we had been talking, the computer had taken up its doodling, and a number of polygons were now rebounding around the display. Lara Krohl was obliged to go and shake the thing out of its daydream. The photograph from the Internet appeared once more in front of us.

'I don't have any f---ing idea who it is,' she said with a certain relief in her voice. 'So I think, whatever is going on here … I think you might have got the wrong end of the stick, Graham.' With the deployment of my name came a shift of her tone into something more wheedling than aggressive. 'Why don't you just let me have the computer back and we'll pretend this never happened.'

'Yes, you are good at pretending things never happened,' I said. 'I shall enlighten you. The reason you have never seen that person is that he is dead. He was shot dead at the age of eighteen. He was in Belfast, with the British army.'

Lara Krohl looked between me and the smiling Winston Richards in absolute bafflement. Her next words were delivered in a tone of careful forbearance as if she were trying to talk a psychopath down from a roof.

'I'm sorry for this – this man's death,' she said, 'but I'm afraid I don't understand at all why you are … '

'His mother worked here,' I said. 'Agatha Richards. She was a friend of mine. She had had to live with the terrible absence of her son – her only child – for a very long time.'

I paused. I had not expected to make quite such a song and dance of this. Even though she was involved in army recruitment, and in defending the war, it was rather a stretch to connect her with Winston's death. It was just that Lara Krohl had come to stand for everything that was not right: all the lies, the substitutions of the fake for the real, of machines for men. She had become accountable in my eyes for the fact that Ed's job had been wiped out by a website; for the fact that Christopher was out of my reach and Pattie was always sitting with her back to me typing messages to someone else. I felt as if I were settling a score with the whole of the world, with everything about it that had disappointed me. However unfair to her, to me it was exhilarating to have a single person serve as a culprit for all of it, and to have her in my clutches now.

All the same, I was only really here – had only really taken the computer – for one reason. With an effort I made myself return to the real business. Lara was leaning against the queen-sized bed and staring at me as if at an apparition. The time since her computer had disappeared must have seemed like a strange dream to her; as indeed it did to me.

'I want to know something,' I said. 'If you tell me, I will give you the laptop computer. I will never breathe a word about anything I may have discovered, and I will not bother you again.'

She prompted me to go on with the slightest twitch of her eyebrows.

'The mother of this boy was named Agatha Richards,' I said. 'She left, along with Ella Flanders – Chas's tutor – somewhat abruptly.' If any doubt had remained in my mind that Lara had been concealing something about their disappearances, it vanished now; at the mention of the two names her face drooped. 'I believe that you might know why,' I said.

She swallowed. 'Why are you doing this?'

'Because I was never told why Agatha left,' I said. 'And I miss her, and I want to know what became of her.'

Lara Krohl muttered something I could not hear and went suddenly into the bathroom, drawing the lock across with violence. When she returned, her arms were folded in the usual way but the gesture had lost its command. Her face was sickly even under the soft light that came in from the window. It looked like an overcast day after yesterday's blazing sun; but it was difficult to engage with the idea that a real world was outside.

'If you ever repeat a word of this – ' Lara Krohl began.

She sat down on the edge of the bed again and looked away from me as she spoke.

'I got Howard to fire her,' said Lara Krohl. 'I told him she had taken something from my room.'

'Good God,' I said, 'she would never in a hundred years … '

'I had no choice.'

'Because?'

She was turned away from me still, but I had the impression her eyes were closed.

'I had a, a relationship.'

'A romantic relationship?'

'Yah, Jesus Christ, a "romantic relationship",' she snapped. 'A romantic relationship with Ella.'

There was a noise from the corridor, a trolley rattling along, the buzz of a walkie-talkie and Mrs Davey's curt voice answering it. Lara held her tongue until Mrs Davey had knocked at a door and been admitted.

'That woman – Agatha,' she said eventually, 'she caught us one time. We'd found a room that was unlocked. After a party. Chas's … his birthday or something.'

It was very strange to think of them in Room 25 together. Lara went on.

'We would see each other after she came to work sometimes. But I told her, I eventually told her it couldn't happen any more. After we were seen doing … we were doing some out-there things. I needed to keep my privacy.'

She coughed. 'Ella was destroyed. She thought it could have worked. But I didn't want people chattering. And I didn't want to go on having a secret, either. She begged me. I told her, I'm sorry, we can't do this. So she left, and she said she was never coming back. And she hasn't. She never has.'

All this came out in a mumbled torrent, and I began to feel that she was unburdening herself of it as much as I was forcing it from her.

'So Agatha had to go,' said Lara. 'She was the only person who knew the relationship had ever happened. And had seen what we got up to. I persuaded Howard she was up to no good. He said he'd always had his suspicions about her. That she seemed the type.'

These last words filled me with a loathing so strong that I produced a terrible shout. Lara Krohl started and turned to look at me.

'*Seemed the type*,' I said. 'He said she *seemed the type*, did he! That woman did not have a bad impulse in her. She would never have dreamed of taking anything. She—'

'Were you in love with her?' asked Lara.

'As a matter of fact,' I said, 'I suppose I was.'

As soon as I had said this, out loud for the first time, I felt that I had to walk away. I went into the bathroom and dried my damp palms on a towel, glancing at my lined face in the mirror. When I came back into the bedroom I could see that Lara Krohl was also staring at her reflection. There was a long silence.

'I'm sorry,' she said. 'About your friend.'

My anger had taken on a different shape. I could feel it fizzing in my limbs. I had defeated Lara Krohl, perhaps, but that did not mean I myself had won.

'I don't suppose ...'

I hated having to ask this, and it took two attempts. 'I don't suppose you, or Howard, have any idea where she went to. Where she might have gone.'

Lara looked away again, out of the window, across all the miles, all the strangers. 'I'm sorry,' she said again.

The signs of remorse had wrong-footed me. She rummaged in her bag, brought out a packet of cigarettes and looked almost imploringly at me. 'Can I smoke in here? I guess not?'

Though normally I would have been seen dead before I allowed this to happen, I told her that it did not matter. She stayed on the edge of the bed, blowing clouds of smoke into the air. She kept beginning to say something and then breaking off from it. The figures of the clock on the bedside table read 09:12. Lara Krohl and I had been in this room for more than an hour, neither one of us attending to a single one of the tasks that would normally obsess us. Suzie would be wading through the morning rush of check-outs. I could not remember when I had last missed any part of a morning shift. Yet, once more, it did not seem all that important.

'Yesterday is, was Ella's birthday,' said Lara. 'For a couple of years after she left, we had this thing where on her birthday we were allowed to send each other a message. Then she stopped. I don't know where she is now. But every year, the birthday comes, I think maybe I'll hear from her, I never do. So I get drunk instead.' She snorted. 'Oh-five-oh-six. June the fifth.

'And you see,' she added, 'I've only got one photo of her. It's on the laptop. That's the main reason I was s----ing myself when I thought I'd lost it. I just want the picture. That's all.'

I made a gesture to say that she should take the computer. She rose from the bed as if she had not moved for ten years. I watched as she closed the computer screen. She put the machine under her arm, where it had spent so much of its time, and it felt momentarily as if none of these extraordinary events had occurred.

At the door, she paused.

'You could try Friends Reunited,' she said.

'I'm sorry?'

'There's a site called Friends Reunited. It's mostly for school and uni mates or whatever. But, you know. You could try looking for her there. People do use it to get in touch. After a long time.'

As she opened the door, I asked: 'Have you tried it? With … '

'The difference between your situation and mine,' said Lara in a low, almost threatening tone, much more like her usual voice, 'is that Ella does not *want* to be found by me.'

Our eyes met for a final time as she stood there with the door half open. Hers conveyed the acknowledgement of a new respect, even a trace of the mutual fondness that nests secretly in the hearts of rivals. The look also contained the understanding that nothing like this would ever occur again. We were not friends, and never could be. All the same, after what had passed between us, we were not really enemies either. For the real enemy I had to look closer to home.

∽

There were echoing footsteps which could only belong to one person. The Alpha felt empty; it was a quiet midweek night with no late-night blow-ins, no Olympic bigwigs. A week had passed since my confrontation with Lara Krohl. Sarah-Jane had gone down to visit friends on the coast. Chas was busy working, as he ensured he always was these days. And that was why I could hear Howard clumping across the chequered marble like a chessman with no one to play with. He had never known what to do without company.

I was sitting in the dark, only that half-glow of the screens casting my fingers in milky neon. Each time I had typed 'Agatha Richards' into one of these devices over the past months and years, it had felt like a foolish exercise. This latest venture, onto the page called Friends Reunited, was in some ways no less so: there was nobody of her name; I established that quickly enough. But the point was that, after this, there would be another website; there would be another lead. I could see why Chas called it the 'web', this thing. It was intricate and many-layered. It might lead anywhere. I was only just getting started with it.

The door burst open and, even though I had been expecting him, I jumped a little.

'Madman!'

'Good evening, Howard.'

He shambled in and threw his jacket onto one of the rotating chairs. There was a shot glass in his hand and a cigarette poked between two fingers. He blew a lazy draught of smoke into the air between us.

'Madman!' he said again. 'F--- me! Wouldn't have thought to find you here at this time.'

'I suppose not,' I said.

'Up to anything interesting?'

I hesitated for a moment, but hesitation would serve no purpose. Since the business with Lara, I had known that we were to have this conversation.

'Looking for Agatha,' I said. 'Do you remember her?'

'Agatha? Of course I do. I never forget a—'

'Well,' I said, 'I gather that you allowed Lara to persuade you Agatha was a thief. And then got rid of her on Lara's advice.'

Howard scratched his head as if this idea were quite unfamiliar to him; as if he were having trouble even understanding what I said. I stayed very still so that he had to turn his face to look at me. The nearest computer threw a chink of light across half of it; the other half stayed in shadow. I saw him mentally audition some nonchalant remark and then abandon it with a slight deflation of the shoulders. When his voice came, it was flat, without the usual mischief.

'How the hell did you find that out, mate?'

'I got it out of Lara,' I told him.

'My God,' Howard muttered. 'That must have taken some doing.'

'We came to an understanding.'

Howard's left-hand fingers drummed on the worktop, but they seemed not to break the silence; not to make any noise at all. He coughed a couple of times and reached out with the stub of his cigarette, but there were – of course – no ashtrays in here any more.

'I had to go along with it,' he said in the end. 'I didn't want to get on Lara's bad side. Also, I thought … I thought perhaps … '

'You thought perhaps Agatha *was* a bad sort.'

'Maybe. But more to the point, I thought she might get to know our secret. From … well, for example, from you.'

'You were right. I told her.'

Howard nodded slowly. 'I was scared that if she knew, anyone might find out eventually. I've lived with that fear a long time.'

'Kathleen knows now,' I informed him.

This, of course, was a much more serious revelation. The cigarette stub dropped from its perch.

'Agatha, you see, left a note when she went all those years ago. Which Kathleen eventually found.'

Howard lowered his head slowly into his palms.

'Kathleen must have told Chas,' he said faintly.

'She did not,' I said, 'because I persuaded her not to. But their relationship ended partly as a consequence, Howard. She just could not take the strain of it.'

He began to reply, and thought better of it.

'An awful lot,' I pushed on, 'has been sacrificed to make sure that your secret has been safe, Howard. Agatha left. Kathleen left. I have been biting my tongue for years. And Chas has been lied to. His life has been founded upon a lie.' I remembered sitting in this same room and reacting angrily when Kathleen used almost this same phrase. But she had been right. 'Sarah-Jane and JD have also been lied to. They have all been lied to for more than twenty years.'

Howard had been swallowing hard and clasping his hands together for the latter part of this speech.

'But you knew all this,' he said. 'You've always known this. And you went along with it. You protected me. When did you change your tune?'

His eyes were frightened, just as they were on the night it all happened: the night it all began to go wrong. Looking into those eyes, I saw him as I had seen him over the years – as the man on the Euston Road who changed my life, as the figure regaling audiences in the atrium whom I felt proud to know; and as the person in whose company Chas had for years been most alive, most himself. I saw him as a person who had made one terrible mistake and spent the past decades fleeing it.

'I didn't say I had changed my position,' I said, retreating. 'I am just wondering whether perhaps it is time, finally, to tell the truth. Even if you only told Chas. Not Sarah-Jane, even. Not the rest of them.'

'It wouldn't work.' Howard's eyes glimmered. It was so difficult to maintain anger against him, especially when you were not sure you wanted to. 'Chas would be knocked over by it. He wouldn't be able to keep it from the others. It's all or nothing, Madman. It's always been all or nothing.'

He had swivelled the chair round so that our knees were touching as we sat there, and both of his hands were on my arms.

'If there was a way I could have told Chas without my whole life collapsing, the whole bloody ... house of cards collapsing.'

He shook his head. 'There has never been a way. I would be done for.'

Then he stood up, so suddenly that I scooted back a little way in my chair, and gestured at the computers. 'But, you know what,' he said. 'These things will have me, in the end.' We both looked at the machines, so bland in appearance. 'I was all in favour, mate. I knew computers were the next big thing. I wanted a piece of that – you know me. But now ... now it's out of hand. Anyone can write anything they want.' I thought about the first time I had made the computer search for 'Hotel Alpha'. 'It only takes someone out there. Everyone gets caught in the end. No one's luck holds forever.'

Even after everything that had passed, I could not be sure whether he really thought this rule applied to him, or whether – as always – he felt that he could be the exception. There was a silence. I had a strong desire to be out of the room, to be somewhere I could think. Howard seemed to be driven by the same impulse; he went as if to open the door, but then stopped and put his hand out and touched my shoulder.

'No one could have been a better mate. Whatever happens now.'

I listened to him walking away. For several minutes I did not move a muscle. Eventually I went to reception, leaned against my walnut desk and looked up at the skylight.

Kathleen had wanted the job in China very much, for sure, but I believed she had really left Chas because it was intolerable to keep a secret from him any longer, and yet impossible to reveal it and watch everything disintegrate. She had chosen, as it were, a third way. I would have to do the same. I could not stay here and continue lying, but I did not want to rip the place apart with the truth. And so I was going to have to leave the Hotel Alpha.

As I clocked off that night and watched the cedars' branches frisking in the gentle night breeze, I repeated it to myself. I must leave this place. More than that: I must go and find Agatha. She was out there, or she might be. I had done this job as well as I could for forty years. I had approached it like a life's work. But it was not; not quite. I had lived most of my life, but not all of it. There was a little left.

When the bus appeared, I imagined getting off at Muswell Hill, putting my key in the lock, going to the oven and finding a plate ready for me, getting into bed with the warmth of my wife there beside me, coming back tomorrow to this place where I belonged. I thought of these things, and it was hard to believe that the same mind had been thinking with such hunger of their opposite. The closer I got to home, the more it felt as if the idea of walking away from it all had simply been an old man's ridiculous fantasy. With each minute that went by I had more work cut out to hang on to it, not to let reality whip it from my hands.

ↄ13ↄ
CHAS

It was only in the week leading up to the Olympic announcement that I realized I really wanted us to win. It was strange, given that for six months I'd directed most of my time to writing propaganda with that aim in mind. But it was only time, not emotional energy. I had done it like a machine.

The world in one city! That was where we lived. *An ancient city with a very modern sensibility*: that was us. *A nation of sports fanatics.* Glittering phrases written by someone who had never seen Big Ben, never watched a sporting contest. People could run or jump or throw things as far as they wanted without it having much meaning to me. Since Kathleen had gone, it was even more the case that I lived in words, not solid things. With Kathleen I had tasted the real world beyond the hotel walls and even come to think it could be mine. Without her, that was gone. She was like Ella in my mind – someone who had once existed because I could reach out and touch her, and now did not. All the places we used to go had vanished with her. I didn't want to go running or go to the cinema with anyone else. What was left was the virtual world, and I had thrown myself head first back into it.

Of course, it wasn't quite the same as when Ella had left. Technology had come a very long way. There was a program called Skype which allowed me to keep in touch with Kathleen for free: she could even look at me.

'And what do I get out of this?' I grumbled.

'You get the satisfaction of me being able to see you and check that you ... ' she said, the voice distant, random phrases snapping off on their way down the tunnel. 'And you look very nice.'

'Thank you. How's work?'

'It's OK. It's hot here. Hot and sweaty.'

'I've been reading your articles. Getting someone to read them to me. You know.'

'Sorry? I lost you there.'

'Oh, I just said I was reading your stuff.'

'You're lovely. Did you see the one about ... ?'

'Sorry?'

After a short period of disjointed interactions like this, we had concluded that they were not a good idea. It was hard to discuss her work, because it was what had taken her from me, and hard to discuss mine, since it had been part of the cause of our separation too. I didn't really want to know where she was living, who she was drinking with, who might be kissing her. And so we reverted to emails, functionally cheery, full of gossip and irreverence, keeping alive a friendship which could only be the ghost of something a hundred times better. Then the emails themselves dropped away, and now we were down to the odd text. If we weren't going to be together, we had to be meaningfully apart.

Still, dozens of other things might trick me into imagine-seeing her: hurried footsteps in the atrium, or profanities, mentions of China or of running, particular people's smells, songs she had played me. She was still out there. That was probably why I felt the first stirring of my wish for London to win. I wanted something to happen that was mine alone, something she had been opposed to, to show that this was a new time.

Ten days before the announcement there had been a strange conversation with Lara. We were in the Alpha Bar at lunchtime. When I sat down, Lara was blowing her nose, and when she began to speak her voice was hoarse and dry.

'So listen, Chas. After Singapore I'm going to take a little break.'

'A holiday?'

'More of a sabbatical.'

'For how long?'

'Six months, nine months.'

'Christ. Really?'

'Yah.' She went on in her bland tone as if the astonishing

notion of her disappearing from work – she who slept with her phone next to her pillow – were something anyone would have expected.

'So I'm more or less saying you will be in charge.'

'In charge?'

'Yah,' she said, and I had a giddying mental rush, something like a flashback combined with a premonition. On one side was the day I had met Lara, the feebleness of being floored by her trivia question. On the other, up ahead, was the reality of being her equal – being in her confidence, if anyone could ever be in her confidence. As the two extremes appeared at once, it felt like being an explorer looking back with sudden wonder over the mountain that has been conquered.

'That would be ... '

'I mean, of course someone would need to be across all the stuff as it came in, someone would need to help you with the admin. But you'd be the brains of this thing.'

Howard reacted as if it was the least I could expect. 'Makes sense, mate. She's grooming you. She rates you second to none. I wonder what she's playing at, though. Tell you what I think it probably is.'

I wasn't really listening; I was imagining myself as Chas York, Chief Executive of Lara Krohl PR. Krohl York PR. Krohl & York?

'Midlife crisis,' Howard went on. 'She's at the age where

people can't help wondering why there's no man. It comes to everyone. Even someone like her.'

Without knowing why, other than that we were on the subject, I asked him suddenly: 'Was there ever anything between you and her?'

'Anything between us?' Howard scraped his chair back along the floor.

'I don't care either way,' I added hastily. 'It wouldn't change my opinion of … I'm just asking.'

Howard's voice was a little different; it was hard to say how. It was a fraction thinner, higher, perhaps. It might be, I thought, the first time I had ever heard him speak without total conviction.

'There never was, no,' he said at last. 'What made you ask?'

What made me ask, I thought, is the nagging idea that there's something I'm not being told.

'Nothing. Just wondered.'

'A lot of people thought it,' Howard mused, 'because we worked so closely together. And because – well, I guess people thought I might have my own midlife crisis.'

'Which you never did?'

'I'm only sixty-six, mate,' said Howard. 'I haven't reached midlife yet.'

It was a typical Howard joke because it was only eighty per cent joke: you could believe, sitting here in his castle, that he really did mean to live a couple of centuries and that everything he had built would still be standing around him. Soon the question about him and Lara, and its curious aftermath of ambiguity, had gone out of my mind. It had been replaced by the idea, swelling with every moment, of the place my life might go from here.

That was why, as we stood in an atrium thickening with bodies by the minute, I found myself jangling with nerves. Victory would give us dozens of new contracts; it would mean huge amounts of new work, all of which I would be first in line for. If I needed a top-up of excitement, Howard was so full of it that it would have infected someone a mile away. He patrolled the atrium, gathering up anyone in his path. A projector screen had been hung from the top balcony. It was a new screen – not the one which had shown the Moon landing and the World Cup matches of old – but the Alpha tradition was the same as ever.

Sarah-Jane was wandering around with trays of champagne and snacks; I could hear her offering them as more and more people appeared, in the way they always did on these big occasions. Howard was discussing a Plan B for the eventuality that Paris won instead. 'What we'll do,' he said, 'if they're insane enough to give it to the French, is we'll get on the Eurostar. We'll go straight down there this afternoon and we'll ruin the celebrations. Get some eggs. Or pour buckets of cold water over people from the fucking Arc de Triomphe or whatever. Or – right, this is a good one, mate … '

'Christ,' someone muttered behind me, presumably pointing

up at the screen, 'look at the French guys. Look how happy they are.'

'They've been told already,' said someone else. 'I bet you. They already know.'

Within half a minute this idea had begun to whisper through the audience around me. How flat the party was going to fall if we didn't win. In Howard's cocky speech I could detect a note of melancholy. This was bigger than him, after all, this decision. He could not really make everything happen – it only seemed so within this building. I had a sudden wrenching feeling that I was about to see the power of Howard – and Lara, of course, but especially Howard – cut down to size.

'Shall I investigate train times and the availability of buckets?' asked Graham. Howard was revived by the joke. 'I can see Lara! There she is. *This* close to Beckham. They're all at a big table, black tie, very swish. There's still a lot of people shaking hands, and …'

'Shush!' Sarah-Jane commanded. 'This is it!'

The volume was turned up and an accented voice filled the Alpha. It was Jacques Rogge, the president of the committee, who had once stood in the bar.

'Before opening the envelope,' he said, 'I would like to thank our wonderful hosts and the people of Singapore, who have worked so hard to make our meeting possible.'

'Oh, for God's sake,' shouted Howard.

There were more preliminaries. I was pacing back and forth,

I realized. Howard's hands were on my shoulders. Finally the moment came. For ten seconds there was absolute silence in the atrium. There was the prolonged noise of an envelope being opened: an absurdly small noise to captivate so many people.

'How can he still be opening the fucking thing?' I blurted out, causing a small ripple of nervous laughter.

'The International Olympic Committee has the honour of announcing,' read Rogge, 'that the Games of the 30th Olympiad in 2012 are awarded to the city of London.'

I only heard the first half of the word, the first quarter of a second; then Howard hollered so loudly into my ear that I thought I was going to be thrown off my feet. There were the squeals of the people in Singapore coming through the screen; there was the uproar around me, and Howard's hands were under my armpits. He was lifting me off my feet, and it turned out he could do anything after all.

∞

It was going to be a long Alpha night. Friends were all around. Howard kept me by his side, topping up my glass as we rolled from room to room. Sarah-Jane got onto the balcony and sang her old favourite, 'That Ain't No Way to Treat a Lady', while the audience in the atrium below whooped up at her. JD had showed up with a girl he described as a 'seriously talented erotic dancer' and addressed as 'baby doll'. As I shook her hand, which was cold and slim, he began excitedly to describe me. 'This guy, my brother,' said JD, 'is a fucking miracle-worker.' It was a while since JD and I had spent any time together, but in the glow of this moment I could trace a straight line back to when we were boys. 'This guy produced ad campaigns for the whole Olympics thing, and for the army, and – seriously, all sorts of things.'

I remembered, with this talk of work, that Howard and I were meant to be attending a reception at the Park Lane Hilton in the morning to celebrate the win. In the morning. But it was already the morning.

'You are completely blind?' asked the girl. Her accent was Eastern European, I thought. An age ago I would have asked her country of origin and informed her of the capital.

'Completely blind,' JD said. 'Howard rescued him from the fire, you know? He—'

'Yes,' said the dancer. 'I know about fire, yes.'

'I didn't actually do that much with the Olympic thing,' I began to say, 'I—'

'Oh, shut up.' Howard had been attending to another conversation, but now he muscled back into this one. I got a waft of that ages-old leather aroma. 'Imagine this place in 2012, when those Olympics are on. I'll be an old man.'

'Shut up, you idiot,' Sarah-Jane heckled from somewhere behind us.

'I will,' Howard insisted. 'That's just the way it goes, that's … '

'I'm not arguing,' said Sarah-Jane, 'I'm pointing out you are *already* an old man.'

He let her have her laugh before continuing. 'I won't be running this place by then,' Howard said. I heard Graham's cough and breathed that old-fashioned hair-cream smell floating into the gaps where Howard was not. 'JD will be in charge,' said Howard, 'and you, Chas, you will be in charge of Krohl's company, and between you two, you will run this city.'

'We'll run this *country*,' JD corrected him, slapping me on the back with enough force to dislodge a breath of surprise. 'There's going to be no stopping us. We'll have an empire.'

'That's enough empires, Hitler,' Sarah-Jane said. There was more banter in this vein. Feeling a sudden dizzy rush, I asked JD to show me to a chair. There I sat, with all the noise swimming round me like clouds of smoke in the air. I thought about the years ahead. It was impossible not to feel, at least for now, that this was my victory after all. I'd tried the virtual world and the real one, and finally I had settled on my own version of life which seemed to have everything, and it was stretching in front of me like a walkway.

⚬⚬

Eventually the smell of coffee wafted up from the Alpha Bar, followed by frying meat. Howard had barely stopped talking all night: stories even I had never heard about the Alpha, tales of the famous and the forgotten, more brash pronouncements about the future. He threw himself in the way of people who were thinking about leaving; he made drinks appear. The hours between three and seven were torn away like layers of tissue paper. Not long after the coffee came the everyday footfall, the sound of ordinary business at the desk. It was only then, shortly after eight, that I turned on my phone's automatic reading function to find a message from Kathleen. *Jesus in the long jump! Well done.*

'Fuck it!' Howard exclaimed, seemingly reminded by the text. 'We're meant to be at Park Lane!'

I stood in the shower thinking about Kathleen, allowing myself to daydream an Olympic future in which she was back here, or in which I was with a girlfriend whose imaginary form was heavily based upon her. By the time I got back down to the atrium, Howard was as battle-ready as if he had just woken from a long sleep.

'All right, let's make this happen. Madman reckons it's going to be quicker on the Tube with the way traffic is at this time of the morning. Ready?'

This was something we had never done together; I had only ever done it with Kathleen, in fact, and it was inevitable that I thought of her again as Howard strong-armed me down the steps, down the escalators and into the throng. The platform was packed; on the train, bodies pressed in on all sides and there was sweat and irritation in the compressed air. Opposite us, Howard told me, a wall of *Standard* front pages proclaimed our win.

'You wouldn't know it from people's miserable bloody faces,' he added. 'But give it time … '

He was interrupted by a terrible noise, an explosion. The train stopped dead. The noise had been so loud that twenty or thirty seconds disappeared into it. There was no room for reaction or thought; there was just this moment, and now smoke, and now voices were raised.

'Fucking hell.' Howard had grabbed my arm with alarming ferocity. 'What the hell was that?'

There was panicky talking and shushing and, eventually, as if by appalled consensus, a complete silence. More smoke, and Howard's voice broke the quiet.

'We have to get out of here!' His voice horrified me. It was a plea. 'We've got to get out!' he said again. 'Something's happened!'

Words from different languages rattled against one another. A woman next to us was talking at ferocious speed and volume in a foreign tongue. There was Spanish from the other side. People were starting to cry. I reached out and found Howard's arm; it was shaking violently.

'We've got to get out,' he said again, but once more in a voice which asked for somebody else to make it happen. I was hammered suddenly in the guts by fatigue, and by the cold-water shock of what we had walked into. I stood up for a moment, thinking I was about to be sick. A plan had almost emerged to break a window. A woman was saying that we should stay here, the track was dangerous. They'll turn off the power, said one of the men. We should really wait to be told, said a different man. Howard was nowhere in this debate, and I had the horrible idea that he was contributing to the ongoing stink of shit which was all around us. I still felt nauseous. I tried to tell myself to take it one moment at a time, as Kathleen would advise if she were here.

'Ladies and gentlemen,' said the driver over a crackling address system. The announcement died away again, intensifying the dread. It was a minute before the man's voice came back. 'I apologize for this,' he said. 'There has been some sort of incident which we believe is a power surge. As I say, there has been some sort of incident. We are going to evacuate the train and we would just ask you to remain patient until we're able to do that.'

The voice vanished; conversations rose up again. My limbs were fizzing with pins and needles as I forced myself to take gulps of air. I had sunk back into my seat. I could hear myself breathing very loudly. But it wasn't me; it was Howard.

'Are you all right?' I asked him.

'Listen, son,' he said, and I felt the touch of his leather sleeve on the back of my neck as he slung an arm round my shoulders. 'I just want you to know. I've been a long way from perfect. I've let you down in certain ways. I've let you and Sarah-Jane and everyone down in certain ways. You need to know that.' His voice was a notch above a whisper. All around it was a sort of drizzling half-noise which had replaced real conversation in the carriage.

'I don't care what you've done,' I said.

'I'm not everything you think,' Howard said, 'but I did my best.'

'I know you did.'

'It doesn't matter,' said Howard, 'I love you.'

I could hear a vestigial, worn-out snuffling like the light rain after a big storm. Eventually there was the sound of the doors being wrenched open and we were getting out of the train. Howard seized my arm and we stepped down onto the tracks. Ahead of us, people's voices – giddy and weightless – ricocheted off the tunnel walls, plotting out our path. We were getting out. We walked in line, the strange hardness of metal planks beneath our feet. We were heading back to King's Cross, said Howard. 'We'll just go back to the Alpha, eh. We'll sack off the reception.' And as he said it, with his hand on my arm, I could feel the hotel around me so strongly that we could almost have been there already. We would go back into the cocoon. I would have a coffee; I would let myself call Kathleen.

But as we came up the stairs towards air and the everyday, I was suddenly aware of the crush of people behind us, and, as the ground levelled out, ahead of us as well. Voices were being raised in what could be taken for aggression. 'Let's keep moving, please,' someone was yelling into a loudhailer in the sort of monotone used to conceal official alarm. 'Let's keep moving, please.' Sirens were keening in the street outside. We were pressed in among bodies on every side.

'Oh my God,' said Howard faintly.

'What?'

'Something's wrong, mate.'

As he piloted me out of the station, there were noises everywhere: the buzz and hiss of two-way radios, people shouting for one another, instructions bellowed through megaphones. Somebody crashed into me and Howard pulled me away. Rain blew in our faces. Over everything was the wail of sirens coming from every direction at once and sounding like the city itself crying out in despair.

'All right,' said Howard, steadying his voice. His grip on my arm tightened still further and he set off at such a pace that I nearly tripped over. 'Let's get home.'

'What's happened?' I asked.

There was an eruption of sound not far off. I writhed in fear and felt Howard's body tighten. My legs felt as if there were nothing in them at all, no bone or muscle, just a mush of matter supporting the heavy rest of me. I slumped against him.

'Come on, mate.'

With that massive bulwark power that he'd seemed momentarily to lose in the tunnel, he hefted me over his shoulder like an infant. We staggered on a hundred metres. I was half here and half nowhere, and we were going down a side street with a familiar taste in the air, and there were the cedars stilled by the city's shock, there was the looming invisible front of the Alpha. I slithered down from Howard's grasp and walked shakily alongside him through the double doors.

So often in these years it had been a place where London disappeared, but not today. Voices chattered at an urgent pitch. Feet fell heavily. From the big screen which had beamed the Olympic win down to us there was now state-of-emergency talk. 'It does now look as if these incidents are the result of … and we're just hearing reports, in fact, of another … '

Sarah-Jane was on top of us, weeping as she grabbed my face, a hand on each side. 'Oh, Jesus,' she said, 'as soon as we heard, I thought you two were dead. I just had a feeling. I just knew it.'

'But we're not, Captain,' Howard muttered as she gathered him into the bundle and the three of us stood there listening to each other's heartbeats. Sarah-Jane was trying to speak, but her voice kept breaking up. Graham's clean smell came ghosting into the frame. He gave a sort of low, long groan of relief, the kind of noise I had never heard from him before. Somebody had turned up the volume on the big screen. 'It does now look as if terrorists … ' someone said in an efficient voice.

'I would never have forgiven myself,' Graham said. 'I could have driven you.'

Sarah-Jane was talking on the phone; through the handset, not far from my face, I could make out the muffled responses of

JD. 'They're here, they're here, they're here,' Sarah-Jane said. He told her not to panic, he wasn't far away. He had ended up going home with the dancer last night. He'd come back. We would all be there.

We stood there with noise lapping at us like dirty water. I felt long, hard hands on my shoulders. Graham was holding me in a tight squeeze. I allowed myself to relax into his unaccustomed grip.

'Oh, God alive,' he said again, 'I would never have forgiven myself. If you had never come out of there. If you … if you had not come out of there.'

'Well,' I said, it'll take more than a few bombs to blow Howard up.'

'Yes,' Sarah-Jane came in, and I could sense her arms going round Howard, 'say what you like about this guy, but he can certainly get out of a tight squeeze.'

I wanted it all to be true, that Howard was indestructible, and I was already dismissing what I remembered from the train: the panic in his voice, the childlike desperation. He had saved me. It was better like that. 'That's twice we've escaped from death,' I said. 'What have you got planned for the next one, Howard?'

Howard seemed, for a few seconds, not to have heard. Then he cleared his throat, gave a half-laugh. 'I think we'll leave it there,' he said. 'I think two of those is enough, mate.'

Among the partly zoned-out backbeat of TV commentary

and the calls echoing around the atrium, Graham cleared his throat.

'Actually, I was the one who saved you from the fire,' said Graham.

There was a frozen moment before Sarah-Jane gave a little laugh, high and half scandalized, as if at a joke which was risqué but slightly too silly to cause offence.

'I was the one,' Graham said again. 'Howard ran away. But we had to keep it a secret. We had to keep it a secret.'

A single word from Howard, that was what I was waiting for. Sarah-Jane too, and everyone else there, all the sudden listeners whose presence I gleaned from the changing of the air, from the Alpha sucking in its breath, the whole building seeming to freeze. We were all awaiting the magic word.

But I could feel what had happened to Sarah-Jane's face as she realized. And I felt straight away as if I had always known.

༄14༄

GRAHAM

'Breakfast is served in the restaurant between half-past six and ten. For service in your room, you need to fill this out and hang it on your door before two a.m. I'll give you two key cards – here. You need to swipe it in the lift before you put your floor in. Did you need a wake-up call or a newspaper?'

'I think we will be fine, thank you.'

'If you have any questions or you need anything, we're here twenty-four hours: just put a call down to reception.'

'I certainly shall,' I said, with a smile for the lady who looked extraordinarily young to be wielding this responsibility. 'Thank you very much.'

'And can I get someone to help with your bags?'

A beefy dark-skinned porter whisked away my suitcase and Chas's things and loaded them onto a gleaming trolley. Chas and I got into the lift together.

'What can we see?'

'There are mirrors on each side,' I informed him, 'so there are an enormous number of versions of us.'

'An infinite number.'

'Well, I couldn't say for sure. I haven't had time to count them. Ha, ha!' At the second attempt, my card in the key-slot brought the flash of a green light and the lift began to climb. The doors popped open on the fourth floor and we were in a corridor whose carpet, patterned with red and blue zigzags like little lightning-strikes, sat uneasily beneath walls painted pale green and decorated with pictures of English stately homes.

'And now?'

'Now things are rather hard on the eye,' I said, 'but this is jolly fun.'

The plastic card sparked another green light on the electronic sensor. I pushed open the door and led Chas into the room, in this hotel that was not the one we knew.

❧

No sooner had I heard whispers of a problem on the Underground than I was plunged into a depth of fear quite foreign to me: not because of Pattie or Ed, who had gone away together for a few days, but for Howard and Chas. I felt, as if it were already a confirmed fact, that they had been caught up in a disaster. Why had I not taken them in the Mercedes! It was precisely the sort of irrelevant decision to which hindsight gives a terrible weight. People were talking about further explosions. There was the ominous rise of conversation, and finally those first grim rain-spattered pictures of ambulances arriving only a hundred yards from where we were standing.

Sarah-Jane went out, charged up the Euston Road and came back again with frantic eyes and hair blown chaotic in the breeze. They weren't letting anyone past. There were police everywhere. Something awful had happened on the Tube. They were down there, she said, her tone pleading to be contradicted; they were down there. It was my job to be composed, and I went into the appearance of composure as smoothly as I might switch into an exaggeratedly English voice to please an American visitor. But real calm existed nowhere in my body.

Minutes went by. Howard and Chas could not be contacted on their telephones. The front desk received a torrent of calls. 'I know he's in London. I know she's at your hotel. I've just heard … I've just seen on the TV … I wanted to check … ' Suzie was alongside me. We directed the calls to the desired rooms; I tracked a couple of guests down in the bar or not far beyond. 'I knew you'd panic,' said a girl with sentimental reproach into the reception phone. 'I'm absolutely fine. I love you too,' she said. 'It's all gone a bit crazy here but I'll make it home by bedtime.' I felt a sort of fury at her, her and everyone else who had survived. It had been a scare, but everyone was fine. Everyone except Howard and Chas.

So it went on in my brain. Sarah-Jane was calling Jonathan for all she was worth, but he was not responding. She was almost out of her wits that he had somehow got caught up in all this too, that all her boys were gone. 'Where are they?' she appealed to me, frantically tearing at the sleeve of my jacket. A fingernail caught the skin of my palm and nicked a graze. The strangeness of the red beneath the atrium's spotlights made me feel unwell, and I realized I would have to go to the lavatory. Afterwards I caught sight of myself in the same mirror I had stared into on the night I let Kathleen in on the secret. Then, everything had been – as they say – to play for. Now I had left it all too late. Chas would never know what he was to me, just as Agatha probably never had.

I walked back into the atrium, sheepishly drying my hands upon my jacket and assembling a checklist of comforting things to say. It is too early to be sure. We must not panic. I was so busy rehearsing them, I did not even notice at first that Howard had walked back into the Hotel Alpha, flushed and wild-eyed with the glow of another successful escape about him. When I saw that he was alive after all, and Chas alongside him, I sank into my chair behind the reception desk.

The terror of the past hour was disintegrating, the shock would follow; but their by-products would not fade so easily. I watched Chas and Howard and Sarah-Jane embrace directly beneath the skylight, in the very heart of the hotel. Friends and admirers looked on with customary glee. Howard had done it again. I realized that I was distancing myself on purpose in order to let the Yorks have their moment. I was not a part of it. I was the man who stood by and allowed things to happen.

Howard might have got Chas home today, but he had not been the one who saved Chas when it really mattered. Yet Chas himself did not know that, he could not know it. He would always think of me as a well-wisher, a faithful old chum. I saw myself in the burning room that night, clutching him to my chest. I could see even further back than that, in fact: back to the time I threw a bouncing ball across the chessboard floor and watched him toddle intently after it and bring it proudly back to me. I wanted more than anything to grab Chas round the shoulders and steer him away from everything that surrounded him here: away from the story he had been told, towards the one that had really happened. I wanted to keep him close to me.

There was one remark too many about Howard's powers of survival, and I saw everything going on once more as it always had. Then I heard myself blurt out the truth, and it was the end of one life and the beginning of another.

∽

The day of the bombing would have been a very peculiar one even without my revelation. The added twist of events made things stranger still, and as I walked out of the Alpha that afternoon and settled Chas into the passenger seat, my head was so woolly that I felt as if I were sitting behind the Mercedes' wheel for the first time. It did not help that the streets were still full of improbable sights: people huddled, comforting one another, at zebra crossings and in shop doorways; a man with a brief-case trailing blood from a head-wound as he walked, slowly and without apparent acknowledgement of his situation, over the roundabout at Archway. Chas sat mutely next to me. I kept asking him if he was all right. He kept saying that he was.

I took him back to my house. Pattie was away for a couple of days; I made us some ham and chips. We sat and talked until well after midnight. Chas asked me many questions about the night of the fire; about my decision to go into the room on my own, and to go along with the story of Howard's having saved him. He did not castigate me for having strung him, and the whole world, along; nor, somewhat to my relief, did he try to thank me for the fact I had got him to safety. He seemed to weigh up all the bewildering new information with a certain calm, as if he were a reporter investigating a matter not directly related to his own life. He remarked more than once that he had 'almost seen this coming'; that 'something had not seemed right'. I could not tell whether all this was what he really felt, or whether it masked a sense of betrayal. He slept in Ed's room, latterly Christopher's, under the map of the old world. In the morning – for the first time since I had met him as an infant – neither of us set foot in the Hotel Alpha.

There, things were progressing as might have been expected.

There had been ferocious arguments, in the course of which Sarah-Jane apparently struck Howard several times on the head, while JD sat numbly waiting for his hero to do something: to summon a defence which never came. I heard all this from JD the next day, and heard also that he and his mother had gone to the South of France. They would be staying there for a while, he said. I was to keep an eye on Chas.

This order was, of course, quite unnecessary. Chas stayed at my house the next two nights. The following day Pattie came back, and I had to tell her everything that had happened.

'Why the hell,' she asked, after a full minute of silence, 'didn't you ever say anything to me?'

'I don't know,' I said – truthfully. 'It was easier just to pretend that the whole thing was the way Howard said.'

'And what are you going to do now? You can't go back to work there now, can you? Could you not have hung on just a few more years and—'

'No,' I cut in. 'I am not going back to work there. I am going to – well, to be frank, I don't know exactly what I shall do. But the first thing is that I am going to take Chas for a little trip up north. Up to Inverness, to see Caroline and Christopher.'

'For how long?'

'Well,' I said, 'I don't really have a plan.'

'You always have a plan.'

It was true; or had always been true. There had never been a week of my life in which I could not predict, with absolute certainty, where I would be the following week. Now there were no certainties; just possibilities.

⚯

After a couple of days spent taking stock of our changed situation, through long conversations – sometimes about what had happened, sometimes about trivial things – we went back to the Alpha. Howard came to meet Chas in the atrium, clutching him – as always – as if he had been away for years. Chas returned the embrace, his head angled down at the floor. I studied Howard's face over the jumble of their arms. For the first time ever, I was seeing him unshaven: the coating of hair on his chin was surprisingly thick and as white as Father Christmas's. He looked poorly rested and his suit jacket was rumpled as if from several days' consecutive service. When he spoke, his eyebrows seemed to labour into their normal playful elevation; the light in his eyes flickered for a moment and then dimmed again.

'I guess we have some talking to do,' he said.

'We do,' said Chas very quietly, and the two of them retired through the corridor to the living room.

Since it felt too odd to be there without working, I took what had always been my place alongside Suzie at the reception desk. Bright blue oozed through the skylight and a big group of laughing holidaymakers took turns to photograph each other in the atrium. I went down to the cellar and found my old check-in ledgers in a retired filing cabinet, not far from a case containing several magnums of champagne. I squatted down and leafed through one of the books from the 1980s; the patterns of names arrived and departed belonging to people now dispersed in a thousand different directions. There had been some idea in my mind that I might want to take some of them with me – to salvage the original Bakelite telephone, perhaps, or the typewriter, or one of the old thrillers Agatha used to pore over. But when it came to it, they were only objects.

I stood for some time in the cool of the cellar, listening to the hotel above as if it were some great creature which had swallowed me. It was churning through its daily excitements and routines as it had done all this time, and as its predecessor had done in Victorian days, when some errand boy or chef's mate now long dead must have stood upon this exact spot in the bowels of the building. The hotel would be perfectly all right without me. It was a sorry thought, but in a certain way also a comforting one.

Chas came back into the atrium in the evening; Howard patted him on the back before heading into the Alpha Bar.

'How did it go?'

'It was all right,' said Chas. 'He wants to see you in the bar.'

'How all right was it?' I could not help asking.

Chas smiled. 'I'm still coming with you, if that's what you mean.'

Ray had reserved an area of the bar with a bottle of wine on the table. Howard was very still. As I approached, he half rose from his seat as if for a formal greeting, and then seemed to think better of it. We shook hands across the table and sat facing one another with the wine between us. Howard sloshed it out into two oversized glasses: almost the whole bottle gone in one go. I studied his face.

'So, Madman.'

I glanced towards the bar, where Ray was making a show of fiddling with his telephone; he caught my eye and immediately took a glass down from a rack and began to polish it with something. I wondered how many of the Alpha's staff knew what had happened, knew now the truth about the man sitting opposite me.

'I'm sorry,' I said, 'for all the trouble I must have caused.'

Howard gave a sort of grimace, almost amused, and inclined his head. 'You could make a case that I caused it, mate.'

'You could indeed,' I agreed, 'but – well, there it is.'

'Been a rough few days, certainly. The Captain isn't answering the phone. JD is answering his, but ... '

'But not in the way you would like.'

'Precisely.' Howard scratched his new stubble, took a gulp of wine and wiped his lips with the back of his hand. 'He's angry. Everyone's angry, obviously. Everyone's going to be angry for a long time.' The wine, sliding down inside him, seemed to give him a brief shot of courage. 'But, well, I'll just have to wait it out.' He rested his hands on his knees and looked steadily at me; but his voice betrayed a waning of the defiance.

'So you and Chas are going away?'

It sounded more realistic each time I said it out loud. 'Yes, he and I are going for a little trip. Up to Scotland, to see my daughter and grandson. We'll stay there for a while, I think. And after that …'

I tailed off. He reached out to touch my sleeve.

'I'll sort you out, you know, mate,' he said. 'Finance-wise. We'll come to whatever arrangement you want in terms of – you know. A golden handshake. Whatever they call it. We can make that—'

'You don't owe me anything, Howard.' My hand had turned cold, and I moved it up from the stem to the body of the glass for the sake of having something to cling to. 'Indeed, without you …'

A couple of young businessmen came in, shiny fellows with well-pressed suits and short, fashionably spiky hair. One clapped the other on the back making some remark about a long night's drinking ahead. Howard watched them with what looked like wistfulness for a moment. I cleared my throat.

'I am hoping to track down – or at least take steps to track down – or, anyway, I—'

'You want to try and find Agatha.'

'Perhaps.' I felt my cheeks warm.

'And Chas says he wants to see if he can find his real dad. His biological dad.'

'I don't think he will ever replace you.' It was as painful as ever to be reassuring Howard; it felt, as always, like an inversion of the way things ought to be. I saw, with a qualm that crept all the way through my body, his eyes seeking further comfort from me.

'Do you think he'll come back? When he's done all that, when he's ... worked out whatever he needs to? Do you think he'll ever want to live with me again?'

'You must have asked him that yourself.'

'He said it was too early to say. Which it is. Of course it is.' Howard shrugged wryly, lowering his eyes to the table with a small smile like an ace card-player finally accepting defeat. 'God knows, I had things my way for twenty-one years.'

Really he had had his own way a lot longer than that, I thought; he'd had nothing but his own way. I thought it without resentment: even with a certain admiration, or sympathy, at least. We sat there for quite some time in silence, watching more latecomers filter into the bar, listening to the rising hum of their conversation. It was a scene so familiar, my brain could not accommodate the idea I would never see it again.

For old times' sake, I came in the following morning and handled my final check-ins with much the same routine I had introduced on a bright morning forty years before. Breakfast is served at these times. We can make restaurant bookings. Suzie stood by with an encouraging smile, knowing this was the last time she would have to watch me plod through this rigmarole. I swept my hand for the last time through the rack of A-shaped keys, and bade farewell to the Mercedes, patting its chassis and the steering wheel as if it really had been alive all this time and would miss me. People kept dropping by to wish me good luck. I spoke on the telephone to the man at Fortnum & Mason, concluding a friendship which had run along quite nicely considering that we never managed to meet. Finally, the hire car was delivered outside and Chas was ready with his things. I glanced up at the skylight, grabbed his wrist and walked through the mahogany doors one last time.

The cedars in the forecourt seemed to look down at me in surprise or reproach. All sorts of things are still to happen here, they said, and you will have no part in them. And indeed, as we stood there, a couple came gliding past arm in arm, guests I had never seen before. They pushed open the doors and went inside, and it struck me powerfully that new people would come here every day, that laughter would ring out in the bar and events would take place in the rooms quite as if I had never been there at all.

'Are you OK?' said Chas.

'I am,' I said. 'Shall we … ?'

The doors flew open and Howard stood there, with one final trick in his bag. 'Listen,' he said, 'are you absolutely sure about this?'

I tried to turn away.

'I did a bad thing,' he said, 'but I tried to make it good, you know. You're the best friends I've had. The only ones I've got, now.'

'Don't start talking like this, Howard.' My voice came out gruff and uneven.

'I tried to make it all right,' he said again. 'I don't know how I'm going to go on without you two. I honestly don't know what to do.'

His voice shook. I went up to him and held him against me, breathing in his leathery aroma. I took a step back and allowed Chas to grab him in turn. My heart was beating very quickly; as quickly as it had when I made the decision to tell the truth. I thought for a moment that Chas would be dragged back into the hotel, but he turned to me and said, 'Come on, then.' I led him to the car without looking back at Howard. And I piled our belongings into the boot and started the engine, knowing that he was still standing there; knowing that I had never been so fond of anyone, but that the end had come.

∞

I locate what is grandly called a 'minibar': a squat brown refrigerator containing only a carton of milk and two cans of beer. We sit sipping at the beers. Chas has already called down to reception to connect his computer to the Internet, at a cost of fifteen pounds which I told him I would pay. I watch him now; he's like a shopkeeper setting out his stall, running briskly through all the button-presses which will configure his laptop for action. It chats away to him in its robotic tone. *Voice-aid enabled. Left-click to open window. You are now connected.*

There is a slab of cheap wood which passes for a desk, and the two of us are perched upon black plastic swivelling chairs like the ones that invaded the Alpha's computer room. Chas gives me directions to get onto the Internet and check the route we will be driving tomorrow as we proceed from here, somewhere in the Lake District, to Inverness. The computer program is ingenious. It includes diagrams of the locations of speed cameras and service stations. You can get live traffic reports, Chas says excitedly. You can find out how the traffic is looking before you set off. He begins to demonstrate another feature of the website; he refers to the merits of 'googling' something. Then he looks up from the computer and straight ahead, as if staring right into the wall: one of those looks of his which, with the pupils motionless, are so difficult to read meaning into. Our neighbours' television is in good voice; it broadcasts a noisy argument, a soap opera, perhaps. I put a hand on Chas's shoulder.

'Are you missing Howard?'

Chas rises as if in response to the question. 'Can you start the shower running for me?'

We stand together in the bathroom, where halfway up the wall a shower head dangles from a perch over a bath which looks too small for a moderately tall guest. For a moment I fight off nostalgia for the place we have left, its free-standing tubs, its mosaic tilework, the tranquillity of its rooms. It serves no purpose to think about it. I reach up and start the water.

'I suppose I am missing him,' says Chas.

'I can take you back, you know,' I say, not wanting to do any such thing. 'You can go back whenever you want.'

Chas's eyes rove sightlessly over the plain walls as the water batters the base of the cheap bath. 'What I miss is Howard as I thought he was.' I lean over the side of the tub to check the water with one hand; it is still running cold. 'I miss that,' he repeats.

'You will feel differently, in time.' I am well practised in saying the right thing. 'You will come to forgive Howard.'

'Maybe.'

'You will see him as what he has always been; what he has really been. As your … '

But what is Howard now? The two of us stand there with the sound of the water and of voices and slamming doors in the corridor outside.

'I'm more interested in what comes next,' says Chas.

The hair stands up on the back of my neck, which is a phenomenon I have heard people describe before. I ensure that Chas can feel his way into the shower before I withdraw, shutting the door behind me, and sit at the desk, looking at the computer.

You like to live in the past, don't you! Howard said years ago. No, I retorted: the present. And yet he was right, as he so often was. I have lived a great part of my life in homage to my own past. Now, however, it feels as if everything lies in front of me. Tonight, looking out of the window at night falling over the motorway which will carry us forward tomorrow, I can say that I have moved forward. Yes, we are living in the present now, all right.

AFTERWORD

Hotel Alpha is designed to be read in two stages. There is the novel which you have just finished and, I hope, enjoyed – unless you're one of those people who always flick to the back first. Then there are one hundred extra stories, which appear on a website: www.hotelalphastories.com. You will find eight of them here, once you turn the page. The extra stories span the same time period as the novel. They shine an alternative light on the plot, show the hidden links between some of its main events, solve mysteries, and give voice to some of the thousands of minor characters and dramas which make up the life of the Hotel Alpha while the main story is playing out. They can be read in any order and in any quantity. Or, of course, you can ignore them altogether – it's entirely up to you.

Everyone knows that human stories are always bigger and more complex than they appear – the relationships and connections between us all are infinite, and a book can only do so much. The Internet, though, removes the physical limitations of the novel, opening up possibilities that have never before existed for readers and writers. We can now choose how much of a story we want to tell, and how much of it we want to know: in theory we can keep going forever. The one hundred extra stories of Hotel Alpha don't quite go that far, and you as a reader probably have other plans for the rest of your life. But it's a start . . .

Mark Watson, May 2014

RESTAURANT AND ELSEWHERE, 1964

Anthony and Rosalynn won't meet for fifteen years, but tonight they came within yards of one another in the Hotel Alpha's restaurant. Anthony and Rosalynn, who will one day sleep together as Tony and Roz, are going to set eyes on each other tonight as seven-year-olds without either of them thinking twice about it. Strange how often life teases you with these film trailers, these little hints as to what lies ahead.

Tonight, both seven-year-olds have peeped at the new Post Office Tower, nearly finished now, an exoskeleton of shiny steel covering the spine of disc-like innards which were once vulnerably exposed to the sceptical brown-grey city. It doesn't look vulnerable any more: it looks, now, like the sort of weird, excitingly modern monster the future is meant to consist of. There's a lot of construction going on. The Hotel Alpha itself is new. Actually, the building is old; it was built in the 1870s and the exterior is much as it always was, but inside, everything is modern: the informal manner of the owner, the self-consciously late hours of the restaurant, the garish floral shirts and long hair of the bar crowd. Even the things which follow the existing grand-hotel tradition – the marble floor and chunky reception desk, the chandeliers – exhibit a note of cheeky subversion. The hotel isn't all that grand, in fact, except in its ambitions.

None of this is of interest to Anthony or Rosalynn, the two

children whose paths cross tonight. Not only are they both too young to care how hotels look: both are unhappy.

Anthony is lying on a camp bed pretending to be asleep, as he has been for the past couple of hours. His parents have been arguing the entire time. The mood between them was scratchy all day. They're in London to visit his uncle Ken, his dad's brother; but Ken didn't have room for them all to stay because of some problem with his landlord. This annoyed Anthony's mother, because it meant a late change of plan. Then they couldn't find a hotel, and, not knowing London at all, ended up booking into the Alpha. Although pretty reasonable (his mum's view) it's still a sight more than they should be spending (his dad's), and so he too got annoyed. They ate dinner in near silence in the restaurant, and Anthony didn't dare ask if he could have dessert, even though he would have given everything in his piggy bank for an ice-cream sundae like the one that arrived for the girl on the next table. Then they came up to the room and things worsened. His dad shouted at his mum for taking too long in the bathroom taking off her make-up. She said something about how she hadn't wanted to come on this trip, and some things about his side of the family which Anthony didn't understand. He washed his face and brushed his teeth as quickly as he could, got into the camp bed the hotel concierge had set up for them, rolled over onto his side facing away from his parents, towards the window, and wished he was asleep.

But it didn't happen; his brain felt as if it were tossing and turning, flipping over in his skull and jumping at every sound – a siren on the street below, a fly buzzing in a corner – like a nervy kitten. He lay there for half an hour. Anthony's mum was reading a book while his dad tried to sleep. There was the buzzing of the fly and the flick-flick of the pages and a series of peevish coughs from Dad. Then, when their bedside light had clicked off, and when they presumably thought Anthony was asleep, they began to argue in whispers.

'Finished with the bloody book, have you?'

'What's that supposed to mean?'

'Thought you were going to be reading it all night.'

'Why do you care how long I read for? I'm not doing it to . . . *get* at you, am I?'

This little exchange ended with a sarcastic little sniff from Dad, a noise he'd honed over the years to be absolutely unbearable to Anthony's mother. As usual, she went for it.

'What the hell is that noise supposed to mean?'

Anthony could feel himself getting hot. He wriggled from his side onto his back and lay flat, looking up towards the ceiling as the occasional traffic rumbled below. They didn't seem to care any more whether he was sleeping or not. He rolled onto his front and buried his face in the pillow, which was really a cushion from the sofa since this wasn't a real bed but a camp bed. Somehow he was in the way just by being here: he was somebody you had to get a special bed for. He plunged his face right into it so all he could feel was the cushion, its slight roughness, the contours of its patterning. He lay like that for a few minutes, trying to make sure they couldn't hear that he was crying. The secret tears stole into the pillow-mush around his face. He sniffed accidentally a couple of times, but nobody reacted. When he felt like he might be about to suffocate and finally raised his face to lay his head down on top of the pillow rather than plumb in the middle of it, the conversation had changed. It was quieter now, more menacing.

'Do you see why I can't trust you?' his father was asking.

'For fuck's sake,' Mum said, and although Anthony didn't recognize the word, he could tell that it was a wrong thing to say. Dad's reaction confirmed it for him.

'Don't you dare use that language with him in the room.'

'He's asleep.'

'Do you see why I can't trust you?' Dad said again, and this time Mum let out an answering breath, a gasp as redolent of despair as any words could have been.

'I'm just telling you what it feels like,' said Dad.

'When are you going to give me a break?' Mum asked. 'When are you going to accept what happened?'

'It's not as simple as that,' said Dad.

Then there was silence, or at least no talking. For a little while Anthony thought he could hear someone crying through the wall in the next room. Then he realized it was coming from the bathroom and it was his mum. He felt that whatever his dad had been accusing her of – and he couldn't begin to guess what, specifically, it was – her crying in the en-suite bathroom proved that it was true. And in any case, Dad is Anthony's hero. He has a collection of cigarette cards with Leeds United players on, and told that frightening ten-year-old that he'd be 'dead meat' if he messed with Anthony again, and can do such a good impression of Fred Flintstone.

So it has to be his mum's fault that things are like this: that his parents are fighting and Anthony's pillow-cushion is wet with his own tears. He likes Mum, but it has to be someone's fault that he feels this lousy, so it has to be hers.

The girl who was served the ice-cream sundae on the table next to Anthony's earlier this evening is now at home in her bedroom in Barnet, which has a name plate on the door with the name ROSALYNN, a name she already dislikes, painted in rose petals. Here too an argument is in progress. But there's no doubt what this one is about.

Earlier tonight, Rosalynn played in the North London Schools' Orchestra (under-8 division) as part of a concert given by seven- to eleven-year-olds and attended by a score of parents whose enthusiasm ranged from lukewarm to alarmingly fervid. Rosalynn's daddy was meant to be there. He swore he would be there – that's the phrase her mummy is now using as she screams into the telephone downstairs, the words muffled by the plasterwork so Rosalynn can only pick out her fury in the shape of them. She was playing second violin. Her dad made some joke about 'second fiddle' which she didn't understand;

that was last time he was here, a fortnight ago. He's away a lot, her dad, because his work is important – whatever it is. But the understanding was that he'd be there tonight.

When the lights came up on the stage, they were brighter than Rosalynn expected, and as she played it was impossible to make out any figures in the dimness beyond. It was only when they finished, and the whole audience was illuminated, that Rosalynn looked over at her mother, a few rows back, with a new haircut, and learned what she felt she had already known: Dad was not there. He had missed it. Like he missed the sports day and the nativity where her brother Simon was Joseph. And always for the same reason, Mum muttered between her teeth as she swung the Mini out of the car park, not waiting to drink coffee and receive sympathetic glances from the other parents. Work.

'But where is he?' Rosalynn asked.

'He must have been delayed,' said her mum, not taking her eyes from the mirror.

'But he said . . .'

'HE MUST HAVE BEEN DELAYED,' Mum repeated.

Then she was sorry for shouting, and as a treat and to make up for his absence, she and Mum and Simon went to a hotel and had dinner. They chatted about how well the concert had gone, and Rosalynn enjoyed the fact that it was late to be eating, and that even Simon (three years older) was impressed with her playing. They talked about the concert and about some of the other musicians and about everything except Dad, the lack of Dad.

Now Rosalynn rolls out of bed, feet first, and creeps in her nightie to the top of the stairs. She stills every muscle and tries to hush even the feathery sound of the breath creeping through her nostrils. She rivets herself to the ground, wanting to be stone. She is very good at this: in 'musical statues' at Flora and Linda's parties she proved almost unbeatable. Her mother has stretched the telephone wire into the study, but Rosalynn can make out her words now.

'Well, if you can't make your daughter a priority . . .'

What's a priority? Rosalynn wonders, the question pressing at her throat so she gives a little involuntary noise. Why can't she be one?

'I don't care, Patrice.'

Patrice is an unusual name for someone's dad. He was born in Montreal. Rosalynn doesn't like the way Mum says the name now as if to dwell on that strangeness.

'I – listen, Patrice. I don't care. Either you make that sacrifice for your daughter, or you don't. Either we can rely on you – this family can rely on you – or we can't.'

Rosalynn knows what 'rely' means. It means you can trust someone. You know that they'll love you. It constricts her breathing for a moment, that her parents can be talking like this. She looks down at her nightie, which has pale blue ponies on it, and hates it for its childishness. She doesn't feel seven years old;

she feels much older, sadly older, pinned down by the gravity of real things. The conversation makes everything in the bedroom behind her – the doll's house with its ever-content residents, the primary colours of the Enid Blyton collector's set on the shelves – seem absurd. The only real thing is that her parents don't like each other. There was a time, there were lots of times (the beach in Brittany, the Easter-egg hunt at Grandma's) where they liked, loved each other. But now they don't.

Rosalynn creeps back along the landing, fearful of being heard: her mum never misses anything. She gets back into a bed which feels cold even when she bundles the blankets around herself, thinking in vain of the phrase 'snug as a bug in a rug' which has always cheered her up, but now seems as childish and as suddenly outmoded as everything else around her. She thinks again of the holiday in Brittany, only a year ago: how grown-up it felt to be drinking cocoa with the rest of the family. She considers going to knock on Simon's door, but he wouldn't understand. This is for her to suffer alone, the fact that they cannot rely on Dad. She is the only person who knows.

She stares up at the ceiling, with the glow-in-the-dark stars Dad put up for her, and thinks about what she's learned. Ten miles south, Anthony is still not asleep, although his own warring parents now are. The two of them, who sat at neighbouring tables this evening, stare now at different impressions of darkness: Anthony's studded by the fuzzy orange of the big-city lights outside, Rosalynn's broken up by the pinpricks of white on her ceiling.

When they meet, in fifteen years' time, what happened tonight will still be important. Anthony – Tony – will have an instinctive distrust of women which he will never acknowledge, but which will cloud many of his interactions with the opposite sex. Rosalynn – Roz – will again unconsciously see men as deserters, or betrayers, or people who don't show up when you need them, but she will have the added complications of low self-esteem and a wild would-be defiance caused by having run away from home. Their romance will, predictably, not last long. But it will produce a child, called Chas, whom Roz loves with the abandon that she applies to every emotional choice, and whom Tony sacrifices the chance to meet, choosing to flee instead, confirming Roz's opinion of men.

All this is years away. Tonight, the two seven-year-olds lie at the mercy of sleep.

They approached me the usual way, the fellow in his grey suit and tie and big glasses, hair smartly combed. 'Did you see what happened, darling?'

I don't care to be called darling by a man I don't know, but that's what happens when you're a certain age. Anyhow, it's worth it. 'Yes,' I said, 'I was up there. I was on the third floor. As soon as I smelled smoke, I came out of my room and ran down the stairs – well, as fast as someone my age can run! – because you're not to use the lift in a fire. I looked up at the balcony and everyone was . . .'

'This is wonderful,' said glasses-man, giving a signal to his camera crew and his producers. 'Save this, love, this is just what we need.'

I kept on chatting away, like some ditzy bird, as they set up their equipment, making sure they got shots of all the evacuated guests milling about, and the beautiful old brick of the building, which they'll use at the start of the report. Then the reporter said to me, 'Just tell me what you saw, love, and don't worry about the cameras, and don't worry, this isn't live, so we can always do it again.' All the things they usually say.

They asked me to sign a form and the sound man held a big microphone on a boom pole over my head, while the reporter pointed the handheld one – which is really just for show – at me.

'Brenda Rogers,' I said, when asked to say my name into the microphone. They never use that. It's for their records, and to check the sound levels.

Then it began.

'Can you tell us, in your own words, what you saw?'

They often say that. As if I'd be about to use anyone else's words! Well, I suppose they thought they were putting me at ease.

'I was just in my room,' I told suit-and-tie, who nodded sympathetically. 'I heard a commotion and came out onto the balcony. You could smell smoke.' I'd changed this story from my original one – that I was alerted by the smoke first – because I wasn't sure if you would be able to smell it with the door shut. 'I came down the stairs,' I explained, 'because you're not to use a lift in a fire.' The reporter smiled, thinking what a dear lady I was. 'There was absolute chaos,' I said. I've used that one three or four times. You can say it about more or less any disaster. 'There were people screaming.' That, too, has never let me down.

It was all over quickly. The crewman put the boom pole down, muttering about the weight of it, and lit a cigarette – which I thought was funny, in the circumstances. The same thing happened after the Deptford fire. You can never stop people lighting up.

Suit-and-tie thanked me and told me to look out for it on the news tomorrow morning. As if I wouldn't know where to find it! He couldn't say for sure whether they would use my bit, but he said it was likely. I'm sure it is. An old lady is precisely what they're looking for. Even though I'm only fifty, in fact – not old at all. But I look much older, and that's what they want. Someone who looks like she's been around London a long time, seen it all, but never seen anything quite like this. Then they'll have a young man, probably. Yes, I go well with a perky younger witness. I think that's why I have the record I do: five disasters, and five appearances on the news.

With this one, it was very easy to get here in time to pose as a witness: I was only in Marylebone, and someone at the bus stop had actually seen the smoke coming out of the top windows. I headed straight over in a taxi. Speed is very important. With Deptford, I nearly didn't make it; but they were short of people to talk to – nobody was keen to be on. The Brixton riots were easy because they went on for so long, and of course no one was expecting to see someone like me in the middle of it. But yes, this one could hardly have worked out better. I shall warm up the television a few minutes before the news to make sure it comes on all right.

Assuming that I am on, I suppose I shall have to leave it a few months before I do this again, just in case anyone smells a rat. I'm not sure if they will, though. Besides, it could be that long before anything else happens. It's not as if I'm in control of the disasters, is it! All I do is hear about them, get there as quickly as possible, and give the best account I can.

CONFERENCE ROOM, 2001

It's quite frankly fucking astonishing that I am still at this party, this so-called engagement party for which they hired this swanky room in a hotel which everyone's heard of. It's quite frankly pretty mind-blowing that I didn't just toss my champagne in Lloyd's face when that ginger bloke handed it to me and stomp off out of here. I'm quite frankly, and I don't use the word lightly, flabbergasted.

The idea that Alistair, who they didn't even know until three years ago, is a better candidate for Best Man than me is absolutely – and I use the word advisedly – obscene.

There is a lot to dislike about Alistair, not least his self-consciously modern hairstyle, as if he were twenty-two, not closer to forty, his claim to support a football team he manifestly knows nothing about, the galling affectation which leads him to address people as 'bro' as if we were living in Harlem or some such place, the volume of his laugh, which has nothing to do with real amusement and everything to do with signalling his appreciation of the joke to as wide a constituency as possible, his habit of striking up conversation when one is at the next urinal. There is the fact that he claims not to smoke other than as a 'social smoker', as if this were a morally superior position, and also the way he rolls cigarettes, as if this were self-evidently better than buying them in packs; worse, as if it were some almost forgotten skill which he alone, among humanity, is in possession of. There is his tendency to introduce himself to women as 'Ali' in order to make himself seem younger or more likeable, the implication in his claim to work for 'the Civil Service' that he is some sort of governmental high-roller when really he inspects roadworks for the council. There are his fucking 'designer shirts'.

But, after all, live and let live.

Obviously Lloyd and Anita see something in him which – well, no doubt he has his . . . well, everyone is different, aren't they, and it would be a dull world if we all agreed. Whom they choose to call a friend is their prerogative. Nobody would try to argue that he does not deserve to be at the wedding. He and his woman, his girlfriend or whoever she is, the person he irritatingly refers to as his 'partner': they ought to be there, if that is what Lloyd and Anita want; it is their day. It is their day.

But to conclude that, on the basis of his measly three years' acquaintance, Alistair is better placed than I am to fulfil the role of Best Man. Well, it is – and I do not use these words lightly – an absolute motherfucking obscenity of a decision.

Where was Alistair when a mix-up with the IKEA delivery men led to Lloyd and Anita's being without furniture until a certain somebody, aka myself, turned up with folding chairs? Where was he during the now notorious tournament of Travel Scrabble which filled the four-hour delay to the flight home from Alicante, but which might have brought about the end of their relationship if a certain somebody, myself, had not suggested a compromise re proper nouns? Is he familiar with the full sweep of Lloyd's nicknames, which include Android, the Cheesemaster, Lloyd Annoyed, many of them coined by a certain somebody, myself, and does he understand the derivation of all of them?

Fourteen years of friendship to Lloyd; only for six of those was Anita on the scene. So naturally the finger of suspicion, if I may use the phrase, points at Anita, who perhaps does not understand the calibre of Best Man that she is turning down here. Not, of course, that that calibre has ever been proved. This – and I am loath to dwell upon my personal disappointment, but it has to be said – this was my best chance of a Best Man opportunity. I confess I had regarded it as being almost a foregone conclusion, based on my credentials. The moment tonight when Lloyd tapped his glass and announced Alistair as his Best Man, and Alistair accepted with a mock-modest gesture, and the hair-ruffling and arm-grabbing that went on; those were low moments, very low moments. I waited for somebody to speak up. There was a sense of injustice in the air. Of a palpable injustice. But nobody looked at me. They were embarrassed to, perhaps. They felt that, even by being present, they were complicit in what had happened. In the mistake. In the – and I use this phrase advisedly – in the crime. In the gigantic fucking atrocity of making Alistair Lowden Best Man instead of a certain somebody, me, self-evidently better qualified for the job.

It is frankly fairly pissing-well unbelievable that I am still here, smiling indulgently at moronic conversation, nodding my agreement that they are a great couple and it will be a lovely day. Explaining what I do for a living, and patiently clarifying that, no, a cornet is not the same as a trumpet, and – ha-ha – yes, a cornet is a word for an ice-cream cone as well.

But the final word on this subject has not yet been spoken. The wedding date is set for some eighteen months hence. That leaves time for things to change. That is ample time. Alistair Lowden believes that, tonight, he has been confirmed as Best Man at the wedding of Lloyd and Anita. Certainly he has been offered the role. He is not quite there yet, though. The wedding day: that's the day we will know who the Best Man is. Not before. Until the day, everything is still up for grabs. Philip Lennox – that certain somebody, yours truly – is not quite out of contention yet.

SMOKING ROOM, 1985

It's a meeting. Smoke dirties the air. In twenty years or so it will be illegal to smoke in this room, or in most parts of the building, but if you suggested that at the moment, no one would believe you.

'So we basically need to decide literally this minute so I can get this faxed off. Are we putting the date on or aren't we?'

They are designing the publicity for a film, not a particularly good one, in which a guy is living with a girl who gets a pet tiger – which leads to considerable awkwardness. It's had frosty reviews in the States: one critic described it as having 'the kind of undercooked goofball premise that even the writers seemingly got sick of after about twenty minutes', and a notable reviewer (admittedly something of a snob) only dignified it with four words: 'Do not see this'. Luckily, the Internet isn't around yet, so people here generally don't know the critical history of a movie when it comes to London. With a spirited enough campaign you can make it look as if it's already been a great success, and isn't rubbish. The studio has put some money behind that job, and this poster will go on the side of London buses soon. It just needs these two people to finish the design.

'Um, I think . . . I don't know. What do you think?'

Florian can't concentrate because of the buzzing of a fly which has been grizzling its way in and out of nooks and corners for twenty minutes, its low, repetitive noise somehow impossible to unhear because, even in the act of deciding not to acknowledge it, you are making a pact with its existence. It's like – well, it's a bit like that thing with the tree falling down in the forest. If they didn't listen to the fly buzzing, it wouldn't be buzzing. But in order to think that, you have to admit that the fly is buzzing. And then it is . . .

'Did you even hear any of that?' Florian's colleague is asking testily, and quite rightly so.

He raises his palms at her in apology. 'I'm sorry, I . . . it's this bloody fly. One more time. What are our options? Sorry.'

She sighs. It's not like she cares about this film any more than he does. But she's more of a professional. In five years both of them will have left the industry and she will be a tour guide in Peru.

'Basically what I think we should do is leave the date off, because then we can have the title in bigger type, which I think would be better.'

'OK,' he says.

'Sure?' she says. 'Because it could be that we get our arses kicked for this. It might be that they desperately want the date on there. There's just no time to check.'

He starts to say that maybe they ought to stick the date on after all. Just to be on the safe side. Just to avoid getting told off by some jerk in LA who thinks nobody goes to see a film unless the release date is spelled out to them. But there's the fly, buzzing quietly and then loudly, never quite in the part of the room you expect. The fly, and the smoke. Above all, the fly. He can no longer stand it.

'Oh, it's fine,' Florian says. 'Don't worry about the date. It doesn't matter.'

It actually does matter, but it's done now. Within five minutes she's gone off to the fax machine in reception and the design is off to the relevant people. It does matter. A man will miss out on his dream job because that date isn't on the poster. Someone else will spend so long staring up at the poster, wondering when the film will be released, that he will be run over by a bicycle and end up meeting a nurse with whom he'll fall in love. In a way all this is down to the designers, but you could argue it's really down to the fly.

The fly buzzes out of the door when the designer leaves. Over the week to come, it will go on to have a hand in several more important decisions.

Along the road he bounds in the spring sunshine, Matthew Gillett, the outstanding candidate for the vacant job at the Hotel Alpha, handsomely dressed in a suit and tie and shoes which have been buffed by a Nigerian man in the station. He checks his watch: forty-five minutes till his interview. He's left the perfect amount of time – long enough that there's no chance of being late, but not so long that he'll be embarrassingly early and look as if he's been preparing for weeks. Time management is very important. It's a phrase he picked up from a book, *The Moment*. You have to have a plan for every minute. Well, Matthew has done that. He planned today, the interview day, precisely: rising with the alarm clock at seven-thirty, showering for ten minutes, eating a breakfast he pre-planned for its energy-providing qualities. Then he spent precisely an hour doing what he's done for an hour every day: rehearsing the answers to questions the interviewer, a Mr Adam, might ask.

What are your best qualities?

'(*Modest laugh.*) This question is a bit of a minefield, isn't it! I suppose there's my modesty, to start with! (*Mental note: judge whether it's the sort of situation where a joke would be appropriate.*) No, but seriously. I think I'm a good team member. I put my organization before myself. That's what I did at Lloyds, and

352

before that at the Planetarium and Spar, my previous employers. I would also say that I'm well-organized and efficient. I've been to see the hotel in action and I notice how smoothly it all runs. You need someone who can fit into that, who can be a part of that well-oiled machine – an important part, but unobtrusive. I think that's me. Also, I particularly pride myself on my time management.'

And any weaknesses?

'Well, we all have weaknesses, of course. I think one of mine is that I set myself unfairly high standards, and perhaps sometimes do the same to people around me. At the Planetarium I was occasionally told off – it sounds funny – for working intimidating amounts of overtime, or for keeping my own department in such good order that other areas of the museum looked a bit shabby. I'm always trying to learn from criticism, and I've learned from those experiences that you always have to make allowances for others in the team.'

Where do you see yourself in ten years' time?

'Where you are now! (*Deferential laugh.*) No, but seriously. I think the main thing I foresee is that I will be doing what I'm doing now – operating at a very high level – but within a position of increased responsibility. I would like to think that I'll have proved my worth to this hotel and, God willing, will be a major part of its hierarchy. I don't see the Hotel Alpha as some sort of stepping stone to a bigger place. I see the next decade as being a process of—'

A woman hurries past him, newspaper under her arm, an umbrella in her other hand – an umbrella she surely won't need on a bright day like this. It catches the fold of his jacket and the two of them look briefly, crossly at each other, and that is the only time they will ever meet. Matthew looks down at the jacket in case there's a blemish left by the encounter, but there's nothing, and he settles back into his interview rehearsal as the sun runs like spilled juice over the brickwork of King's Cross station up ahead.

What in particular attracts you to the Hotel Alpha?

'Of course, I've been aware of the reputation of the hotel for a long time, like anyone interested in London life. (*Mental note: try to say this as if you've always lived in London, rather than moving down from Kettering four years ago.*) I've always been fascinated by the idea that it's a place, not just to stay, but to do whatever you want. And I would like to be someone who can help guests to—'

A double-decker bus rolls past, and Matthew instinctively takes a couple of steps away from the road as if the bus might lurch onto the pavement. He glances up at its red body, bathing like everything else in the generosity of the sun, and vaguely notices the banner advertising a romantic comedy which is in the cinemas now. He saw the same ad last week. The design was sketched out – by coincidence – in the smoking room of the Hotel Alpha, where he's headed now. Because of various distractions, the two people responsible for the design omitted to include the date. If they had included it, Matthew might have taken notice of what day it was when he saw it last week, and it might have triggered the realization that his Alpha interview was actually meant to take place then. As it is, on he goes now, the perfect candidate, mentally rehearsing his finely chiselled answers to questions that will never be asked. In the hotel, now one hundred yards away, the person who got the job is already happily at work.

ALL OVER THE HOTEL

Top ten reasons for sleeplessness in the Hotel Alpha, occurring in guests between 1965 and 2005:

1. General, unfocused sense of unease.
2. Noise from another room, or from the atrium.
3. Worries connected to work, finances, etc.
4. Worries related to romantic relationships, including marriage.
5. Woken up by strange dream or by unknown circumstances and unable to relax back into sleep.
6. Thinking too hard about need to sleep, paradoxically making goal unattainable.
7. Misjudgement of food or alcohol consumption leading to disturbed physical equilibrium.
8. Miscalculation of fatigue levels leading to too-early bedtime.
9. Body's instinctive dread of relinquishing consciousness, as sleep too close a sensation to ultimate negation of death, against which human instinct automatically rebels.
10. Dripping tap.

Ten reasons for sleeplessness that have occurred just once in the Hotel Alpha between 1965 and 2005:

1. Allergy to detergent used to wash sheets, causing succession of 46 sneezes in two minutes, causing state of wakefulness impossible to shake off.
2. Fear of dark which cannot be admitted to new girlfriend.
3. Visitation of ghost, presumably in a dream.
4. Gout.
5. Hypochondria leading to conviction about imminent illness.
6. Partner's wetting of bed.
7. Obsessive desire to solve riddle about getting a goat and some other items from one side of a river to the other.
8. Nostalgia for homeland, Transnistria, a part of Moldova which asserts its independence.
9. Person next door laughing indecently loud, and all through night, at rerun of 1970s sitcom *On The Buses*.
10. Once killed a man.

ROOM 68, 1966

'I advise you to stay in the wardrobe for a little longer,' says the concierge in an undertone. 'Until the moment they knock on the door.'

'But what if . . . ' the Rolling Stone begins.

'Don't worry, there is no way of opening the doors. Not even for the police. Ha, ha!'

The rock star hears the mutter of mirth and wonders how old this guy is. He seems ancient, but he doesn't look it.

'Now listen,' the voice continues. 'When they knock, I shall detain them with some questions, affecting not to believe that they are the police, or, anyhow, some sort of shilly-shallying.' He must be in his fifties, thinks the Stone, and just be one of these geezers with that condition where you look like you never age. 'That door at the far end,' the concierge continues, 'communicates with the room next door. Normally it cannot be opened, but I have taken the liberty of unlocking every such door on this floor. While I am busy with the police in this room, you should steal away quickly through the door, and then the next door, until you come to the end of the balcony.'

'There's cops down in the lobby as well, though,' frets the celebrity.

'The atrium, yes,' the concierge agrees. What the fuck is an atrium? wonders the Stone. It reminds him of Latin at school.

He can just about remember school – it's not many years ago – but Christ, things have happened since then. More than enough has happened even in the past twenty-four hours. He can't entirely remember how he got here, or when he last woke up in a bed. A phrase comes into his head: light years from home. A thousand, two thousand light years from home.

' . . . and that is Room 44,' says the concierge. 'You should be safe in there for as long as necessary.' Shit: he hasn't been concentrating. He heard 44 at least. He'll head there. He can hear the footsteps of the cops outside, their low conversations. They sound as nervous as he is. More nervous, probably. What can they do to him, really? He only mentioned that he needed to 'keep his head down' for a while, but the hotel staff have taken it really seriously.

A silence follows; then the policemen guess the wrong way, heading towards the far end of the balcony. It will a few minutes before they've knocked on all the doors and ended up here. It's going to work perfectly.

The concierge clears his throat.

'My boss – Howard – is very fond of one of your songs,' he says, 'the one named "Satisfaction".'

'That's cool. Thanks.'

The Stone doesn't mean to sound lukewarm, but he's always at a loss to know how to respond when people mention specific stuff they've liked. He always says thanks, but it tends to sound a bit half-hearted. He prefers just to sign his autograph rather than gas about the songs. The worst thing is when people sing them back at him. He doesn't reckon this guy is going to try and do that.

'I suppose . . . I suppose the song is about trying to – obtain satisfaction in one's life, really?' the man ventures.

'That's pretty fair,' says the Stone.

He's spared from adding to his comments by a hard trio of knocks at the door. The concierge opens the wardrobe without a sound, a finger to his lips as he points towards the communicating door. The Stone winks and begins to walk with exaggerated delicacy across the carpet. The two men's lives will not intersect again after this, although in the years ahead Graham will occasionally glance up at a screen and see the man cavorting about, his face a little older each time.

ROOM 76, 1970

Every time someone knocks on any of the bloody doors in this place, it sounds like it's yours. This is the third time he's sprung to his feet, gone to jerk open the door, and not found her there. Once it was a visitor for the person the other side of the wall: a visitor who ought not, from the look on her face, to be there. Once it was a housekeeper in a uniform so white it looked brand new; she glanced wryly at him before being admitted two doors down. And this time there is nobody there at all. Whoever made the knock has been noiselessly admitted to a room, or was the product of his imagination. Or a ghost.

It's not as if it could be her, anyhow. She isn't coming back. He has lost her. She is with somebody else; or she's with nobody else, but happy; she's happy without him, that's the point. And that's how it has to be. He doesn't deserve another chance, probably. It's just that a hotel promises everything, or at least rules nothing out. Anything, in its neutrality, can be imagined. Nobody made of the ordinary human stuff can hear a knock on a door, even the wrong door, without believing for a few seconds that the impossible has happened, and the person they have longed for is here after all.

picador.com

blog
videos
interviews
extracts